Chapter 1

It was nearly 5 PM and Kristen was beginning to feel pangs of hunger as she had eaten nothing since breakfast. Had she known in advance what her new life as a homeless runaway would be like she probably would have eaten a larger breakfast. But when you run away from home you usually do not have a detailed plan. Your only goal is to get away from what you see as an intolerable situation and you do not think about the long-term future.

Kristen hadn't planned even beyond the first day. She had simply packed her bags with a few of her meager possessions and all of the money she had saved up from working at McDonald's and whatever she could steal from her worthless junkie father. She hardly considered that theft at all seeing as he stole any paycheck she could not hide and would spend most of the family income supporting his drug habit. Stealing drug money from a person who stole it from you in the first place is hardly any crime. Her father was so hung over last night she wondered if he even noticed she was gone yet. He probably won't even realize anything is missing until he goes to buy more drugs. That was the type of person that she was running away from.

She turned to the man she had been riding with for the past several hours. "Are we going to stop for dinner soon? I'm beginning to get hungry. I haven't eaten since breakfast."

"We'll stop at the next diner," he muttered as he stole yet another glance at her cleavage. Although she was grateful for the ride, she was about ready to ditch this guy. In the five hours since they left California he had been leering at her on average every 5 minutes. Probably the only reason that he picked her up at all was that he was hoping to get lucky. If that was his intention, he was sorely mistaken.

"Where are we?" she asked. "We've been driving for hours."

"Nevada," he said 'accidentally' brushing his hand across her left breast with a look of perverse satisfaction in his eyes and the scent of his last meal lingering in his beard. She felt like slapping him and shouting "eyes up here buddy!" but she held her tongue. If she could just endure a little bit longer she would be rid of this perv soon enough.

Finally, after what seemed like forever but was probably more like an hour, they arrived at a diner called Ma's Roadside Burgers. It was a small restaurant but hopefully she would find someone there who she could hitch a ride with that was more tolerable than her current companion. She didn't even know where she was heading; she just knew she wanted to get as far from home as she could.

They got out of the truck and went into the restaurant. She made sure to take all of her things with her. She told her traveling companion to go ahead and order something while she used the ladies room. After answering nature's call, she checked herself out in the mirror. She looked okay under the circumstances, but her lipstick could use a touch up. She preferred the darkest red lipstick to match her dark red hair. That had been her look since high school.

She emerged from the restroom and surveyed the restaurant. There weren't many people there at the moment. An elderly couple at one table, a big fat guy sitting in the corner, a middle-aged looking man, and a group of guys having a beer. She saw her traveling companion and went to tell him she wanted to eat alone. He did not seem happy about this but simply nodded his head with his eyes fixated clearly upon her breasts.

That was when she saw *him*. Sitting alone in a dark corner of the restaurant was a guy with spiky hair and dressed in a black leather jacket. He was wearing dark sunglasses that obscured his eyes and was very pale in complexion. He looked like some punk rocker from the 80s. Despite all of that he was probably the most attractive person in the restaurant and the only one who looked to be around her age. What did she have to lose?

"Excuse me," she said, "mind if I sit here?" He looked up without removing his sunglasses and nodded. As far as she can tell he wasn't ogling her breasts, but with the sunglasses it was hard to tell. In any case she didn't feel she would mind. Being ogled was only bad to her when she was ogled by people she found to be unattractive. To be ogled by the right man is perhaps the greatest form of flattery.

"I'm Kristin," she said as she took a seat across from him.

He didn't say anything in response. That was when the waitress came over.

"What'll you all be having this evening?"

"I'll just have a burger and fries, and to drink I'll get a Coke." Kristen looked over at the man across from her.

"And what about you, Sir?"

"I'll have a steak, as rare as you can make it. I like to be able to taste the juices." He licked his lips ever so slightly and smirked.

The waitress left and Kristen decided it was best that she try to make some small talk. "So where are you from?"

"California," he replied, again without looking up.

"I'm from California as well." She noticed a cross and some dog tags hanging from his neck. "So are you religious or something? Cause I noticed you have a crucifix around your neck. That's why I asked."

"Not exactly," he said with a small laugh. "I mostly do it to be ironic."

"What do you mean by that?"

"Nothing." He laughed again, which made her a little bit nervous.

"So are you a veteran? I noticed you're also wearing some dog tags."

"Yep, served in Iraq."

"What years were you in Iraq?"

"91."

"91? Wait, you mean you were in the first Gulf War?"

"That's the one."

"But you don't look older than 20. I should know because I'm 18. There's no way you could possibly have been in the first Gulf War."

"Well, I was."

"Why would you make up a lie like that when it is so obviously not true? Do you think I'm some kind of idiot?"

"I'm not lying. You asked me a question and I answered honestly."

"You honestly expect me to believe that you are in your

40s? Okay, I'll humor you, when were you born?"

"January 17, 1970. I was in Saudi Arabia when I turned 21. I couldn't even have a drink to celebrate because of Muslim prohibition of alcohol. It really sucked."

"Riiight." Great, the one guy she decided to talk to was delusional.

"You don't believe me, do you? Well, whatever." He started to look down at the table, not even at her breasts like most guys. For some reason that bothered her, was this guy trying to play hard to get? Just what exactly was his deal? She had to admit that she was intrigued.

"So did you read my thoughts to figure that out?"

He smiled. "No, I'm not a mind reader. Any more questions?"

"If you're not a mind reader, then what is your deal?"

"Do you really want to know?"

She nodded.

"I'm a vampire."

"Of course! You're a vampire. That makes perfect sense. Why didn't that just occur to me, it should have been obvious?" She couldn't help but roll her eyes.

"You still don't believe me?"

"Sure, I believe you. I know there are lots of people out there who like to live that vampire lifestyle, those Goth kids and stuff. That's why you're wearing all black. So you're not really an actual vampire, you are just one of those vampire people."

"No, I am a real vampire."

"Yeah, right...you are a real vampire. I didn't mean to put down your lifestyle. I'm a big fan of Twilight too. So what kind of vampire are you? Are you like Edward Cullen?"

"Noooo, I'm not like Edward Cullen. I'm not a vegetarian and don't know any vampires who are. I never feed without killing. And I definitely don't sparkle. I'm also heterosexual. But my name is Eddie. Believe me; after Twilight came out I've seriously considered changing my name. People have a certain reaction when you tell them you're a vampire named Edward."

"I'll bet." This conversation was beginning to get awkward. But she's dated worse. So this guy believes he's a vampire, she had no problem with vampires. She was pretty weird herself. "So, what type of vampire are you?"

"Type?"

"Yeah, like what type of rules do you follow?"

He smirked. "I don't follow any rules. I'm my own person."

"A rogue vampire, eh? But what type of vampire rules do you need to follow...biologically? You obviously must be able to tolerate sunlight as you haven't burst into flames."

"Sunlight won't cause us to burst into flames, but we don't like it, thus the sunglasses and the pale skin. It may seem like a cliché, but it really is very practical. But believe me; it takes a lot more than a little sunlight to kill a vampire. Most of what you see in Hollywood is just myth, though some of it is true."

"Such as? Perhaps this is an awkward first conversation topic, but if sunlight doesn't kill you, what does?"

"You don't want to find out. Let's just say killing a vampire isn't very easy. We are already dead after all."

"Right." He was really into this. At least he was an interesting conversationalist. She could put up with him for a couple hundred miles if worse came to worse.

"I can prove it to you if you'd like."

"How exactly would you do that?"

"Feel my pulse. Or a lack of one, rather." He extended his pale hand to her. She grabbed it. His hands were as cold as ice; it even gave her a chill. She squeezed his wrist and felt for a pulse, but could not find one. She held on for a full minute, but still did not feel any pulse.

"So, have I convinced you yet?"

She frowned. "I know there are people who can stop their heart and can control their bodily functions for a limited amount of time. Mind over matter, mind over body. Whatever."

"So you still don't believe? Well, that's fine. Most people don't. I don't even know why I told you. I guess I was just making conversation. I don't talk to people very often. Vampires tend to have few close associates."

"There's no vampire country club?" She smiled. He may

have been crazy but she was enjoying this conversation.

"Not exactly, no. There aren't very many of us and most of us stay in stealth mode, living off the grid and whatnot. I've been staying at a motel."

He had a motel! At least that means he had a place to stay for the night. It was better than nothing. If she played her cards right maybe she wouldn't be sleeping outside tonight. Although, did she really want to sleep in the same room with a person who thinks they are a vampire? She might wake up with more than just a hickey. A lot of these people were into biting and blood tasting. But she was open minded about those things. As she said, she has dated worse. But it was getting late, so what did she have to lose? She had pepper spray in her purse if she needed it.

"So you have a motel? This may be a bit forward of me, seeing as we have just met and all, but I have no place to stay tonight. If your motel is not too far do you think perhaps I could stay with you for the night? Now, I want to make it clear that this isn't a hook up or an invitation to a booty call, I just need a place to stay for the night."

He smiled a big grin. "You don't have a problem sleeping in the same room as a vampire?"

"I'll admit that at first I found you to be a bit strange, but after talking to you I have become intrigued. I still don't know precisely what exactly you mean when you say that you are a vampire, but I'm willing to keep an open mind about these things."

"What I mean is exactly what I say. I am a vampire, an immortal member of the undead who sustains themselves by drinking human blood, nothing more, and nothing less. If you still don't believe me there is one more test that you could do."

"And what is that?"

"Do you have a mirror in your purse?"

"Yes, I do."

"Then take it out and point it towards me."

She slowly took her compact mirror out of her purse and opened it. As soon as she did so she saw the reflection of the truck driver who had brought her to this diner glaring over her shoulder. She quickly closed the compact and turned around.

"You know, I was thinking," began the truck driver, "you

never said thank you for giving you a ride here. And now I catch you here putting the moves on this pale skinned faggot over here."

Her heart began to beat rapidly and she could feel her pulse begin to quicken. "Look, I don't want any trouble. Thank you for giving me a ride this far, but I think this is where we should part ways."

The truck driver grabbed her right arm. "I think that that's being a little disingenuous, don't you think?"

Her heart began beating faster and faster. "Look, if it's money that you want, I don't have much. But I'm willing to pay what you feel is fair."

The truck driver smirked at her and leaned forward as he pulled her arm toward his crotch. "You know there are other ways of paying a person that don't involve money." She tried pulling her arm away, but he pulled it closer towards him. "Come on, honey, I haven't had a good release in a good long time."

She managed to jerk her hand free. "Gee, I wonder why that is!" She went to go and slap him but he grabbed her hand again. He raised his other arm to go and strike her but turned around to see Eddie had grabbed his arm.

"I don't think you want to do that, I've stuffed a lot of faggy Goth kids in a lot of toilets."

Eddie smiled again and twisted the truck driver's arm and with a single motion picked him up by his arm and threw him over his shoulders and onto the table. Everyone in the restaurant turned to look.

"I think that you owe the lady an apology." Eddie leaned forward, getting right in the truck drivers face.

"I-I'm s-sorry," muttered the truck driver. Then he reached for his pocket, drew a knife and stabbed Eddie right in the arm. Eddie lunged backwards as the truck driver got up from the table and punched Eddie in the face, knocking him to the floor and knocking off his sunglasses. The truck driver turned back towards Kristen with a lecherous gleam in his eye. She began to move backwards and looked over to the floor where Eddie was getting up. He looked straight at her with glowing yellow eyes - like those of a cat - and then leaped up knocking the truck driver flat on his ass. Eddie slapped the knife out of his hand and pinned him, staring him straight in the face.

"P-please," choked the truck driver, "just let me go. I didn't mean anything by it."

Eddie laughed sinisterly as he stared directly into the truck driver's face. "Oh really now, you didn't mean anything by it when you stuck a knife into my arm? I find that hard to believe. It sounds like the kind of thing that a sniveling coward says right after he has picked a fight that he cannot win as he senses he is about to die. I can smell the fear on you and feel your blood coursing through your veins."

"L-look, I'll give you whatever you want, just please, spare me."

"You didn't say pretty please with sugar on top."

"P-pretty please with sugar on top!"

"Isn't it funny, how a dying man will say anything, however stupid and pathetic, to save his own life."

"Please, Mister, I said I'd give you anything that you want."

"But you see, there is only one thing I want."

"W-what is it?"

"I want to feed!" Eddie opened his mouth wide, revealing two glistening white fangs, which he plunged into the truck driver's neck. A fountain of blood began to ooze out in all directions as Eddie began to drain his victim who was rapidly becoming pale.

That was when the waitress came out with their food and dropped it in horror and screamed. She tried covering her mouth, but that was when Eddie looked up, his eyes glowing yellow, and his fangs dripping red with blood all over his shirt. As she began to run Eddie dived forward, knocked her to the ground and bit into her jugular saturating her and him with blood. The rest of the restaurant patrons were all getting up and starting to slowly walk backwards.

A black male, one of the groups of men drinking a beer, dropped his beer, pointed at Eddie and shouted, "What the fuck are you!"

Eddie looked up staring straight forward at the young man as he stood up.

"Well, my good gentleman, I am a vampire."

Everyone stared at Eddie before the middle aged man said, "I don't know what the hell is wrong with you, but I am calling the police." As he went to take out his cell phone Eddie picked up the truck driver's knife from the floor and threw it directly into the man's chest, causing him to drop his cell phone and fall to the floor dead. Someone let out a scream and everyone began running in all directions.

First Eddie picked up a chair and threw it at the door, blocking the exit. As one of the young men tried opening the door the others ran off. Eddie ran towards the young man, came up behind him and bit the back of his neck. He then grabbed him around the stomach and chest and hugged him tightly, crushing his rib cage. He fell to the floor dead as a door nail.

Eddie stood over his latest kill, looking down at him and smiling in satisfaction as blood ran down his lips. As he admired his work, he heard a gunshot and fell to the floor. The black male stood over him with the gun still smoking. He had fired a shot directly into Eddie's back. He slowly approached Eddie's body and kicked it.

"It's alright everyone, I got him. A direct shot to the back."

The others who were hiding slowly came out to see for themselves that Eddie was dead. All of them except for Kristen. She was still watching in stunned silence in the corner of the room. She slowly began to get up as the others gathered around Eddie. As she approached the crowd around Eddie, she saw Eddie's head slowly rise as he cracked a smile. She was about to say something when Eddie leaped up and twisted the black male's arm, causing him to drop the gun. He knocked him to the floor and snapped his arm straight off. He then used the arm to smack the rest of the restaurant patrons in the face before knocking them all to the ground.

One by one, Eddie picked each person up and threw them across the room. He tore the limbs from their bodies, which flew off in every direction, splattering blood all over.

The next couple of minutes were a blur of dismemberment and bloodshed. Soon the entire restaurant was covered with blood and severed body parts. The victims did not even look human anymore. The young, the old and everything in between, now they were just a mangled pile of body parts and blood. They couldn't even be identified without a dental record.

Amid all the chaos, Kristen just sat huddled in the corner watching Eddie. After Eddie had eaten his fill, he began to slowly walk over to Kristen covered head to toe in blood. He looked at her with his catlike eyes and a big bloody grin with protruding fangs. That was when she closed her eyes.

Chapter 2

Kristen's eyes were shut tight as she awaited the inevitable. She felt his cold hand on her shoulder that sent chills up her spine. Then she heard the words, "Open your eyes and get up." She did as she was told and slowly opened her eyes as she stood up. When she opened her eyes she was staring face-to-face with Eddie. She stepped back slowly.

"Are you going to kill me?" Kristen managed to choke out.

Eddie came closer until they were looking eye-to-eye. Looking into his eyes she felt almost mesmerized. The fear slowly left her body. "Get out your compact," he said. She did as she asked. "Now look at me in it," he commanded her. She slowly opened her compact mirror and pointed it at Eddie. His image did not appear. "Now, do you believe me?" he asked her. She nodded. "Good." Eddie smiled.

"Do you need a doctor?" she asked him as she touched his

arm.

"No," he said as he shook his head. "I am already beginning to heal. All I need is blood. So long as I have enough blood in me I'm practically invincible. Right now you can't even begin to imagine how I feel."

"Are you in pain?"

He shook his head. "No, quite the opposite, I feel intoxicated. Picture how you would feel eating the most delicious food you have ever tasted as you simultaneously experienced the most intense orgasm of your life and multiply it by hundred and you wouldn't even come close."

Kristen slowly stepped back a few more paces.

"I can hear your heart beating, and I can see the blood gushing through your veins. It is taking every ounce of self-restraint to control myself right now."

"Are you going to kill me?" she repeated.

"Do you want me to?" He licked the blood from his lips.

"No!"

"Then why didn't you run while you had the opportunity?"

"I don't know, shock maybe. Why didn't you go after me?"

"I don't know." They both began laughing, nervous little laughs at first, until they were in full-blown hysterics.

"Why are we laughing?" she asked as she continued to laugh.

"I have no fucking idea." They laughed and laughed some more until they both could hardly breathe and were in tears. After a few minutes they finally managed to settle down

"You know," began Eddie, "you're the first person I have ever met who did not run away when I began slaughtering people. It is rather unusual, wouldn't you say?"

"Yeah." What else was there to say? She still didn't know why she hadn't tried to run yet. Maybe she knew it was hopeless, or maybe it was something else altogether.

"Now there is the question of what we are going to do about it."

"I won't tell anyone what happened here."

"Well, that isn't an issue. I somehow doubt anyone would

believe your story about a vampire killing spree."

"That is true. I think if I told them that story I would find myself in a mental asylum."

"Most likely."

There was a long and awkward silence before Eddie finally spoke up. "So do you still need a place to stay for the night?"

"What?"

"I don't think that any of these others are in any condition to give you a ride. And I don't think you want to stay here, correct?"

"True."

"The way I see it, you really don't have any other options. As far as things go, I'm the only ride in town."

Kristen couldn't believe what was happening. But he was correct, what other choice did she have? If she stayed here she would seem like an accomplice to a mass murder and no one would believe her story. If she talks to the police they will probably send her back home, assuming they didn't arrest her on the spot. It's possible that her father even has an arrest warrant out for her for stealing 'his' money. That is, if the bastard has even realized she's missing.

"So what do you say?" Eddie offered her his hand, and she took it. It wasn't as cold as the first time. She could feel the fresh new blood warming his cold body.

"But wait," she said grabbing his arm, "what about this place? Are we just going to leave it like this, with blood and guts all over the place?"

"I don't think anyone is going to be able to track down a dead man." He laughed and she laughed as well. "Shall we be going?"

Eddie put his glasses back on and they walked out the front door carefully stepping over the dismembered body parts strewn across the floor. He led her to a black car and told her to get in the front. She did as he ordered her. "Buckle up," he said, "the last thing we need is to get stopped for a ticket."

They drove off with the diner quickly receding into the background as the sun finished setting over the horizon. Kristen did not know what she should be thinking. She was now driving across the Nevada desert after sundown with a mass murdering vampire, still covered in the blood of his latest victims, and she was going to spend the night in a motel with him. This is not what she anticipated when she left home this morning, though she doubted that anyone could ever expect something like this to happen. How are you even supposed to react to a situation like this?

Was this even real? Maybe she was just suffering from heat stroke. No, however unbelievable this may be she couldn't deny that it was really happening. She wasn't sure whether she should be terrified or exhilarated. Although it defied common logic, she somehow felt safe with Eddie in a way that she had never felt safe before. She knew that he was a mass murderer and a monster, but the fact that he has not killed her means that she is pretty well protected with an invincible being watching over her, unless of course he is planning to save her for a midnight snack.

Before she could think about it for too long her thoughts were interrupted by the very sound that they most dreaded – the sirens of a police car.

"What are we going to do Eddie? They want us to pull over."

Eddie smirked. "Well then, I suppose we had better comply with their wishes."

What was he thinking? As soon as they saw him covered in blood they would surely arrest him and possibly also her. But maybe that would be the best thing under the circumstances. She really had no idea what Eddie was planning for her, and at least in police custody she would be safe.

Eddie stopped the car as the police pulled over behind them. A police officer got out and Eddie rolled down the window. "What seems to be the problem officer?"

The police officer took out his flashlight and shined it on Eddie. "Well," he began, "for one thing you were speeding, and for another..." The officer looked closely at Eddie. "Son, are you covered in blood?"

Eddie began to laugh. "That's very observant of you officer. With deductive reasoning like that you could be the police officer of the month." Eddie laughed more. What the hell did he think he was doing, she wondered.

"Alright, both of you out of the car, now!"

Eddie smiled at the officer and pulled down his glasses to make his eyes visible. "You know officer, I'm pretty God damned fucking comfortable right here."

The officer drew his gun and pointed it at Eddie. "I'm serious, out of the fucking car right now!"

Kristen opened her door and got out and put her hands up. "Please, don't shoot. We'll do as you say."

"Fine," said Eddie, "we'll do it your way, then." Eddie opened the car door and came out with his arms outstretched and slowly put them behind his head.

"Now put your hands on the car!" the officer shouted.

"Aw, do I have to?" Eddie said, imitating the voice of a small child.

"I'm warning you, Mister, hands on the fucking car right now!"

Eddie stretched his arms outward. "You didn't say Simon says."

The officer raised his gun towards Eddie. "This is your last chance."

"Eddie I think he is serious," pleaded Kristen, "just do as he says."

"Listen to your girlfriend mister, she's talking sense."

"She has no idea what the hell she's talking about. If there's anyone that she should be worried about, it's you."

"This is your last warning." The officer pointed his gun straight at Eddie's chest.

"You shouldn't have done that." And with that Eddie leapt forward and before the officer could do anything the gun had been knocked from his hand and gone off. When he looked up Eddie's knees were digging into his chest and he was staring down into the officer's face, his eyes glowing bright yellow.

"W-what are you?" the officer managed to gasp out.

"I'm the last thing you're ever going to see!" Eddie kneeled down and began to chew the officer's face off. His bloodcurdling screams echoed in the night and all Kristen could do was stand there and watch as Eddie devoured the officer. In one final stroke Eddie reached down, tore off the officer's head and began drinking the blood dripping from his severed head.

"How rude of me," said Eddie, his mouth dripping with blood, "I didn't even ask you if you would like any? Where are my manners?"

"That's okay; you go ahead and finish it on your own."

After drinking the blood from the officer for several more minutes Eddie finally had finished feasting. He got up and wiped the blood from his mouth and put his sunglasses back on. He then went over to the police car and flipped it over on its side and kicked it over. He tore the doors off and began smashing them against the rest of the police car. He didn't even break a sweat, if vampires even sweated at all.

"Sorry," said Eddie as he walked back towards his car, "but I really hate cops. Also I stole that car off the last guy that I killed. Shall we be on our way?" All Kristen could do was nod and get back in the car. It looked like she wouldn't be shaking Eddie off so easy.

Chapter 3

They arrived at the motel. It was an off-road area in the desert with nothing else nearby. It was probably several miles from the motel into the nearest town. It was small and very inconspicuous. As soon as Kristen saw it, it occurred to her that it is probably the perfect place for vampire to go in order to live off the grid. Few people would pass by or take notice of it, so the odds of him being discovered there were slim.

"We're here," Eddie said.

They got out and went to room 13. It seems like vampires weren't superstitious. As soon as she walked in Kristen was shocked at just how mundane it was. There was a crappy small screen television, a bed, a desk with one chair and a nightstand. There was also a small closet and a door leading into the bathroom. Above the bed was a painting of a lighthouse that seemed out of place in a desert setting like this.

"Welcome to casa de Eddie, what do you think?" She frowned and Eddie took notice. "What's the matter? Not to your liking?"

"It's not that, I was just expecting something more, I dunno..."

"Something scarier, maybe a room full of skulls and spooky black candles?"

"Yeah, kinda. I guess I was expecting it to be weirder."

"You know vampires are still people. We may live an indefinite lifespan and feast on human blood, but we were all human beings with normal lives at one point. No one is born a vampire, you become one. Besides, vampires are mostly nomadic. It is suspicious if we stay in any place for too long, so we don't put a great deal of effort into the decor. People tend to notice things such as you not aging and the fact that people go disappearing shortly after you arrive in town."

"So what do you do for a living?"

"Some vampires manage to hold down respectable jobs, but the majority of us are criminals. We live from day to day and from kill to kill. We only need to feed occasionally, although most cannot resist the desire to feed frequently. But beyond that we have few needs. Money, health care and other things of that nature are not necessary, once you have abandoned mortality."

"So you've been living like this since you were turned?"

"For more than 20 years."

"It must get lonely."

"It does." Eddie threw off his jacket and began taking off his blood soaked shirt. His chest was as pale as the rest of his body and she could not see any heartbeat. He was in reasonably good shape for a person who has technically been dead for 20 years.

Eddie began to take off his pants and underwear and tossed them to the side. Kristen was taken by surprise to see Eddie's pale nude body illuminated by the dim light of the room. His body was still stained with the blood from his latest killing spree. He definitely did not sparkle, and she couldn't help but find herself aroused.

"Like what you see?" Eddie snickered as he walked slowly towards her. She began to blush but couldn't deny that she liked very much what she saw. Eddie threw his sunglasses to the floor and gazed at her with a penetrating stare as he slowly walked towards her with the blood dripping down his thighs.

"I-," she began as she started to feel weak at the knees.

"Do not lie to me. You can't hide your excitement. I can see your heart beating faster and the blood rushing through your veins. I can practically taste your warm sticky blood. I can smell it, I can feel it. And I can't control myself. A vampire drunk on blood needs no aphrodisiac. Blood is an intoxicant to us. Nothing excites our passion more."

Eddie walked up to Kristen, staring her directly in the eyes, mesmerizing her. She fell backward onto the bed. Eddie moved forward and lifted her shirt over her head. He began to feel her breasts and tore off her bra, tossing it aside. He started licking her nipples. He could feel the blood through his tongue and could barely restrain himself. He wanted to bite into her but did not want to destroy her.

He pushed her down on the bed. He began licking her face and kissing her. He began to pull down her jeans and panties to her ankles. He climbed on top of her staring deeply into her eyes. She was practically paralyzed. The rush of adrenaline and arousal was causing her heart to beat rapidly and Eddie could feel the blood through her flesh. He caressed her naked body and it took every ounce of self-control he had at his disposal to keep from tearing her limb from limb. He spread her legs and entered her. She moaned as waves of pleasure cascaded through her body. Eddie thrust his blood stained body violently against her, squeezing her breasts very hard. Then, as he stared directly into her eyes, he bore his fangs. Kristen looked up and prepared for the inevitable death blow.

It did not come.

The next several hours went by in a blur and Kristen awoke to the rays of the sun peering in through the windows onto her naked flesh. She felt weak and saw that the sheets were covered in blood. Eddie was nowhere to be found. Did she dream the whole thing? No, it was real. And not only was it real, and despite the terrifying nature of it, last night was by far the most intense and pleasurable experience of her life. She felt like she hardly had the strength to get out of bed.

She reached over to the nightstand and knocked over a beat up old notebook. She opened it in the middle and began to read:

October 3, 2006

Today I feasted well. I was driving down the highway at around midnight and saw a hitchhiker. She looked cold and young. If I had to guess I would say she was probably about 20 years old. I picked her up and brought her to a motel. After making small talk for a while we got down to business. She fought with me but was no match for my strength. I tore her clothing off and sunk my fangs into her delicious pale flesh. The ecstasy! I have not eaten so well in weeks. I drained every drop of blood in her body and then disposed of it in the desert. If I had not been so hungry it would have been nice to keep her alive and have my way with her for a while. But she would've run away if I hadn't killed her then and there. But I suppose it's not good to play with your food. You might become too attached and not want to eat it, much like a farm girl cannot bare to devour her favorite piglet. But people will be surprised just what they will do when they are hungry enough.

She heard the door opening and threw the journal down on the nightstand. Eddie opened the door and Kristen covered up her bare breasts with the sheets. He was dressed in his typical outfit but it looks like he managed to get the blood stains out, that or he had a whole wardrobe full of the same outfit.

"Bashful are we?" Eddie snickered. "You weren't very bashful last night."

"Well I–" she blushed.

Eddie picked up his journal. "Doing some reading?"

"I was just curious and-"

Eddie waved his hand at her. "It's okay; curiosity is only natural under the circumstances. You're probably wondering what kind of man it is that you have gotten involved with. Since you're curious I will answer your next question. I've never been the introspective sort, but I keep a journal of my kills. It is useful to keep track of one's diet."

"How many people have you killed?"

Eddie sat down on the bed and whispered in her ear, "A lot."

"How many is a lot?"

"More than just a few."

"A number Eddie!"

"I never counted. But believe me when I say it is a very large number. But I do keep record of when and where I eat. I try not to hit the same place too often. We vampires must make some effort not to draw attention to ourselves. Most rookie vampires make that mistake and pay for it with their lives. The majority of vampires don't even make it through their first year. It's rather ironic, you are granted immortality only to have it lead you towards an earlier demise than you would have likely had, had you simply remained mortal."

"What about what happened at the diner? That wasn't very discreet, or the police officer. People are going to get suspicious Eddie."

"I lost control. It was a temporary lapse of judgment due to being blood deprived. I was originally just looking around for a single victim to satiate my hunger. Sometimes I'm tired of being so restrained. Sometimes I grow tired of always hiding the truth."

"Why did you tell me?"

"I don't know. Most people tend to avoid me. I'm not exactly a person who looks the most approachable. You asked, so I decided to tell the truth. And you didn't run away in fear after I lost control. Why is that?"

"I don't know. I honestly don't know."

"I don't think it was shock. Shock is a temporary state. You're still here. If you were truly afraid you would have fled by now."

"Maybe I still will." Her heart began to beat faster.

"I don't think that you will."

"What makes you so sure of that?"

"Because you're too afraid of trying to leave, but beyond that it has been my experience that anyone who stays this long is probably willing to stay with it for the long haul. Besides which, there was last night."

Kristen blushed again and drew the sheets closer to her chest. "Eddie, about last night..."

He waved his hand at her again. "There is no need to explain."

"But there is. Eddie, what you did, what we did, was wrong. You are a mass murderer."

"And what does that make you?"

"W-what do you mean?"

"Surely you do not see yourself as entirely innocent. You were witness to a mass murder. And, after witnessing it, you went to a motel and made love to the killer who was still drenched in the blood of the victims. That hardly leaves you as an innocent and neutral party to this event."

"Well, I, I mean..." But she realized that he was right. If she were to give an honest account of the events of the last few hours she certainly does not come across innocent of any wrongdoing, and aside from not being totally innocent...

"You enjoyed it. Do not deny it. I may not have several centuries of experience like some vampires do, but I am not a fool. For better or worse you're now an accomplice. Whatever reason that you could convince yourself of you know deep down that part of you enjoyed it. You have tasted the exhilaration of the life that I can offer you and even if you are still afraid of me some part of you does not want to escape."

As much as she would like to deny it, everything he said was true. The last 24 hours have been the most exhilarating experience of her life and not something that she would just want to walk away from.

"Let us see what the damage is," said Eddie as he flipped on the local news channel. As he suspected their little massacre had made the news.

"A scene of carnage is what greeted restaurant patrons last evening," began the news lady. "Mr. John McHale and his wife were passing by and looking for a bite to eat after a long day on the road and decided to stop at Ma's Roadside Burgers. As soon as they looked in the window they met with the site of unimaginable horror – bodies torn limb from limb and completely drained of blood. The bodies were so thoroughly mutilated that they still have not been identified. It is being called a massacre." She pointed the microphone at John and his wife. "Mr. and Mrs. McHale, can you tell us in your own words what happened?"

"Well, we were just stopping in for a bite to eat, like you said, and we looked inside to see if it was crowded and we saw all of these bodies just strewn about the place, with blood splattered all across. I took one look and I just threw up, as did my wife. Then, once we had composed ourselves, we immediately got out of there and called the police."

"Who or what do you think could have done this?" the news woman asked the police officer at the scene. "Do you think it could've been some kind of animal?"

"Well, I don't really know. Whatever or whoever did this was a monster, like some kind of a werewolf or something."

"A werewolf!" laughed Eddie.

"What's so funny?" asked Kristin.

"There's no such thing as werewolves." Eddie laughed some more.

"This coming from a vampire. You mean vampires don't have a secret war going on with werewolves?"

"Not that I am aware of," snickered Eddie. "I have yet to encounter a werewolf, and if they existed I'm sure I would've been informed of it. Most of the things you see in Hollywood or read about in the fantasy section of the bookstore aren't true."

"But apparently vampires are."

"I'm the nonliving proof. But now, be quiet, I want to continue listening to this report."

"In a possibly related case," continued the news woman, "a police officer was found not far from the burger joint, likewise drained of blood and decapitated. His police car was found completely destroyed just a few feet away. Authorities are still looking into it, but whatever we are dealing with is clearly something or someone highly dangerous."

Eddie turned off the TV and smiled.

"What are you smiling about?"

"I'm just very pleased with my work."

"Aren't you worried that you will be caught?"

"I haven't been yet. And I don't intend to anytime soon. They are never going to suspect a man who has been dead for more than two decades of committing a murder in the middle of nowhere. And if they did I would have little trouble taking care of them."

"But what does it mean for us Eddie? Are we just going to stay here?"

"For the time being,why, do you have someplace more important to be?"

"No, you know that I don't."

"So are you going to stay put for now?"

She nodded.

"Good then." Eddie stood up and walked towards the door.

"Where are you going, Eddie?"

"You must be getting hungry. Am I correct?"

She nodded. It was true that she was rather hungry as she never had dinner last night, given Eddie had to eat and run. Plus she had had a very physically exhausting evening.

"I don't suppose you like blood as much as I do?"

"Well I do like red meat. But no, I would prefer some actual food. Do you need any money?"

"No, I'll take care of it. You just get some rest. I'll get us some snacks at the nearby convenience store."

And with that Eddie left.

After a couple of minutes Eddie arrived at the convenience store. He noticed a police car pulled in in the parking lot. Perhaps this was not a good idea. But he was already there so he might as well get what he came for.

Eddie walked quickly up and down the aisles just grabbing whatever snacks and drinks he could find. He didn't bother asking Kristin what specifically she would like and it had been a long time since he had gone food shopping for himself. He almost forgot what it was like to consume something other than human blood.

He saw a few other people in the store. And then he spotted the police officer. The police officer looked suspiciously in his direction, but then turned back to the cashier. He would prefer to wait until the police officer had left before he went to the counter.

Eddie could not resist eavesdropping using his superior hearing abilities. From across the store he could hear the police officer asking the cashier if he has seen any suspicious characters recently. The cashier replied that he had not.

After a few minutes Eddie saw the police officer leave and went up to the cashier to ring up his purchases.

"That'll be $21.95."

Eddie checked his pocket. He only had $15. This was embarrassing. He could just put something back but he felt something welling up inside of him. He began to make tight fists.

"That'll be $21.95," repeated the cashier growing impatient. "Is there a problem? Other people are waiting you know."

Eddie began to tremble. Suddenly the bloodlust was uncontrollable. It was taking all of his concentration to restrain himself.

"What the hell is wrong with you, you freak."

That was when Eddie lost it. He grabbed the cashier by his throat and picked him up with one arm. "Who are you calling a freak?" Eddie began choking him as the cashier's face turned blue. That was when he felt something hit him in the back. He turned around to see a man pounding his back with his fists. "Leave him alone freak!" shouted the man hitting Eddie. Eddie let go of the cashier and threw him up against the wall. He then turned to the man hitting him and grabbed both his arms. "Don't call me a freak!" It was no sooner than he had said that that Eddie tore the man's arms from their sockets.

The cashier began to run and Eddie stopped him before reaching the door. "Where do you think you're going?"

The cashier froze. "Look, mister, I don't want any trouble."

"Well, well, it's a little bit late for that now isn't it?" Eddie lifted the cashier up by his shoulders and bit into his neck. He savored the taste of warm blood wet against his lips. But then he saw that other people in the store were fleeing out the back entrance. He threw the cashier to the side and ran out to the parking lot.

He saw the first person running to their car and leaped on

him from behind and bit into his jugular vein, splattering his blood all over Eddie. Eddie wished that he could savor the experience for much longer, but he saw another customer starting up their car and beginning to drive off. Before he could get more than a few feet away, Eddie jumped on the roof of the car and smashed through the windshield with his fists. The driver stopped the car abruptly throwing Eddie forward. He grabbed the car by the hood and flipped it over onto its back. Eddie tore the door off the car and pulled the driver out. He bit into his neck and this time took a nice long drink, savoring every moment until his victim was drained.

He didn't see anyone else in the area. But just to be sure he went back and finished off his first two victims until he had drained them dry. He searched the store to make sure there was no one else there. He then went through the pockets of his victims and stole the money and credit cards from their wallets. He decided that he might as well stock up on snacks for Kristen while he was there because he wouldn't be coming back, obviously. He also didn't want to leave as much of an obvious trail. This time he would cover his tracks. After looking around for a few minutes he found some lighter fluid which he doused the store in. As he was leaving he lit a match and threw it on the floor in a puddle of the lighter fluid. The place caught fire pretty quickly as Eddie got in his car and sped rapidly away.

What was he thinking committing such an obvious crime in broad daylight? Why was he getting so sloppy? His bloodlust was getting out of control. Usually he could restrain himself, but now his craving for blood was beginning to take control. He would have to be more careful in the future.

Kristin heard Eddie's car pull up at the motel. He quickly ran in after checking to make sure the coast was clear. He slammed the door behind him and Kristen bolted upright in bed. She noticed that he was covered in blood again.

"Here," said Eddie as he threw her a bag of potato chips.

"Eddie, what happened?"

"Nothing, I just got delayed."

"But you're covered in blood! You killed more people didn't you?"

"I lost control. I couldn't help myself."

"What happened?"

"It doesn't matter."

"Of course it matters!"

"Just shut up and eat your damn potato chips. I'm horny and you're going to have another busy night."

Kristen just smiled and began to eat her potato chips. Eddie was right, it doesn't matter what he just did. And that was when she knew that her old life was over and her new life had begun. And she was looking forward to that.

Chapter 4

Reginald was watching the latest on the news from his den as he slowly sipped blood from a wineglass. He turned on the TV to see an image of a burning building in the desert. He turned up the volume.

"And yet another tragedy has befallen a small area in the Nevada desert. A convenience store was found completely burned to the ground with three people dead. Two of the bodies were burned beyond recognition, but a third one was found right outside completely drained of blood with his car flipped over. This report comes just a day after a nearby diner was found to be the site of a massacre, as well as a police officer drained completely of blood not far from there. Investigators believe that the three incidents are related, but so far they have no leads. These killings are being dubbed the vampire slayings and some suspect it may be the work of vampire cultists or Satanists."

Reginald turned off the television and put down the remote. "Eddie," he said under his breath. "I'll bet this is that bastard's work." He pounded his fist on the end table, knocking over his glass of blood. "Dammit...blood stains."

"So you think that it is your young protégé yet again?" asked Thomas as he turned to face Reginald. "I always knew it was a mistake for you to turn him. He always was sloppy and undisciplined."

"I thought that he had changed. I tried to get him under control and it has been years since he has slipped up."

"Well now he has slipped up big-time. This isn't just a drained body here or there of some anonymous person who will not be missed. This is multiple counts of mass murder in a very public manner. He has struck three times in just a few days, pathetic."

"Eddie never was my best work."

"Best work," scoffed Thomas, "he is by far your worst. He is worthless garbage. Of all the people to be granted immortality he is by a wide margin one of the least deserving of such a gift. He is the kind of scum that is only good for feeding on. And even there he isn't the greatest. A disease infected hooker would have been a better meal than him. He wouldn't even qualify as fast food. Had I been there I would've never let you turn him, junkie swine."

"I felt pity for him."

"Pity is something that you leave behind when you cease to be a mortal. It is a quality of human weakness. Those at the top of the food chain should not take pity on their prey."

"Becoming immortal does not mean we should abandon all human qualities."

"Humans are food, nothing more. If we believed that we shared anything in common with humans we would not murder them. But we do. You can pretend to cling to your ancient code of chivalry, but you know as well as I that we are no better than common killers. We all feast upon the living in order to sustain ourselves. Unless you completely disregard that fact there is no way you can see yourself as anything other than a predator."

"But we do have something in common with humans – we were all once human."

"But then we evolved into something above them. But even we have rules and Eddie has failed to play by them. You know what that means."

"Let me talk to him."

"Sure, talk to him, but don't leave him alive once you are finished."

Reginald nodded his head, ending the matter. It was time to pay a visit to Eddie.

Chapter 5

Kristen woke up to find Eddie sitting up in bed, staring at her.

"What's wrong Eddie? Having trouble sleeping?"

Eddie gave her one of his characteristic smiles.

"What are you smiling about?"

"I don't sleep."

"You don't sleep at night?"

"I don't sleep, ever."

"Never?"

"Not usually. It's unnecessary. Sleeping is something you do when you are still alive. The dead have no need for sleeping, why would we? It's not like our body needs to rest."

"So you never rest?"

"There's only one circumstance. When we are badly injured or severely blood deprived we sometimes enter a sleep like a coma. You know all of those legends of the vampire asleep for centuries in his coffin?"

"That really happens?"

"Sometimes, but usually not for centuries. Usually it is a very brief period of time. When we are blood deprived our craving for blood will generally keep us in a very restless state. But past a certain point, especially if injured, we will rest as our body heals. Although I have heard tales of people, or other vampires, who imprisoned troublemaking vampires in coffins for extended periods of time."

"Centuries?"

"By some accounts, although I'm not sure if that is really true. I really don't want to find out. To be imprisoned away from any blood for such extended periods of time could well drive one insane. But I prefer not to sleep. Even before becoming a vampire I never looked forward to sleep. It was one of the things I was glad to get rid of."

"Why?"

"Let's just say I have a lot of issues, issues unrelated to being a vampire. Ironically enough becoming a vampire was the thing that ended my nightmares. If you don't sleep you can't have nightmares. Being dead can be a very restful experience in that regard."

Kristen shot him a puzzled look. "Hmmm...so vampires have nightmares. I never would've thought. What do you have nightmares about? Is it about all of the things that you've done as a vampire?"

"Strangely enough, no. As I've said, vampires don't sleep, so my nightmares ended the day that I died. I feast on living people regularly but that has never bothered me in the least. I do have nightmares about my childhood and my service in the Gulf War. My father was a cruel and abusive man, and it turned me into a cruel and abusive child. He would beat me and my mother when he would drink. He built himself up by putting others down, by making them feel weak and worthless. I hated him, I hated him with all my heart, until it stopped beating, and then I went on hating him."

"My father was the same. He would drink, he would steal from me and he would cheat on my mother until one day she just up and left. We never saw her again. I learned from her example and that is why I ran away as well."

"So I guess we have something in common. We're practically soulmates."

Eddie laughed hard, but Kristen just managed a slight smile. But she couldn't deny that she did feel some kinship with Eddie. She wasn't sure whether it was just a physical attraction or something deeper, but whatever it was it just felt right. Here she was fucking a mass murdering vampire and now they were having a heart-to-heart.

"But it probably suits me to be a vampire. Even if I had never become a vampire I feel that I was naturally inclined towards killing. I was born to be a killer. It was in my blood. As a child I killed animals, in the war I killed enemy soldiers and as a vampire I prey upon the innocent and guilty alike. Killing is all I ever did. If I wasn't a vampire, I would still be a killer, I just wouldn't devour my victims."

Perhaps not the most encouraging thing to hear from the man you're sleeping with, but for some reason she did genuinely feel safe with him. He hadn't killed her so far and it is unlikely that they would encounter anyone that Eddie couldn't handle. So long as he didn't start seeing her as his next meal she was probably safer with him than with anyone else she has ever been with. She always was attracted to bad boys, although she never would have pictured herself being involved with a vampire. But then until just recently she never would've believed that vampires even existed. But she did find the idea of vampires to be sexy, even when she thought they were just fiction. Now she was living the fantasy that many can only dream of.

Before she could respond to Eddie she heard a knock at the door.

"Who could that be Eddie? Does anyone even know that you are staying here?"

"No, they don't."

"Maybe you should just ignore it."

The knocking on the door grew louder and louder. "Open up Eddie I know you're in there!" shouted a familiar voice.

"Reggie," Eddie cursed and turned to Kristen. "Just be quiet and don't say anything. I have to get this."

Eddie opened the door and there stood Reginald in a black trenchcoat and dark sunglasses just like Eddie's.

"Reggie, long time no see. How have things been?"

Reggie slammed the door behind him and pointed accusingly at Eddie. "Cut the niceties, you know why I'm here. This is a real mess you've gotten yourself into Eddie." He looked in Kristen's direction. "Who is she?"

"A friend."

"Just a friend?" asked Reggie, lowering his glasses and revealing glowing yellow eyes.

"Maybe more than just a friend," replied Eddie.

"Does she know about you?" asked Reggie. Kristen's heart began to beat faster and Reggie had his answer. He looked angrily at Eddie. "So she knows everything, doesn't she? That's just great Eddie. It's a wonder you have lasted as long as you have."

"She's not going to tell anyone anything," began Eddie as he turned towards Kristen, "will you?"

Kristen nodded her head but could not hide her

nervousness.

"Of course," said Reggie throwing his hands up in the air, "because it's not like vampires have gone to extraordinary lengths to keep their existence secretive. You're a real piece of work Eddie."

"Yes, I am, your work."

"Don't remind me."

"But don't worry, she has no one to tell and who would believe her anyway?"

"Haven't you learned from your last screwup Eddie?"

Last big screwup? He's done this before, wondered Kristen.

"I'm getting tired of cleaning up after your messes Eddie. You're just lucky that I came alone. I was supposed to kill you, but I guess my human side, my weak side, still pities you and I honestly cannot say why. I guess every creator deplores the thought of destroying his own creation. You are still like a son to me, in some sense, however reckless and irresponsible you may be."

"For what it's worth, I've always seen you as more of a father than my biological father. He never gave me anything, you gave me immortality."

"And I have regretted it every day since."

"And why don't you just do what you came here to do? Why don't you just kill me?"

"If I was going to go through with it, I wouldn't have knocked first. Consider this a warning – a final warning. If Thomas finds out what happened he may not kill me, but he will certainly track you down and kill you."

"If he can find me."

"You weren't that difficult to find Eddie."

"This was a small area. I'm in the middle of nowhere and this is the only motel anywhere near the massacres."

"You probably should have been expecting me then. But I'm serious Eddie, this is your final warning. Don't make yourself a visible nuisance again, or it will be the death of you and whoever you happen to be with at the time."

Reggie looked at Kristen. She gulped and drew back. Her

heart beat even faster.

"Thanks for the warning," said Eddie with a heavy dose of sarcasm. "Glad to see people are looking out for me."

"I mean it Eddie...no more chances. You won't be seeing me again."

Reggie left and closed the door behind him.

"Bye-bye Reggie," said Eddie as he waved at the door. He turned to Kristen. "Sorry about that. I hope he didn't scare you too much."

"Who was that Eddie?"

"Exactly who he said he was, my creator."

"So he was the one who turned you into a vampire?"

"The very same."

"He doesn't seem too pleased with you."

"He never has been. He sees me as immature for a vampire. I'm pretty young as far as most vampires go."

"So he was a much older vampire than you?"

"By about 600 years. I'm not even one century-old. There are normal mortal human beings out there older than I am. But age doesn't necessarily bring greater wisdom. If you spend time with a lot of these old-timers most of them are pretty set in their ways. Some of their views are positively medieval. I guess you never do fully overcome the environment that you were raised in. Even if I live for centuries, I'll always be a child of the 1970s."

"Somehow you don't strike me as a flower child."

"Well, no, I'm really not."

"I guess that there's a lot that I do not know about you."

"What do you want to know?"

"Everything."

Eddie just smirked and nodded his head.

Chapter 6

February 1991

Every night Eddie had the same dream, the same nightmare rather; more of a flashback in dream form. There was his father standing there stinking drunk, so drunk that you could smell the alcohol on his breath from across the room. And there was Eddie's mother cowering in the corner – weak, frightened with a stare of absolute desperation and resignation. Her eyes blackened, her arms bruised and blood running down her cheek.

"Stop it, leave her alone!" Eddie would shout.

His father would turn to him, take a chug of his alcohol and laugh at Eddie. Then in a mocking tone would repeat what he had said in a babyish voice, "Stop it, leave her alone." Then his tone would become more hostile. "Oh yeah, what are you gonna do about it you little faggot. Are you going to just put on mommy's dress and cry like a little girl like you did the other night."

"I mean it," Eddie would yell, "leave her alone."

Eddie's father opened his arms wide and laughed hard as he took another chug from his alcohol bottle. "Why don't you make me then, you weak little piece of shit. What's the matter, tough guy?" Eddie's father moved closer. "Run out of smartass things to say?"

Eddie made fists and looked down at the ground trying to hide his tears.

"That's what I thought. Now come here Eddie. Come on over to daddy."

Eddie shook his head.

"Awww, what's the matter? Don't you wanna give daddy a big hug?"

Eddie shook his head even harder.

"C'mere you little fag. I'll give you something to really cry about."

Eddie began to back off and started slowly walking backwards away from his father.

"Just like I thought, you're totally incapable of being a man and standing up for yourself. You are weak, just like your mother. A weak and pathetic little girl. And you know what a big strong man does to a weak pathetic little girl?"

Eddie shook his head violently as he turned to run.

"Let me show you!"

Eddie's father grabbed Eddie by the back of his shirt, turned him around, held him up against the wall and smacked him hard across the face. Eddie's nose began to bleed and tears streamed down his face.

"Stop crying you weak little faggot!"

Eddie backed into the corner and could not stop his crying.

"Alright then, if you want to act like a little faggot, I will treat you like one."

Eddie's father began to take off his belt and pull down his pants.

"No daddy! Please don't. I'll be good, I promise."

"Weak right up till the end, begging like the weak little worthless vermin that you are."

As Eddie's father came towards him that was when he would wake up screaming in a cold sweat, his heart pounding a hundred miles a minute. His screaming would wake up most of his bunk mates.

"Dammit Eddie," said his bunk mate Walter, "we're in a war zone, but you wouldn't know it over the sounds of your late-night screaming." Walter went over to Eddie and put his hand on the shoulder. "We're all scared Eddie, it's only natural under the circumstances. Anyone could have a nightmare under these conditions. War does that to people."

Eddie shook his head. "It wasn't the war that I was having a nightmare about."

"So you're having nightmares in a war zone, and it's not even about the war? What could be more frightening than a war?"

Eddie put his face in his hands and wept. "My father."

"You're having nightmares about your father?"

Eddie nodded.

"Well, God damn it man. You shouldn't be having nightmares about your God damned father. You should be having nightmares about God damned Saddam Hussein! Are you trying to tell me that you come halfway around the world like this only to have nightmares about your father. Is your father more frightening to you than Saddam freaking Hussein!"

"To me he is. I don't know Saddam Hussein and will probably never see him in person, but I do know my father up close and personal. It is the small, petty tyrannies that confront you in your own life that are more frightening and real to you and some foreign bogeyman in a land you know little about."

"So you've got daddy issues, lots of people do. There's nothing all that strange about that."

"That bastard is the reason why I'm here. All this talk about being a man, proving you're not weak and that you could stand up for yourself."

"So you want to prove yourself to your father?"

"I wanna kill the fucker!"

"Okay, so your issues are a little bit deeper than most people's."

Eddie shook his head and made his hands into fists as he slammed his bed. "You have no idea, you have no fucking idea."

"Normally I would just tell you that you should try and get some sleep, but if you go to sleep I suspect that the majority of us won't get much sleep. So I suggest you just take a chill pill and try to relax and not scream your God damned head off every time you wake up. Think you could try and do that, Eddie?"

Eddie nodded his head and Walter went back to his own bed. Eddie laid back down and stared at the ceiling. He would show the world that he was not weak and he would never allow himself to be weak, to be bullied and bossed around by anyone anymore.

It was a hot day in the desert the day that Eddie's unit had moved into Kuwait. The sky was blazing with the Sun as red as the depths of hell and the background noise was a constant bombardment of explosions that could give anyone an earache in 5 minutes flat. Eddie did not like the heat, nor the noise. He could feel himself sweating like a pig and worried that he was dehydrated as every other breath was labored.

"What's the matter, Eddie," asked Walter smacking him on the back, "can't take the heat?"

Eddie drank from his canteen and wiped the sweat from his forehead. "It's hotter than Satan's colon out here! How the fuck can anyone stand to live in this hellhole?"

"We're liberating these people Eddie."

"Liberating them from what? Once we leave they still have to live in this place, so I hardly consider us to be doing them any great favor."

"It's a noble thing Eddie, to die in order to set others free."

"What about dying to set yourself free?"

"You wanna die Eddie?"

Eddie took another chug from his canteen. "No! I want to kill. I want to kill to prove to myself that I am strong. I'm afraid to die."

"If you're afraid to die then I think you picked a lousy choice of career. There is nothing noble about killing Eddie. Sometimes we have to kill, but killing for the sake of killing is a sin."

Eddie rolled his eyes and drank some more. "Sin," he laughed.

"What's so funny Eddie? I see you wearing that cross all the time, I took that to mean that you're the religious sort."

"You assume wrong."

"Then why do you wear it?"

Eddie wiped away more sweat. "Because it belongs to my mother. It's the only thing I have left of her."

"So you're the sentimental type. You admire your mother?"

"My mother was weak... I won't make the same mistake that she did."

"Damn man, you really do have some family issues. When you get home you should really consider therapy."

Eddie just shook his head and laughed.

The POWs were lined up kneeling on the ground with their hands behind their back. Eddie looked up and down the many rows and counted 120 of them. All of them surrendered. So much for the great Iraqi Army. In Eddie's eyes they all exemplified the cardinal sin of weakness. Looking at them all stacked up like a row of dominoes Eddie fantasized about kicking down each and every one of them and putting a bullet in their heads.

"Pathetic," he said as he spit in one's face. He turned to Walter. "We should execute each and every one of them."

Walter looked at Eddie and shook his head in disapproval. "That wouldn't be right Eddie. They surrendered and are entitled to protections under the Geneva convention."

Eddie scowled. "We risk our lives trying to stop these assholes after they invade an innocent country and we are supposed to treat them with dignity and respect. That's utter bullshit."

"Those are the rules of war Eddie. We are supposed to teach by example."

Eddie began to laugh. "The rules of war, ha! There are no rules to war. There are only two types of people – predators and prey. We have caught our prey because they were weak. We should be able to do whatever the hell we want to them."

Walter was about to respond when one of the POWs leaped up, pulled out a knife and threw it straight into Walter's throat. Blood spouted from his neck like a fountain. It had hit him directly in the jugular. He pulled the knife out of his throat and fell down dead on the ground within seconds.

Before he even knew what he was doing Eddie raised his gun and shot Walter's killer several times in the stomach, causing him to fall down on the ground. Eddie walked over to him, pointed the gun straight in his face and shot him multiple times until he had nothing left that would resemble a head. Then he shot the body several more times and kicked it repeatedly with contempt.

Eddie stood there, covered head to toe in blood. He wiped the blood from his face and licked it from his lips. He began to laugh and laugh before breaking down in tears.

Chapter 7

October 31, 1991

It was a cold night. Eddie had not been with a woman since he had returned from the war a couple of months earlier and on a chilly night like this Eddie sought the comfort of another warm body lying next to his. Her name was Lydia. She was a pale skinned brunette.

"So why were you discharged again?" asked Lydia as she began to undress.

"Temporary insanity and mental disturbance," replied

Eddie as he sat in his bed waiting for her.

"Well, that's certainly reassuring. Tell me again why I agreed to fuck a basketcase."

Eddie laughed.

"You sure laugh a lot, is everything a fucking joke to you?"

Lydia stood there naked with her hands on her hips.

"You aren't fucking a basketcase, you're fucking a Marine. Besides baby, you know that a military psycho has got to be creative in bed."

She rolled her eyes at him. "And didn't you tell me you had your own place?"

"I do."

"This is a shitty apartment Eddie, and the place is a total pigsty."

"Hey, are we gonna fuck or just talk? My roommate will be back in another hour or two."

She began to tap her foot in annoyance. "Well, he better not think that he's going to join us. I don't go out for threesomes."

"Tonight it's just us and baby I'm going to rock your fucking w-world."

Eddie leaned over his garbage pail and began to vomit. Lydia stepped back in disgust.

"What's wrong with you Eddie?"

"N-nothing," choked Eddie before vomiting some more.

"This isn't exactly a turn on you know."

"I'm sorry. I've been like this since I got home. I must have picked up a bug or something while I was overseas."

"And what are all those skin rashes all over you. Did you get those in the war as well, or is it some sexual disease?"

"No, it's nothing like that. I'm f-" Eddie began to choke "-ine." Eddie leaned over and vomited a ton more into the garbage pail.

Lydia began to get dressed. Eddie looked up with vomit drooling down his chin.

"Where you going baby?"

"I'm getting out of here. You clearly have some kind of disease, you live in a rundown filthy apartment and you're a psycho."

"Wait, don't go baby." Eddie puked up another load into the garbage pail.

"Goodbye Eddie." And by the time he looked up from the garbage she was gone.

Dammit, he thought as he pounded the wall behind his bed and vomited some more. He had been sick for a long time and doctors weren't quite sure what was wrong with him. There was only one thing that would help him when he was feeling this sick. He needed to go see his dealer.

Eddie's dealer was a shady looking man in a black trenchcoat named Roscoe. Eddie approached him in a darkened alley not far from his apartment.

"Eddie," said Roscoe walking towards him with outstretched arms, "so good to see you again so soon. What can I do for you this evening. Would you like uppers, downers?"

"I've been feeling sick again."

"Well, I'm no doctor, but then I can get you the stuff they won't write you a prescription for."

"Just give me $300 worth of the works. And none of that low-grade crap you gave me last time."

"Watcha talking about Eddie? You know my stuff is always good."

"Yeah, last time I had a really bad trip and came close to overdosing."

"Well, all things in moderation my good Eddie. Here," he tossed Eddie a small bottle and a needle, "this stuff is good. It'll really fuck you up good. You'll be so high that you'll forget you are ever even sick."

"Fine, but if anything happens to me my roommate knows who you are."

Eddie paid Roscoe and began to walk home, eager to inject his new goodies. What he did not see was another man following him home. The man was dressed in a stylish black suit and worn old-fashioned looking bowler hat like you would see someone in the Mafia wear in all those old gangster films.

As Eddie went into his bedroom he noticed that his

roommate wasn't home yet. It looked like he would be tripping solo tonight. But he couldn't help but feel that he was being watched. But he was probably just being paranoid he thought. He eagerly opened the bottle and grabbed it with his trembling hand as he began to fill the needle. He looked away as he injected it because he did not like the sight of blood.

The drugs began to take effect almost immediately. Eddie began to feel a pleasurable rush as his feelings of sickness dissipated. He started to feel numb like he were floating. His heart began to beat faster and his nausea was replaced by feelings of relaxation and euphoria. Everything in the room began to sway.

That was when Eddie heard his window open. He looked up to see a man dressed like a gangster standing over him. He assumed he was just hallucinating and ignored the man.

Eddie was not hallucinating.

The man looked upon Eddie shaking on the floor. He looked pathetic, drooling like an imbecile. He was the type of person that the world would not miss if he were to die. He was already in the process of overdosing. He looked at Eddie shitting and pissing his pants as he began to choke on his own vomit. He preferred to feed on worthless people, but he never did particularly like junkies. Their blood always tasted rather off, tainted by the drugs.

As he continued to look at Eddie, already in the throes of death and minutes away from his final demise, he suddenly felt an overwhelming sense of pity for the poor pathetic and weak creature writhing on the floor in front of him. He could sense Eddie's heart beginning to fail as Eddie shook violently on the floor. It was now or never.

He leaned down and got on top of Eddie. He bore his fangs and with one quick bite sunk his fangs into Eddie's jugular vein. He began to taste the blood on the tip of his tongue and it took all of his effort to restrain himself long enough to inject his venom into Eddie's bloodstream. He withdrew his fangs, stood up and watched Eddie die.

Reggie waited for several hours as Eddie's lifeless body slowly transformed into one that was simply undead. Eddie's body became pale and cold and his eyes took on a bright yellow glow.

And then finally Eddie woke up.

Eddie awoke with a jolt. The sun had not yet risen and the room was dimly lit, but Eddie's vision had never been sharper. He could read the smallest print on the newspapers sitting across the room. Every small amount of light seemed almost blinding. Eddie covered his eyes, because even the dim light was too intense for his newly sensitive eyes.

"Finally awake I see."

Eddie uncovered his eyes and stared straight ahead at Reggie and jumped back.

"Who are you?"

Reggie smiled. "You could say that I am your maker, the one who has brought you back from the dead. Well technically speaking you are still dead, but that doesn't mean you can't enjoy life to an even greater degree than you did before."

Eddie was confused. "Who are you and what are you doing in my house?"

"Forgive my rudeness. My name is Reginald, although my friends tend to call me Reggie. I had followed you home with the intention of devouring you and feasting on your blood. But something inside of me made me feel pity and I couldn't in good conscience just let you die."

Eddie just stared at him with an uncomprehending stare.

Reggie shook his head. "I can see that I am not getting through to you. Let me explain. I am a 600-year-old vampire and now so are you, well except you are much younger, a newborn babe, in fact."

Eddie raised his arm to block the light from his eyes. "Halloween is over and I don't have any candy for you. I don't know who you are or what you're doing in my apartment, but if you don't leave right away I'm going to call the police."

"You misunderstand me. I am here to help you. A few hours ago you were overdosing on heroin and I, taking pity upon you, decided to turn you into a vampire, rather than let you die. You should be a little more grateful."

"What type of crazy shit are you talking about?"

"If you don't believe me see for yourself."

Reggie pulled out a mirror and put it right in front of Eddie's face.

He cast no reflection.

"What is this, some kind of a trick mirror?"

"Vampires cast no reflection. You are a vampire now, so you no longer cast a reflection."

Eddie stared intensely in the mirror and looked up at Reggie with a dumbfounded look.

"Still don't believe me? Feel your pulse or your heartbeat."

Eddie began to panic. He felt his pulse to see that he did not have one. He then felt his chest to realize that his heart was not beating.

"What have you done to me? How am I even alive? Why isn't my heart beating?"

"Like I was explaining to you earlier, you are now a vampire. Your heart will never beat again but nor will it need to. You are no longer mortal nor bound by mortal necessities. You have awakened on to a new life that will be everlasting."

"I need to get to a hospital."

"You will never need another hospital again. From this day forward will never again know sickness, disease, frailty, or aging. You are now a superior life form free of all the human frailties and weaknesses."

"But I'm not alive!"

"Technically speaking no, you are indeed dead. But in being dead you may find life more fulfilling than it ever was before. Take a moment to think about it. You were sickly and dying and now you are fine. Admit it, you've never felt better in your entire life."

What Reggie said was true. Eddie never felt more alert and could feel no signs of his previous sickness. He could feel a new energy coursing through his veins. But along with that he suddenly felt an overwhelming hunger.

"Why do I feel so hungry?"

"Because your body has already used up its entire blood supply in your transformation and now you crave replenishment."

Eddie grabbed his stomach and felt a moment of disgust.

"But I don't like blood. I've had some bad experiences with it."

"I think you'll find that that will change very quickly. Once you have your first taste of blood you won't be able to get enough of it. You like the feeling of being high? Well, from now on all your highs will come from drinking blood, and those highs will so greatly exceed the high that any of those previous drugs could give you that you will wonder how you ever lived without blood."

Eddie's body ached for blood, it was true. As much as the thought of it made him sick, the thought of going much longer without any blood made him feel even sicker.

"I suppose I probably should have saved you some, but blood is always much better fresh."

Eddie clutched his stomach and looked up at Reggie. "Save me some of what?"

Reggie moved aside and pointed to Eddie's roommate lying dead on the floor completely drained of blood. The sight of it made Eddie feel sick.

"W-what did you do to him?"

"Well I was going to eat you, but since I decided to spare your life I had to find an alternative. I wasn't going to go all night with nothing to eat. I hope you weren't too attached to him."

"He was my only friend."

"I'm the only friend that you need now. The first rule of being a vampire is never to get too attached to people. If they aren't a vampire, you will most likely want to feed on them. And if you have enough self-control to not want to, any given individual you do form an attachment to will eventually die. So I would recommend getting acquainted with solitude as fast as you can."

Eddie felt like he should be mourning his friend but he couldn't concentrate over the overwhelming urge to drink blood that was now consuming his every waking thought.

"When can I feed?"

"I see you are learning fast what your priorities are. You will feed soon enough. But first there are a couple rules to being a vampire that I should probably go over with you. You may want to take notes as today is going to be a long day. But the first day of a new life always is."

It was after sunset that evening that Reggie decided Eddie was ready for his first feeding. Reggie had spent the day teaching Eddie the basics of being a vampire. Now it was about time for him to get some first-hand field experience. Eddie put on the dark sunglasses that Reggie gave him and they prepared to set out for the night.

"So I guess this is sort of like losing my virginity?" asked Eddie.

Reggie laughed. "Something like that. But I don't really think it's comparable. The lust for sex doesn't even come close to the feeling that the lust for blood will now take. Admit it to yourself Eddie, have you ever lusted for a woman with the same level of intensity that you now lust for blood."

Eddie shook his head. "No. Right now my desire for blood is so overwhelming that I would gladly take a small lick of blood over every whore in the country."

"Believe me, once you have gotten your first taste of blood sex will seem like a minor pleasure that you could do without. But you will never be able to go without blood, never."

"But vampires can still have sex, right?"

"Yes, but after tonight you'll see why all other desires are secondary to blood." Reggie turned to Eddie. "Do you have anyone in mind for your first victim? Someone special for your first time."

Eddie cracked a smile. "I've got someone in mind."

Within a short time they had arrived at the alley where Reggie first found Eddie. It took them no time to find Roscoe standing alone in the dark alley like he did every night. Eddie tapped him on the shoulder and he turned around, startled.

"Eddie!" exclaimed Roscoe. "You scared me half to death."

Eddie smirked. "Funny that you should mention death."

Roscoe gulped and Eddie could hear his heart beating faster.

"Why should death be funny?"

"Because that shit you gave me the other night killed me. And what did I tell you? I told you if you gave me bad shit again I would come and get you."

Roscoe's heart was now beating 100 miles a minute. "What are you mean that it killed you? You don't look dead to me."

Eddie lowered his sunglasses revealing his glowing yellow eyes and also bore his fangs at Roscoe. "Then perhaps you should take a closer look."

"W-what the hell?" Roscoe drew back. "Is this some kind of a joke?"

Eddie shook his head. "Killing a man is never a joke Roscoe. But since you seem to be the joking sort I'll ask you a question. Trick or treat?"

"Trick or treat? What's this about?"

"You know, I think I'll show you a trick." And with that Eddie grabbed Roscoe and leapt a good 15 feet into the air before slamming him down onto the ground. Roscoe moaned in pain and Eddie thought he heard something snap. He picked up Roscoe and slammed him up against the wall, holding him up by his shirt using just one arm.

"P-please Eddie, I'm sorry," Roscoe managed to choke out. That was when Eddie saw that Roscoe's nose and face were bleeding. The blood glistened in the pale moonlight and the aroma was beginning to make Eddie intoxicated.

"I'm sorry too. But I will no longer be requiring your services and I don't think I can control myself for another minute. I'm afraid I don't have time for any more tricks, but I do have time for one treat."

Roscoe looked Eddie right in the face and saw his fangs gleaming and before he knew what was happening Eddie had plunged his fangs into Roscoe's neck. The blood flowed instantly into Eddie's mouth and tickled every one of his taste buds. The feeling was electrifying. Within just a few seconds Eddie was experiencing a more powerful buzz than any drug he had ever taken had given him previously. As he gulped back the blood his entire body tingled, it was like a full body orgasm. Once he started drinking Roscoe's blood he couldn't stop. The longer he continued the greater his ecstasy became until he had drained him dry.

Eddie wiped the blood from his mouth and licked what was left with his tongue. Reggie stood there smiling as Eddie fell to the floor, shaking with pleasure and foaming at the mouth with blood.

Reggie came over to Eddie. "So, was it good for you?" Reggie laughed.

Eddie nodded with this stupid crazy grin on his face.

"So was it better than sex?"

Eddie continued to nod.

"Better than any drug that you have ever tried?"

Eddie looked up, still drooling blood and laughed. "Blood is the new Coke. It's better than fucking 100 hookers while high as a kite with an electric wire up my ass!"

Eddie was rolling on the floor and laughing, still covered in the blood of his first victim.

Reggie shook his head and laughed. "You're in hysterics. I would say to try and show some dignity, but everyone gets a little crazy during their first time."

Eddie looked up at Reggie with the look of intoxication still on his face. "I want more."

"You will get more. But first we must dispose of the body. A good vampire never eats and runs if he hopes to eat again."

"I want more...now!"

"In time Eddie, but first things first."

But before Reggie could dispose of the body he heard a scream as he saw Eddie tear a woman off the street and begin chomping down on her neck.

"Eddie! Control yourself!"

Eddie looked up at Reggie with his face covered in blood and while still drooling blood shouted, "I don't want to!"

Chapter 8

"So you and this Reggie guy go back a long time," said Kristen. "I guess you had a falling out at some point."

"You could say that."

"So what are we going to do?"

"Do?"

"Yeah. Are we going to stay here? He sounded pretty serious about his threat."

"I wouldn't worry too much about Reggie. If he had wanted to kill me he would've done it by now."

"What about the other guy, Thomas?"

"Well, he hates me even more than Reggie does. But I'm still not very worried."

"I think that we should get out of here Eddie."

"I suppose I have begun to wear out my welcome. I have made myself a bit too visible. Reggie is right about that. Even if I could keep ahead of him and Thomas eventually regular law enforcement are going to come looking for me. Not that I leave much trace of my existence behind, but I have behaved too suspiciously and stayed in one place for too long. But if we are going to leave we might as well go out on a high note."

"What do you mean by that?"

"By that I mean why leave on an empty stomach? There are probably around a dozen people staying here. A dozen people is a lot of blood."

"Maybe we should just leave well enough alone. You've already killed a large number of people in a short period of time."

"Then what's a few more?" Eddie shrugged with a casualty that suggested the thought of killing people meant no more to him than the swatting of a fly.

"It just seems so unnecessary to go and kill all of these people as well."

Eddie scoffed. "Suddenly having pangs of morality? Feeling remorse? Going to play Little Miss innocent now? I have to eat you know. If I don't feed on these people I'm just going to feed on someone else. Sparing them now isn't going to save anyone else later. Killing is killing, so what does it matter who I kill or where?"

"I was just suggesting..."

"No, I fully understand. You still haven't grown used to this yet. You still see this as a game."

"It's not that."

"I should also point out to you that I need to feed in order to get it up. Vampires need blood in order to get an erection. If you want me to keep fucking you then I would advise you to quit moralizing and let me do what needs to be done."

She wasn't sure how to respond. Maybe she really was just trying to deny her role in all of this. At this point it did little help to delude herself as to the situation. She was in every way fully complicit in Eddie's actions and any remorse she might feel after the fact couldn't really be genuine because...

"If you are really so bothered by what is going on you would have left by now. But you can't. You can't just walk away from this. It's not like some vacation. You are in this for the long haul. You'll be surprised how quick you get used to it. We'll wait until tonight and then I will feast and we will have a night of passion that you won't soon forget. But pack your bags, we might have to leave in a hurry."

They waited until sundown after the majority of the residents had gone to sleep.

"It's time for our night orgy to begin," said Eddie with a big smile.

"What are you going to do?"

"I am going to sneak into their rooms and kill them off one by one. That is the easiest way to do it. Just stay here and wait for me."

Kristen nodded, although she still felt apprenhension at the whole idea of what Eddie was planning on doing.

Eddie went out the door and went to the motel room immediately next to him. The door was locked, but it was easy enough for him to push it in. As soon as he did so he saw an elderly man and woman sit up in bed.

"Who the hell are you?!" shouted the man. But before Eddie could answer he ran up to the couple, grabbed them both by the throats and crushed their windpipes. He then bit into the man's jugular and drained him dry before moving on to the woman. He never much liked the taste of old blood as the elderly often had arteries that are clogged with cholesterol from years of self abuse. As a vampire, you tend to notice these things once you have tasted a large variety of people.

Eddie then moved on to the next room, where he opened the door more quietly. Sleeping in the bed was a blonde woman in her 30s in a blue nightgown. He approached her slowly, covered her mouth with his hand and bit into her neck. The taste of her young, athletic blood was much more appealing than the cholesterol coated blood of the elderly couple. It was a much more satisfying feed.

For the next room Eddie decided it would be easier to go in through the window, which he smashed straight through. Sitting on the bed watching TV was a fat single man. He didn't look the least bit appealing and his blood probably had more cholesterol than it was worth.

"Who the fuck are you and what the hell are you doing?" asked the indignant man.

Eddie laughed as he approached the man.

"You think this shit is funny?"

"Yes, actually, I do." Eddie laughed some more.

"Well, you're not gonna think it's so funny when I kick yer ass!" The man slowly started getting up from the bed but fell down flat on his ass.

Eddie burst out laughing. "Somehow I don't think that is going to happen. Because to kick my ass you would have to get up off of yours, and I don't think that you are quite capable of that."

Eddie ran over to him, grabbed him by the throat with both hands and snapped his neck. He decided he wasn't worth draining. Killing him would be sufficient. Eddie just tossed his lifeless body onto the floor and then picked up the TV and smashed it repeatedly into the dead man's face. He didn't even know why he did it. Maybe he was just tired of showing any restraint. Maybe he was just bored. Or maybe he just really didn't like a worthless fat ass like that enough to afford him any dignity in his death.

Eddie listened carefully for heart beats by pressing his ear against the wall. He heard someone snoring in the next room and didn't even bother using the door this time. Eddie just ran in and burst through the wall and into the next room. There was a young couple in their 20s and before they knew what had happened Eddie was on top of them and devouring them. They didn't even have a chance to scream before their lives were over. Their blood was the tastiest of everyone that Eddie had tasted tonight.

By now Eddie was on a full-blown blood high. He had already drank enough blood to satiate his hunger for weeks, but there was no turning back now. He had to finish what he had started.

The next couple of rooms appeared to be empty but then Eddie approached the door of room number three. He could hear breathing but he was pretty sure that everyone was asleep. He decided it was best that he not make too much noise, so he quietly pushed in the door. As he approached the bed he saw a man and woman with a young boy sleeping between them. The young boy sat up in bed and stared straight into Eddie's eyes. "Who are you?" he asked Eddie. Eddie bore his fangs as his eyes glowed a bright yellow. "I'm Count Dracula, the boogie man and the monster under your bed all rolled into one and I'm here to kill you." The boy paused a moment and then let out one ear piercing shriek.

"What the hell!" exclaimed the father as he bolted up in bed. But before his father even knew what was happening Eddie dove forward, grabbed the child by the head, and turned his head until his neck was snapped. Eddie then bit into his neck and began to suck him dry. The boy's mother woke up just in time to see him die and began to scream herself before fainting.

"You monsterous son of a bitch!" shouted the father as he lunged towards Eddie. As soon as he did so Eddie grabbed him by the neck and threw him up against the wall. As Eddie approached him to move in for the kill he heard a voice behind him.

"What the hell is going on in here, I heard screams."

Eddie turned around to see the motel manager standing in the doorway in his pajamas with his beer gut hanging out. Eddie ran forward, grabbed him by the throat and bit into his neck. Much like the fat single man, this man's blood was thick with cholesterol. Eddie guessed that he would've died of a heart attack anyway, if he had not killed him. In Eddie's warped mind he was doing the man a favor.

As Eddie continued to suck the life out of the motel manager he felt the sting of a lamp as the boy's father smashed it onto his head. Eddie threw down the body of the manager, turned around and smacked the father hard across the face, knocking him to the ground.

"You killed my son! You child murdering monster!" The father could barely speak as blood gushed from his nose and mouth driving Eddie wild with thirst.

Eddie laughed. "Do you really think I don't know that I am a monster. I'll tell you this, it is going to take a lot more than a lamp blow to the head to kill a monster like me."

The father rose to his feet slowly. He grabbed a chair and began to hold it up with difficulty and pointed it at Eddie.

"And what are you planning on doing with that?" Eddie grabbed the chair by the legs and with one great pull tore the chair in half and smashed the two pieces together against the father's head, causing him to fall to the floor. Eddie then ran forward and kicked the father hard in the stomach, causing him to cough up blood. Eddie picked him up by his pajamas and began to lick the blood from his face. "Blood tastes more delicious when it is full of passion and rage." And, without hesitation, Eddie began to bite him in the neck.

With the father now finished off, Eddie turned his attention to the mother who was lying unconscious on the floor. It would be so easy to just kill her then and there. Eddie found himself infuriated that he did not get to kill her in front of her husband. But at least she saw him as he snapped her son's neck.

Eddie approached the woman lying there in her thin, white nightgown that was now stained with drops of blood that had splattered onto her. She looked beautiful, almost angelic, and Eddie was uncontrollably turned on by the combination of sex and blood.

He went over to her, picked her up and gently placed her down on the bed. He grabbed her nightgown and tore it in two, exposing her naked breasts. He could sense her heart beating in panic, even though she had fainted. He could see the blood flowing through her veins, giving her a heavenly glow. He could barely control himself. He didn't want her to be asleep when it happened.

Slowly caressing her breasts he bent down and began to lick them. When she did not awake he lifted her arms up with one hand, holding them up over her head, and he kissed her right on the lips. Then he took his other hand and smacked her hard across the face. She woke with a jolt and before she could say anything Eddie covered her mouth with his hand.

"Do not say anything. I want this to be perfect. It will only hurt for a moment, but I want to look into your eyes when I do it."

She tried to scream but the sound was muffled by Eddie's hand. Eddie turned her head to the side exposing her neck. He couldn't wait another minute longer as the warm pumping of her blood pulsed under Eddie's hand. He extended his fangs, slowly approached her neck, and bit into her. He could feel her trying to scream as he began to drink of her blood. It was the sweetest tasting blood that he has had all night. He continued to drink until he could no longer feel her trying to scream.

He got up off of this young woman that he had just drained of life. Her naked body was now paler than it originally was, and appeared completely lifeless. Small bits of blood stained her skin and Eddie went back and slowly licked up every last drop from her body.

Now every inch of Eddie's body was tingling with excitement. He felt completely bloated with blood and was on a high, one so intense that he had not experienced one like it in years. He felt like he was drowning in a glorious sea of human blood. But he had to compose himself. Taking great care, he piled up all of his victims into the bed together as one big happy family; all pale, lifeless and covered in blood. He took a perverse satisfaction in doing this. He almost felt remorse at having to kill them, but his state of euphoria was too intense for him to feel anything but pleasure at this moment.

He felt like a cigarette. It was odd that he should suddenly desire a cigarette. He had quit smoking the day that he had become a vampire. Drugs, alcohol and nicotine no longer had any effect on him in his undead state. You needed to be alive in order to feel the effect of addictive substances. Now the only thing he was addicted to was blood. Nothing else in this world could get him high the way that blood could.

But still, even if it would have no real effect on him physiologically, the situation called out to him to smoke a victory cigarette.

He searched around the room and was in luck. There was a mostly empty pack of cigarettes sitting on the nightstand next to the bed. He had thought that he could taste the vague hint of nicotine in the father's bloodstream.

Only two cigarettes left. Oh well, that was all that he needed. He searched around and managed to find a lighter. He put the two cigarettes in his mouth and lit up. He inhaled deeply, and blew the smoke out in rings. He had been taught that trick in the Army and it was traditional for him to have a cigarette after every kill. He had abandoned that tradition after he got out of the Army, but doing it again after all these years felt oddly appropriate under the circumstances. And, as an added benefit, he didn't need to worry about lung cancer.

Eddie walked over to the bodies while still smoking the cigarettes. He took another long puff and blew the smoke in the faces of the dead. This act of contempt was unusually satisfying.

He moved closer to the dead body of the mother. She still looked angelic, perfect and without flaw. For some reason that made him sad, and then he grew angry.

Having almost finished the cigarettes, he did not see an ashtray. He leaned towards her still naked body, took the cigarettes out of his mouth and put them out on her dead body, one on each nipple. She no longer looked like an object of abject perfection. For whatever reason, this made Eddie feel better.

Eddie began to count out the number of people he had killed. There should still be two victims left for him to finish off, and the night was still young.

He left the motel room and started to walk along the remaining stretch of the motel, carefully listening outside of each door for signs of life. After passing by a few empty rooms, he heard the sound of a man praying. Well, he thought, it would be rude to allow his prayers to go unanswered.

With one kick of his foot Eddie knocked in the door. It fell with a thud to the floor and the man looked up at him with a startled glance from his desk chair. Eddie smiled at him.

"Who are you, and what the hell are you doing here?" The man turned around in his chair.

Eddie smiled even wider. "Why sir, I am your Guardian Angel and I am here to send you to your just rewards."

"Don't you make a mockery of me boy. I am a God-fearing man and I don't believe for one second that a punk like you is an

Angel."

"Well don't be hasty to judge my friend. I was in a real hurry this morning and left my harp and wings at home."

"So you're a smart ass too."

"Amongst other things, but I am an Angel as well."

"And which Angel might you be?"

"Why am the Angel of death and I have come for you."

The man stood up and waved his finger in Eddie's face. "Now you listen here you stupid punk, I'm going to give you exactly 10 seconds, just 10 seconds to get the hell out of here, and then I'm calling the police."

"My good sir, I don't think the police are going to be much help against me. But I will be honest with you, you are correct that I am not an Angel."

"You think?!" The man's anger and sarcasm were unmistakable.

"But I am also not mortal." Eddie stared at him with his glowing yellow eyes and bore his fangs. The man jumped back in fear.

"You're the devil!"

"The devil! You flatter me! No, I am not the devil."

The man began walking backwards as Eddie walked towards him.

"Then what are you then? A demon?"

"I'm afraid not. I am merely a humble everyday vampire. Sorry to disappoint you."

"A vampire! So you are a servant of the devil."

"I serve no one except myself."

As Eddie approached him and had him backed against the wall in the corner of the room, he held up a cross at Eddie. "Look at this demon!" he shouted as he brandished the cross in Eddie's face.

Eddie lunged backwards covering his eyes with his arm and making hissing noise.

"Take that, you spawn of Satan!"

The man began to walk towards Eddie holding up his cross, as well as taking out a Bible. Eddie walked backwards and then stopped walking, uncovered his eyes and began laughing. "Yeah, that doesn't work. I was just humoring you. I like to fuck with people like that before I kill them. They say you shouldn't play with your food, but sometimes I can't help myself."

"Unholy demon! No servant of Satan can resist the cross and the holy words of God." He raised his cross at Eddie again.

Eddie laughed and pulled out the cross that he was wearing around his neck and shook it at him. "Yeah, I'm afraid I've already got one of those, and it's not a cheap dollar store piece of shit like yours is." Eddie swatted the cross out of his hand on to the floor and then grabbed the man's Bible and started tearing out the pages. "This isn't even good as toilet paper."

The man fell to his knees and put his hands together in prayer. He then began to beg. "Please, spare this old man of God."

Eddie shook his head. "Why should I?"

"Please," he continued to beg, "I've done you no wrong. What purpose does it serve to kill me?"

"I am a vampire, I need blood to sustain myself. It's a simple matter of fulfilling a biological need. Besides, if you believe you're going to a better place, then you shouldn't be afraid. Did Jesus not say to feed the hungry? Did he not say to consume the body and blood? Well I am hungry and you shall feed me."

"Please, please," he continued to whimper as he grabbed Eddie's legs.

"Please don't beg, it's so irritating to me. I don't like food that doesn't put up a fight."

"God will not forgive you for this!" he shouted as tears streamed down his face.

"If there is a God, then when you see him please offer him my most sincere apologies."

The man looked up at Eddie one final time. Eddie looked him deep in the eyes, lifted him up and with one fell swoop bit deep into his neck and drank of his blood.

After checking out the rest of the motel Eddie walked back to his room. Kristen was there waiting for him. "Did you get them all?" she asked. Eddie nodded his head. "As far as I can tell I got everyone who is still present at the motel."

Eddie walked over to the bed and sat down next to Kristen. He was soaked with blood again and his head was still tingling from the blood high.

"You should have come with me. It was pure ecstasy. I can't remember the last time that I feasted so thoroughly. It's like every single cell in my body is on fire. You should have seen the looks on their faces, that was almost as intoxicating as the blood itself."

He tossed her a golden necklace studded with diamonds.

"What's this?" Kristen examined the necklace closely to see that there was still blood on it.

"It's a gift."

"Where did you get it?"

"Does it matter?" She stared at him. "Consider it the spoils of war. I picked it off one of the bitches that I killed. I thought that it would look better on you. So why don't you put it on?"

"I don't know Eddie, I feel kind of weird wearing the jewelry of a dead woman. It just feels wrong."

Eddie pounded his fist against the wall, cracking it. He then turned sharply at Kristen. "You ungrateful bitch. I give you a gift that is probably worth more than anything that you have ever had in your entire life, that may very well be worth more than your own life, and this is the thanks I get. Another lecture on morality from the woman fucking the mass murderer. Tell me my dear –" he moved his face in close to hers and grabbed her neck tightly "– why do I bother keeping you around? Why shouldn't I just complete my rampage and finish you off as well. I'm sure that your young, healthy blood would be delicious."

Kristen gulped and her pulse begin to accelerate. "Well I –"

Eddie began to stroke her hair. "Put on the necklace."

Kristen put on the necklace without bothering to wipe off any of the blood.

"There now, don't we look pretty? Pretty enough to eat. But I'm horny, so I would rather fuck." Eddie looked up and down her body. "Now take off all that clothing. But leave the necklace on. It may not surprise you, but many vampires have a neck fetish. Had I not become a vampire I never might realized just how sexy and appealing a human neck could be."

Kristen got out of bed and slowly undressed. Eddie watched her with his excitement growing by the minute. To him the only thing better than killing was fucking, and by an odd quirk of fate, he was now unable to do one without the other. In order to have sex he would have to kill first. His two greatest passions were now forever linked. But he would have to use restraint if he wanted to avoid killing his latest plaything. He was beginning to despise the very word – restraint. Easier said than done.

Soon Kristen was undressed and standing before him naked, save for her new necklace. Standing there completely uncovered he could see the blood coursing through her veins and could hear her heart beating louder and louder with each passing minute. Her blood pulsated over every inch of her naked body, further exciting his passion.

"I can sense your fear. I must say the fact that you are afraid for your life right now only makes this all the more enjoyable."

Eddie motioned for her to come closer. She got into bed with Eddie. Now she was close enough that Eddie could practically feel her blood under her thin soft skin. He felt like killing her right then and there, but he would have to control himself.

He whispered in her ear. "You know there is nothing more sexy than a frightened creature. All of the senses are heightened, every sensation magnified when you feel it may be your last."

Kristen choked back her fear. "A-are, are you going to kill me?"

Eddie smiled and stared her straight in the eyes as he flipped her onto her back and climbed on top of her. "I don't know yet. But why ruin the surprise. You'll enjoy this more if you don't know how it's going to end."

Kristen gulped some more and began to tremble as she felt Eddie enter her. He stared down into her eyes as he began to thrust. He dug his nails deeply into her back, drawing blood. His body felt warm, she could feel the blood of his newly dead victims coursing through his body. Likewise he could feel her blood pumping rapidly through her veins. Her heart was beating faster than ever before from a combination of fear and excitement.

Eddie grew more and more passionate and she could feel herself covered both in the blood of Eddie's victims that he had never washed off, and her own blood, which Eddie was drawing out of her as his nails dug deeper and deeper into her backside.

She didn't know how long it had continued, but soon Eddie began to shake from excitement. He pinned her up against the wall and bore his fangs at her. Before she could even yell out Eddie leaned forward and sunk his fangs into her neck. She could feel Eddie inside of her as he began to drain her blood. She felt her body growing weaker and weaker as a wave of pleasure washed over her. It was the most intense orgasm of her life and just as it reached its peak she suddenly felt her energy draining. Eddie drew back, with blood dripping from his fangs. She looked up into Eddie's eyes for what she felt was the last time and began to feel herself sinking. And then everything went dark.

Chapter 9

It was several hours later when Kristen finally awoke and the sun was just rising. She felt drained. As she went to get up, she found that she barely had the energy to move. Was she dead? No, of course not; if she were dead she wouldn't be awake right now.

The next question that occurred is what had Eddie done to her?

That is when she remembered how last night ended. She instinctively felt her neck. She could still feel the necklace around her throat. In feeling closer around her neck, she could feel a puncture wound. It wasn't very deep and already seemed to heal, but it was definitely true that she didn't imagine what had happened last night.

Was that why she was so weak?

Eddie must have drained her blood. But apparently he didn't drain her completely as she was still alive.

But perhaps there was another option.

Had he turned her?

She tried getting up again, but could barely raise her body. She was still feeling weak. If she had been turned into a vampire, she should be feeling super powerful right now. That clearly was not the case.

She looked up out the window at the bright sun. The sunlight hurt her eyes, that was true, but that didn't mean that she was a vampire. She didn't feel any more sensitive to the sun than she had before.

No, as far as she could tell she was still a human being and still alive.

She checked her pulse and found that her heart was still beating. Yep, she was definitely still a living, breathing human being and not a vampire.

As she thought further on that she realized she was disappointed. Had Eddie turned her she would've felt much more safe.

Speaking of Eddie, she didn't see him anywhere. Had he left her there? No, he wouldn't do that. He was probably just out checking out his latest work.

That was when she heard it – gunshots. Then she heard a scream.

Within a minute Eddie came bursting through the door, still covered in blood, fresh blood. He tossed her her clothing. "Get dressed, we've got to be leaving," he said.

Kristen rubbed her eyes and struggled to sit up in bed. "W-what, what's going on here, Eddie?"

"Someone saw the results of my latest slaughter and called the police. He came at me with a gun but I took care of him quite easily. Look, I hate to eat and run, but we don't have time to pussyfoot around."

Eddie began frantically packing. Kristen just sat there and stared.

"Well, what are you waiting for?!" Eddie yelled.

Kristen tried standing up, but fell out of bed onto the floor.

"Dammit... I can see that you're still weak from last night. Well, we don't have time."

Eddie came over and picked up Kristen's naked body from the floor and carried her out to the car.

"Eddie," she said in a voice that was barely a whisper, "what if someone sees me?"

"There's no one alive to see you. Don't be a prude. You being seen naked is the last thing we have to worry about."

Eddie started to pull out of the motel and began racing down the desert highway.

Kristen was still delirious but managed to whisper, "Eddie Darling, where are we going to go?"

"We'll find out when we get there. Right now we just have to get away from here, as far from here as possible. I would've liked to have cleaned up my mess this time. I guess I am getting sloppy. But that's what happens when you're on a blood high. The intoxication of the blood takes over and it is impossible to think straight."

"B-but, I, I think that we should have some idea of where we are going."

Kristen began to shiver and Eddie wrapped a blanket around her.

"I was thinking maybe we could head down to Vegas."

"V-Vegas?" Kristen managed to mutter beneath trembling lips.

"Yes. I figured that if we could get enough money we could set up somewhere more accommodating and stay off the grid for a while until the panic and media frenzy manages to die down a bit. I also want to try and put as much distance between us and Reggie as possible. This incident at the motel certainly won't slip beneath his radar. And as soon as Thomas hears about the massacre at the motel, he will know that Reggie did not kill me and will be down here very quickly. We have to lay low for a while."

Kristen looked at Eddie and smiled feebly. "I always wanted to visit Vegas, but I could never afford it."

"Well, you don't have to worry about that. Luckily I managed to pocket enough money and jewelry off of my victims to keep us going for a while. And I'm a pretty good poker player. I could probably take a couple of hundred dollars and turn it into thousands. Then we could live good for a while. And Vegas is a big city, it is easy to hide there. It is also easy to find victims who will not be deeply missed by the majority of society. Anyplace that attracts addicts and lowlifes is a good place for vampire to feed inconspicuously."

"Eddie?"

"Yes?"

"Am I going to die?"

Eddie looked at her and shot her one of his big smiles and began to laugh. "No, you aren't going to die. I just got a little carried away last night. I probably shouldn't have drained you so much. But you'll recover, I wouldn't let my latest plaything escape from me so easily."

And even though those weren't the most comforting words he could've offered to her, they somehow made her feel safe. If she was still alive after everything that happened last night it means that he still wanted her around and was able to restrain himself enough that she didn't have to fear for her life. For now, that was comfort enough, and she soon fell into a peaceful sleep.

After several hours, Kristen awoke feeling much more rested and recovered, but still mostly pretty weak. By then the sun had almost gone down and it was beginning to get dark. She rubbed her eyes and looked up at Eddie who had removed his glasses.

"So, you are finally awake. Feeling better?"

Kristen nodded. "Yes, but I think that I have to pee."

"I'll pull over on the side of the road."

Eddie stopped the car and Kristen hobbled out. She hadn't even remembered that she wasn't wearing any clothes but then realized as soon as she felt the cold and attempted to cover herself up with her hands.

"What if somebody sees me?"

"You still worried about that? In all the hours we've been driving I haven't encountered a single person who has noticed. We are in the middle of nowhere. Don't be so shy. I know you're no prude. Just go squat behind the car and I'll stand watch."

Kristen went behind the car, squatted down and relieved herself. Eddie couldn't help but stare.

"Eddie, you're supposed to be looking out for passing cars."

"Don't worry, I-"

But before Eddie could finish Kristen let out a scream and came running towards him. She jumped naked into his arms.

"What's wrong?"

"I saw a rattlesnake!"

"Where?"

"Right there," she said as she pointed to the rattlesnake right near the car tire.

Eddie laughed as he leapt forward and grabbed the serpent by its neck. He then brought it towards Kristen's face and she ran back screaming.

"What's the matter? It's just a little snake." He laughed some more as he walked towards Kristen, who continued to walk backwards until she fell right on her butt.

"Stop it Eddie! This isn't funny."

Eddie laughed even harder. "What's not funny about this? You're sitting there buck naked in the desert sand scared to death of a little rattlesnake."

"Snakes are poisonous Eddie!"

Eddie smiled. "Let me show you a trick." Eddie dangled the snake by its tail and it turned around and bit him right in the chest. He let go of the snake and let it hang there. "Tada!" he exclaimed. "How many snake handlers have you seen that would let the snake bite them right in the chest?"

"Not everyone is immortal, Eddie."

"That is true, but it is also true that some of us are. And those of us who are, aren't afraid of anything." Eddie pulled the snake off of his chest using two fingers and crushed its head. "There, it's dead. Happy?" Eddie threw the snake away. "His venom isn't anywhere near as powerful as mine."

Kristen walked over to Eddie, rubbing her naked body with her arms, trying to warm herself up. "I'm cold Eddie. I'm going to get sick out here."

"C'mere," said Eddie as he motioned with his finger. Kristen came over to him and he pushed her down onto the hood of the car. He looked into her eyes and began stroking her hair with his cold, icy fingers. "It's time that I warmed you up." She began to feel Eddie enter her, thrusting hard and pushing her against the hood of the car. She moaned with pleasure. He whispered in her ear, "You know there are some who say that the snake that seduced Eve in the garden was actually a vampire." She turned and looked into his eyes and whispered back,"Is that true?" Eddie looked at her and smiled,"I have no fucking idea, and frankly I don't give a damn." He thrusted hard one more time and then walked away.

Kristen slowly got up from the hood of the car and hugged her body.

"Still cold even after all of that?"

Kristen nodded with her teeth chattering.

"Then I guess you'd better get dressed. You will catch pneumonia out here. Besides, I know you don't want anyone to see you."

Kristen smiled at Eddie as he tossed her her clothes from the back of the car. "I'm not worried about that anymore."

"You're not? Why is that?"

"Because I know you're the only one I want to see me. And I know if anyone else saw me that you would totally fucking kill them."

Eddie smiled again at Kristen. "C'mon, get in the car. We still have a long way to go and it's getting late."

Kristen got in the car and they sped off into the darkness.

Chapter 10

It was just after 10 PM when they arrived in Vegas. Kristen grew excited as she could see the lights of the city before them. At last she was finally getting to fulfill her dream of getting to go to Las Vegas. Of course, in her dreams she never pictured herself going there escorted by a vampire sociopath, but then no one's dreams are ever fulfilled in the exact manner that they would have imagined them.

"So," said Eddie, "what is it that you wanted to do first in Vegas? You said it had always been your dream to come here. Did you have any specific plans in mind?"

"Well, I always dreamed of coming here and maybe working as a cocktail waitress in one of the casinos." Kristen blushed a little bit after admitting that. She put her hand on her cheek. "You know I never admitted that anyone before. Sounds pretty stupid, doesn't it?"

"Not at all. I think that you would make a very attractive cocktail waitress. It shouldn't be something that would make you blush, although I must admit, it excites me to see you blush."

"It does?"

"Yes, though not for the reason that you might suspect. When you blush I can more easily sense the blood coursing beneath your skin. The closer the blood is to the surface, the more irresistible it is."

"I'm surprised I have any blood left after what happened last night."

"Don't worry, I can control myself. I never take more than I need, usually. I only took a little bit from you, but it was hard to restrain myself. For a vampire on a blood high restraint is one of the most difficult things in the world. Once we start drinking blood it is often hard to stop. That is why we usually only try to take a little bit. But draining a dozen people like that has the same effect that alcohol has on normal humans. Once you drink too much, your judgment begins to fade and rational thinking goes out the window."

"But still, you are able to restrain yourself from killing me."

"Yes, you must have that effect on me. The last time I was on a blood high like that, I had to be stopped by someone else."

"You mean Reggie?"

"Yes. He is a much older vampire and has learned better self-control over the years. Younger vampires, such as myself, often have great difficulty with moderation. Reggie acted as my mentor and was able to to keep me from getting carried away. Before we parted ways, he had saved me several times when I did get carried away."

"Are you getting carried away now?"

"Don't worry, you are safe with me. I may have gotten a bit carried away, but I am beginning to come off of my blood high. You have to understand that even a small amount of blood is intoxicating to us. Most vampires never learn restraint and end up getting themselves destroyed rapidly. Without a good mentor to teach you the ropes it is very easy to slip into bad habits. Many vampires get their first taste of blood and are simply unable to stop. Once the body gets used to it, you can learn to control yourself better, but every time we feed a frenzy sets in. That is why we try to only take a little bit of blood at a time and limit our number of victims. If we feed too frequently we can become intoxicated in the way that I had been after our latest massacre. All things considered, you probably are lucky to be alive."

Eddie laughed, but Kristen did not smile. He could sense how nervous she was.

"Well," she said, "I have to admit that I have given blood before and never was it this exciting."

"There are some vampires who prefer to rob blood banks or feed on animals, but they are a minority. Very few can resist the intoxication that comes from drinking from a live human being. Nothing else fully satisfies the thirst. You can survive that way, but you can't really live."

Kristen managed a faint smile but was still looking rather pale.

"I can see that you are still weak. I probably took more from you than was healthy."

"Well, when you donate blood, you are only supposed to give it once every so often. You're only supposed to take a little bit at a time."

"When we get to a hotel, I will get you some orange juice. Once you have rested for a while and gotten your strength up, we will paint the town red!"

Kristen smiled a bit bigger this time. "I thought we were trying to avoid a bloodbath this time."

Eddie smiled. "Come on, we'll go find a fancy hotel. This is your first trip to Vegas, so we might as well live it up. How does Caesar's Palace sound to you?"

"Do you really think that we can afford that?"

"With all the money that I took off of the people at the motel, I think that we can afford the deluxe suite. As I said, we might as well live it up while we are here."

"Well I guess you only live once." Kristen smiled and ran her fingers through her hair.

"When you are immortal, once is all you need. And just because you have an eternity doesn't mean you should put off enjoying yourself until a later time. That is the first rule of being immortal."

"How long do you think we can afford to stay here?"

"That depends on how much I win. I told you that I am a good gambler. We have plenty of money to gamble with, so we might be able to stay here indefinitely."

"Do you think that Reggie knows what has happened by now?"

"I'm sure if he hasn't, he will soon enough. Word travels fast. With any luck he won't be able to track us down. We just have to lay low for a while. But don't worry, I haven't lasted this long without learning a few tricks of the trade. Now let's get to a hotel so you can get some rest."

Kristen nodded.

Within a short time they had arrived at Caesar's Palace. A bag boy soon came to escort them to their room.

"Welcome to Caesar's Palace, here is your room," said the bag boy as he threw their suitcases onto the bed.

"This is lovely, Eddie," said Kristen, "it's even more beautiful than I ever imagined it. I can't believe that I'm actually here."

Kristen and Eddie surveyed the room. Their accommodations here were a big improvement over the motel where Eddie had been staying for the past couple of weeks. There was a king sized bed, a couch, table, big-screen television and a great view overlooking the city. Kristen went to go and look at herself in a large golden mirror on the wall. Without thinking, Eddie came up behind her and only then did he realize his mistake. The bag boy was looking right at them and they could only see Kristen's reflection in the mirror. He quickly moved out of line with the mirror.

The bag boy turned around and gave a look of bewilderment.

"Is something wrong?" asked Eddie as he backed away even further from the mirror.

"N-no," muttered the bag boy, "my eyes must just be playing tricks on me. If there is anything that you need, don't hesitate to call room service."

The bag boy backed out of the room slowly getting another glance towards Eddie, who lowered his glasses and glanced back. The bag boy ran off clearly looking perturbed.

"What was the matter with him?" Kristen asked.

Eddie walked over to the mirror and stood in front of it. "He must've seen my reflection, or lack of one, rather."

"Oh, no!" Kristen said as she covered her mouth with her hand. "Should we be worried? Maybe we should leave."

Eddie shook his head. "Nah, I wouldn't worry about it. It was a careless error on my part, but I would not worry about it. I've had a lot of experience with these matters. The majority of people, when confronted with something illogical or frightening ,will dismiss it out of hand or convince themselves they didn't see it. I doubt that he will tell anyone what he saw and if he does the response will probably just be laughter and ridicule."

"But what if he doesn't!"

Eddie put his hand on her shoulder as they both stood staring into the mirror at her reflection and whispered in her ear, "then I will take care of him."

A shiver went up Kristen's spine and she sat down on the bed. "I'm still cold Eddie. And I still feel weak."

"Why don't you take a hot bath and then get some rest, and then, in the morning, we will order you the biggest breakfast you have ever had in your life."

She looked up at him, smiled and nodded. "That sounds good Eddie. But what about you?"

"I think that I will go check out the casino. I do all of my best gambling at night. And this is a town that is made for the night life."

"It's the perfect place for vampire!" laughed Kristen. "I'm surprised you haven't come here sooner."

"I never said that I haven't."

"So you have been here before then?"

"Yes, a long time ago. Both as a human and as a vampire."

Kristen looked up at him with a worried glance. "Did, did you feed here?"

Eddie paused a moment before answering. "Yes."

They both sat there enduring an awkward silence before Kristen finally broke it. "So I think I'll be taking my bath and then I'll probably go to sleep." She touched the place on her neck were Eddie had bit her.

Eddie stared at her for a moment, his eyes invisible under his dark sunglasses."That sounds good. You need your rest. I will try to be here when you wake up."

"What if something happens and I need to reach you?"

"I'll be around, don't worry. I am sure that nothing will go wrong. But just to be safe, I would lock the door."

Eddie started to walk towards the door and slammed it shut behind him.

Kristen was shivering so decided to draw her bath. She undressed and carefully hung her clothing on the towel rack. She took off her necklace and put it down on the sink. She slowly filled the tub with warm water and gently sat down. The warm water felt good against her cold skin. She instantly felt it warming her body and she soon fell into a state of deep relaxation. And before long she had fallen asleep.

As soon as she fell asleep she began to dream. She saw herself walking alone on a foggy beach with the water crashing at her feet. In the distance, she saw a man approaching from the shadows. As she walked closer, she saw his face – it was Eddie. She ran to him and embraced him. She could feel her head against his chest, but could hear no heartbeat. He was cold to the touch and that caused her to shiver. "I'm cold Eddie," she told him. He said nothing in return but held her tightly. "You know, Eddie," she said as she rested her head against his chest, "I think that I love you." Again he said nothing. She looked up at him and saw his fangs exposed. He leaned forward, pushed her hair aside, and bit hard into her neck. She could feel the blood dribbling down her neck and onto her naked breasts. She felt the life draining from her body and could feel the water rising around her. She opened her eyes to see that she was drowning in a sea of blood. As she slowly sunk beneath the red waves of blood, she felt herself beginning to drown.

She awoke with a start to find she had fallen asleep in the tub and sunk underneath the water. Her heart was beating fast, and it took her a moment for her to regain her composure and realize where she was. The first thing she did was feel her neck. The puncture wound had almost healed. She then looked around and saw that she was alone. It was just a dream, a nightmare. Yet at the same time, she found it a strangely pleasurable one.

Years ago, she had kept a dream journal, but abandoned it after someone accused her of having her head in the clouds. She had gone through an introspective phase then and had always felt that her dreams were trying to tell her something. Was this dream a warning about Eddie? She couldn't be sure of the answer. But she could be sure, that in spite of everything that has happened, she couldn't deny how she felt about Eddie.

But now probably wasn't the best time to think about that. She had had some of the weirdest and strangest days of her life these past few days, what she needed now was rest. Once he had regained her strength, then she could decide what she would do next.

She got out of the tub, dried herself off and put on a new bathrobe. She then climbed into bed and fell fast asleep, faster than she had ever fallen asleep before.

Chapter 11

Eddie surveyed the casino. Even though it was the middle of the night there were plenty of people still playing the slots. But Eddie wasn't really much of a slot player. With a slot machine, he had no real advantage. A vampire didn't have greater luck than the average person and the odds were just as stacked against him as anyone else. The real advantage that vampires had was in a game like poker. Although he was no psychic, with his ability to sense people's heart beats and pulse he could detect stress and signs of anxiety. You really couldn't fool a vampire with a poker face.

Eddie made his way over to the poker tables. He was one to play with high stakes. Altogether he had stolen over $10,000 from his victims at the motel. He was hoping he could make several times that amount through playing poker. He had done that before, he was confident that he could do it again. He hasn't been around here in a long time, so he figured it is doubtful anyone will recognize him.

He was going to go over to a poker match until he realized that there was a mirror right behind the poker table. That was one disadvantage of being a vampire. He would have to find another table.

After several minutes of looking he found a table in an area without any visible mirrors. He sat down with a group of seven other men wearing suits. They looked like the classy type of high stakes players that he was looking for.

"The opening ante is $100," said the dealer.

Eddie nodded in agreement and put forth his chips. "I'm in."

The dealer dealt the cards. Eddie had three of a kind. He could do worse. He looked around at the other players and listened carefully for the beating of their hearts. He could see that one man's heart was beating very rapidly, so he probably didn't get the greatest hand. He also might have a cholesterol problem and it's a wonder he hasn't had a heart attack yet. He listened closer as he looked over the next man who was scratching his head. Eddie could detect a mildly raised pulse rate, but nothing dramatic. It seems like most of them, whatever they may have gotten, were able to stay calm.

Suddenly Eddie's attention became completely fixated on one man in particular. Like Eddie, he was wearing dark sunglasses and had a pale complexion. He was tapping his fingers on the table but that was when Eddie noticed the most significant thing – the man had no heartbeat whatsoever. The only way that could be possible was that he was a vampire. He could see the man looking over at him. Vampires could always detect their own. He couldn't believe that he didn't notice right away. He really must be getting even more sloppy.

One of the men at the table decided to raise the ante by $100. Eddie decided to fold.

Once the game was over the pale faced man walked over to Eddie and put his arm around him. He lowered his sunglasses and looked Eddie right in the face. "Eddie," he said, "you old bastard, how are you doing?"

That was when Eddie realized who it was. This was

Marcus, one of Eddie's oldest friends and one of the first vampires that he had met after being turned. Eddie could remember the first time that he had met Marcus. It was in 1992, just a couple of months after he had been turned.

Marcus was one of the oldest vampires that Eddie has ever known. He had been a male prostitute in ancient Rome, a sexual performer at Emperor Tiberius's Palace on the island of Capri. It was there that he became a personal favorite of Caligula and kept the emperor's loyalty by helping him to indulge every vice. He became a gladiator, but was tragically injured before the emperor's very eyes. As they dragged his bleeding carcass off of the arena, a strange pale skinned man had come up to him and began to drink his spilt blood. That man then bit him. Several hours later he awoke into his new eternal life. He never saw the one who turned him again.

More significantly, Marcus was the vampire who had turned Reggie, and that is how Eddie knew him.

Eddie looked his old friend straight in the eyes and slapped him hard on the back. "Who are you calling an old bastard? Last time I checked you've got a good two millennia on me."

Marcus began to laugh. "That's true. You are so young that you are practically a mortal. There are old purely human men in nursing homes who are older than you."

Eddie smiled at his old friend. "So, what have you been up to?"

"You know, the same old, same old. A little debauchery, a little bit of murder, and a little bit of gambling."

"Don't you find it a tad bit ironic that you're hanging out at Caesar's Palace?"

"What can I say, you are always nostalgic for the era in which you grew up. This isn't quite the same as Caesar's actual Palace, but it always brings back fond memories to surround yourself with the familiar. But what I should be asking is, what have you been up to?"

Eddie averted his gaze and looked down at his shoes. "You know, same as you. All vampires tend to make a habit of murder."

Marcus told Eddie closer and whispered in his ear, "I know what you have been up to, Eddie. Word travels fast. You have been making yourself very visible, Eddie. It isn't good form for a vampire to get himself this much attention."

Eddie frowned. "I see that you have been talking to Reggie."

Marcus drew back and gave him a puzzled look before laughing. "Ha! I haven't spoken to Reggie in years."

Eddie looked at him with bewilderment. "You haven't? Then how have you heard about my latest exploits?"

Marcus shook his head in astonishment. "It's not as though you have made any effort to hide what you have done. Mass murder on such a large scale and in such a gruesome and grisly manner becomes national news very quickly. You are practically the new Jeffrey Dahmer. Three incidents of mass murder in the same location in a few days of each other, people aren't stupid Eddie. I'm sure that every vampire in the world can recognize this as the work of their own kind. Sure, normal everyday humans refuse to acknowledge the existence of supernatural creatures such as vampires, but you must be extremely naïve if you don't think this is the biggest news amongst vampire kind at the moment. Eventually even the humans will catch up with the obvious. See for yourself."

Marcus pointed to one of the televisions in the bar. News reports were discussing the nationwide manhunt that was being launched to find "The Vampire Serial Killers", responsible for these murders.

Marcus shook his head back and forth."This is very sloppy work Eddie, very sloppy. Had you stopped at the diner maybe people would've believed that it was an animal attack, but three identical attacks; give the police some credit Eddie. They have already put together the pieces and realize that this is the work of a systematic killer or killers. I'm presuming that you're working alone."

"Sort of."

Marcus raised his glasses and looked at Eddie with shock. "What do you mean...sort of? Do you have other vampires involved with you?"

Eddie shook his head and looked away from Marcus. "Not exactly."

Marcus began to grow indignant. "Be straight with me Eddie, what the hell is going on with you?"

"It's a woman, a human girl."

"I should have known! You're not thinking about turning her, are you? Not like last time."

"No, it's not like last time. Right now she is still completely human."

"Does she know...what you are?"

Eddie nodded. "She knows."

"And she's completely fine with that?"

"She seems to have accepted it."

Marcus shook his head violently and put his hand to his forehead. "This is really reckless Eddie, even for you. You've been a vampire for over 20 years and you still haven't learned to stop thinking with your dick. Do you know what would happen if she were to turn you in?"

"Of course I do, do you think I am stupid?"

Marcus smirked. "Do you really want me to answer that?"

"Don't worry, I trust her. She's in this too deep to get out of it now. She has nowhere else to go and no one would believe her story anyway. I'm pretty much all she's got."

"You know Eddie, vampires haven't managed to stay in the shadows for thousands of years by being reckless. We choose victims carefully for a reason, so that no one will miss them when they're gone."

"I didn't just become a vampire yesterday, I know that. She isn't exactly famous. She's a teenage runaway from a loveless home. It's doubtful that anyone is even looking for her, and if something were to happen to her it's doubtful that anyone would care enough to file a report. She's about as anonymous and unconnected as people can get."

Marcus continued to shake his head in disapproval. "Still, how long have you known her for? How can you be sure that you can trust her?"

"I've known her long enough."

"And what are you doing making friends with humans like that anyway?"

"I got lonely."

Marcus snorted a laugh. "Well, hell, we all get lonely Eddie. But why would you want to make friends with humans? To just be more lonely when they eventually die?"

"Because limiting yourself to vampires doesn't leave for a very active social or sexual life."

Marcus slapped Eddie hard on the back. "Well, my friend, you just don't spend enough time with your own kind. Spend some time with me and I will show you the kind of fun that only vampires can have. What do you say? I will teach you how to have a good time and to be discreet about it."

Eddie stood there for a moment, staring at his old friend, before nodding in agreement.

"Good. You don't get to be 2000 years old without learning a few tricks of the trade. It seems I will have to take you under my wing again and give you a refresher course in the vampire basics. And I know just where to begin."

Marcus took Eddie to his limousine. It was a fancy white limousine with steer horns as a hood ornament. The license plate was from Texas.

"So," said Eddie, "I see you have spent some time in Texas. I wouldn't have thought of Texas as a place that would be favorably inclined towards vampires, being in the Bible belt and all."

Marcus laughed and put on a cowboy hat. "Trust me I didn't stick around very long. It doesn't take very long in a small town for people to get suspicious, especially when you do not seem to age. I had spent a lot of time in Texas because I was waiting for an old millionaire to die and leave me his fortune. It pays to make friends in high places. That is the way you can survive incognito as a vampire for so long. You just have to know who you can trust. And one thing that you can always count on is that the rich are willing to give a lot to people that they believe have unlocked the secret of immortality."

Eddie smiled. "So I take it that you promised him more than you eventually gave him."

Marcus tipped his hat and nodded. "As soon as he signed his estate over to me I didn't hesitate to give him the secret of immortality – a tall glass of various poisons that I had mixed together. Just because a person is rich doesn't mean they got rich through their own wisdom. There is much to be said for generations of inbreeding among the nation's aristocracy. As soon as I inherited it all, I immediately transferred all of the money into numerous secret accounts under various aliases. No one will ever trace me and I will continue to live the high life in complete and utter anonominity. That, my friend, is how you stay alive as long as I have." Marcus opened the door to his limousine. "Now, shall we depart?"

Eddie got into the back of the limousine. The windows were one way – you could see out but no one could see in. It also provided a perfect shield against the sunlight.

Eddie leaned back into the comfortable leather seating. "I have to admit, this is a pretty nice life that you have built for yourself, Marcus."

"Well, I try my best. That's one thing that you young vampires have yet to learn. You have yet to learn how to be a vampire in style. Even back in ancient Rome, I knew how to live the high life and I knew who to rub elbows with in order to keep living that life. An eternal life span and a couple of wise investments and inheritances and you can keep yourself living the good life for centuries at a time. I have lived for 2000 years and I have spent most of that time living in a life of luxury. You have much to learn Eddie, much to learn."

"Well I am eager to learn. Where do we start?"

"I will start by showing you how to eat well without being sloppy and leaving a mess behind."

"Where are you taking me?"

"You'll see when we get there. Trust me, you won't be disappointed. It's a little ways away, but we will be there shortly."

After about an hour they arrived at their destination. It was a small brothel in the middle of nowhere called Honey's Honeys.

Eddie looked towards Marcus. "This doesn't look very fancy Marcus."

"Don't be deceived by appearances. It is a matter of quality and discretion. This place doesn't even appear on the map, but the women there are some of the highest quality hookers that money can buy without anyone asking any questions later. Just follow my lead."

Marcus got out of the limo and did what appeared to be some kind of secret knock on the door. What appeared to be the whorehouse madam appeared at the door, dressed in a gold leotard and brandishing a shotgun.

"Hey Ilse, what have you got for me on the menu tonight?"

She raised her eyebrows. "So, back so soon are we? And it looks like you've brought a friend this time." She looked in Eddie's direction and cocked her shotgun.

"This is Eddie. I promised him a good time."

She looked Eddie over carefully, examining him as though she were sizing him up. She nodded in approval. "He looks rather pale, he's one of your kind isn't he?"

"Is he that obvious? It's true he's not the most discreet vampire out there. But he's an old friend and I feel obligated to show him the ropes. So what do you have for us tonight?"

Ilse motioned for them to come in and they quickly shuffled in and closed the door behind them. She led them to a back room where several women were sitting on a gold leather couch.

"These are new arrivals," said Ilse as she waved her arm in their general direction. "Take your pick."

Eddie and Marcus walked up and down the row of women seated on the couch. There was a wide variety of women to choose from. All of them looked rather young and thin though, and one woman in particular reminded Eddie of Kristin. She had long red hair and a pale complexion. He found himself irresistibly drawn towards her.

Marcus came over to Eddie and saw him sizing her up.

"So Eddie, did you find something you like? She looks like a rather tasty little dish. It's all on me, of course. And if one isn't enough, feel free to select more than one."

"No, "said Eddie as he shook his head, "she will do just fine." Eddie licked his lips slightly, exposing his fangs.

"Well then," said Marcus as he approached a petite, dark-haired Asian woman dressed in a purple leotard, "I think I'm in the mood for an Oriental dish this evening." Marcus took her hand and led her away from the couch as she smiled at him.

Eddie took the redhaired girl and led her away from the group.

"So have you made your selection for the evening?" asked Ilse with a devious smile.

Marcus nodded in her direction. "I think that we've got everything we need, right Eddie?"

Eddie nodded. "I'm good here."

"Well, then have a good evening, gentlemen," said Ilse. "And make sure you bring them all back in one piece." Ilse winked in their general direction.

Eddie and Marcus escorted the girls to the limousine and waved to Ilse in the doorway. She waved back with an ominous looking smile.

Eddie sat between the redhead and the Asian woman and Marcus sat next to the Asian woman.

"Comfortable ladies?" asked Marcus. "Would you like anything to drink?"

The two women looked at each other and nodded, happy to be getting so much attention from wealthy men like this.

"We have the finest wine," said Marcus as he popped the cork, "aged to perfection."

"Some of this wine is older than me," joked Eddie.

"I doubt any of the wine is older than me," laughed Marcus.

The two women laughed as Marcus poured them sparkling glasses of red wine.

"And how old are you?" the Asian woman asked.

Marcus leaned in close to her. "Let's just say I'm older than any wine than you have ever tasted."

She giggled as she sipped from her wineglass. "Funny, you don't look like you're a day over 20."

"Why thank you. I guess that I just age well." Marcus laughed loudly.

"So are you going to have any wine?" she asked Marcus.

"I never drink...wine," he responded before bursting out laughing.

With that, they all began laughing. Marcus doubted that she got the reference, but he didn't particularly care either way. He hated having to make small talk.

"So," said Eddie as he turned to the redhaired girl, "what is your name?"

"Kyra," she said.

"I'm Tania," said the Asian girl.

Marcus began to snicker.

"What is so funny?" asked Tania.

"Nothing," replied Marcus, "I just don't much care what the name of my next meal is."

"So do you like to do it anonymously?" asked Kyra.

"After you have lived long enough and devoured as many women as I have, they all start to seem anonymous after a while."

"So you are a regular Don Juan then?" asked Kyra

"I've just been around for a very very long time," said Marcus. "A very very long time."

"Well," said Tania, "like I said, you don't look like you're a day over 20 to me."

Marcus just smiled and shook his head. "Appearances can be deceptive. For example, you probably think we are just two horny young guys looking to get our jollies off with a couple of cheap whores. But it is so much more than that."

The two girls looked at each other nervously.

"Oh really?" asked Tania. "Do you have something greater in mind for us?"

"Yes, in fact we do," said Marcus.

"And what exactly is that?" asked Kyra.

"Well if I told you that, it would ruin the surprise," laughed Marcus. "But first things first –"

Marcus began to fondle Tania's breasts and put his hand between her legs. Eddie began to do the same to Kyra. As soon as they had started they could feel the sweet presence of blood beating rapidly through the girls' veins. It was intoxicating being so close to the object of your desire but having to hold back.

Eddie and Marcus stripped Kyra and Tania until they were both naked, and straddling them in their laps. Eddie was trying to control himself and just enjoy the experience, but the desire for blood was becoming overpowering. As he struggled with all of his willpower to control himself, Marcus began to lick Tania's neck. Marcus could feel the warm blood just beneath her skin pulsating against his tongue. That was when he knew he could hold out no longer. As Tania let her long hair fall back over Marcus's pale chest and exposed her neck and jugular vein, Marcus drew his fangs, and with one thrust bit hard into Tania's neck. She went to scream, but Marcus covered her mouth with his hand as a long stream of blood trickled down her naked body.

Kyra was about to scream as well, but Eddie grabbed her mouth and whispered in her ear not to be afraid. She nodded in complacency and Eddie continued to hold her mouth shut as Marcus slowly drained the life from Tania. Her skin slowly turned from a healthy brown to a much paler tone until Marcus had drank his fill and let Tania's lifeless body fall to the floor of the limousine, blood still leaking from her neck wound.

Marcus took his right arm and wiped away the blood from his lips and licked away the rest. It was a very satisfying feed.

Kyra squirmed in Eddie's lap as he struggled to hold her still. He could feel her heart beating rapidly and the blood gushing through her veins. The feeling of so much blood rushing so rapidly against his skin was almost more than he could bare. He began to hold her tightly, making it more difficult for her to breathe. She began to kick and flail her arms before Eddie squeezed her so tightly that she could not move.

"What are you waiting for?" asked Marcus. "Didn't your mother ever tell you not to play with your food. Finish the bitch off."

"Some of us like to savor the moment."

Marcus laughed. "You certainly could have fooled me with your recklessness. I had you pegged as the type to eat and run; you are a psychopathic thrill killer who can barely restrain himself from killing. So what is the hesitation right now? Did you eat a big lunch?" He laughed again.

Kyra began to struggle more and more and Eddie squeezed

her tighter and tighter until he began to hear her ribs cracking. She tried to yell out in pain, but Eddie firmly kept his hand over her mouth, making it difficult for her to breathe.

Eddie pulled back Kyra's head and looked deeply into her eyes. He could see that she was crying and she looked very helpless and afraid. She reminded him of Kristin, the first time she saw him.

Marcus looked over in Eddie's direction and nodded. "Do it."

After a moment of hesitation, Eddie drew his fangs and plunged them into Kyra's pale white neck. As soon as the blood touched his lips he could feel that lovely feeling of intoxication returning. He squeezed her breasts tightly as he felt her heart rapidly beating until it finally beat its last beat.

He continued to hold her tight for several minutes after she had died. He was still amazed at how quickly the body turns cold, once it has been drained of life-giving blood.

Eddie licked his lips of blood and then let go of Kyra's limp body, which fell to the floor on top of Tania. Two naked bodies pale and covered in blood now sat at their feet.

"Now that is how you feed," said Marcus as he wiped away the blood from his mouth. "And now comes the next most important part – the cleanup." Marcus tapped on the window. "Driver, take us to the middle of the desert." Marcus turned to Eddie. "Don't worry, he is a very loyal driver." Marcus put his arms behind his head and smiled deeply.

A few minutes later, the limousine stopped.

"Get out," said Marcus, "and don't forget to bring Kyra with you."

Marcus opened the limousine door and dragged Tania's lifeless body out onto the desert floor. Eddie picked up Kyra's body and threw it over his shoulder and then threw it on top of Tania.

"Now what?" asked Eddie.

"What do you mean now what?"

"Well, are we just going to leave them there?"

Marcus took out a canister of gasoline and a lighter. "Now we burn the bodies. Then our work here is done. Whatever doesn't burn will never be found or identified."

"It doesn't seem much more thorough than my methods. Won't people come looking for them?"

Marcus shook his head. "Doubtful. These women are all homeless, runaways, people with no families that care about them. No one ever misses these types of people. And if anyone notices they are gone, I wouldn't expect a thorough investigation. It pays to network Eddie. Ilse keeps me well supplied and in return I pay her well. My driver helps me dispose of the bodies and I pay him generously as well."

"I guess it helps to have money."

"Yes it does. This is the vampire high life, Eddie. How are you liking it?"

Eddie could still feel the intoxicating high of the blood rush. "I'm liking it pretty well."

Marcus put his arm around Eddie. "I'm glad to hear it. Stick with me Eddie, and the good times can keep on going. It's possible to have a good time without making a mess of things. That is how you survive for two millennia." Marcus slapped Eddie hard on the back, causing him to spit up a little bit of blood. "Come on now, let's be getting back before the sun rises."

They got back in the limo and drove off into the desert, just as the sun began to rise.

Chapter 12

Kristen awoke after a good night's sleep. She was still feeling very weak but had regained a considerable amount of her strength.

As she got up out of bed, still in her purple bathrobe, she looked around to see that Eddie wasn't back yet. So much for a big breakfast. She guessed she would just call room service. She decided to have pancakes along with bacon and eggs with a big glass of orange juice.

As she poured her syrup on her pancakes she decided to put on the TV. She put on the local news channel to see if anything suspicious had occurred last night. There was nothing in the news about any murders or killings. As far she could tell Eddie had managed to control himself. She always worried when he disappeared like that because usually it would result in another massacre, and she hoped not to have to flee so soon after just arriving.

As crazy as it sounded, she almost felt disappointed that there was no news of another massacre. It was amazing how fast she was getting used to the idea that her boyfriend was a mass murderer. She had never been a perfect angel, and had stolen on more than one occasion, but until recently the idea of being an accomplice to mass murder would have been completely inconceivable. But she guessed that people can get used to anything.

As she was contemplating that she heard laughter outside of the door. She turned to look just in time to see Eddie and Marcus walk through the door.

"Eddie!" she exclaimed. "I was beginning to worry about you." She got up and began to run towards him and embraced him. "Did you win any money last night?"

Eddie looked down into her eyes and had a flashback to the night before. Her eyes looked just like Kyra's eyes and that was almost more than he could bare. He pushed her slowly away.

"What's wrong Eddie?" she said as she stared deeply at him.

"Nothing, everything is fine."

They both stood there for a moment saying nothing before Kristen looked over at Marcus and tightened her bathrobe. "Who is your friend?" she asked as she motioned in Marcus's direction.

"Yes, Eddie," said Marcus as he approached Kristen, "please introduce us. Who is this lovely little dish?"

"Kristen," said Eddie, "this is Marcus. Marcus, this is Kristen."

"Charmed," said Marcus as he kissed Kristen's hand. It took all of his restraint to resist the urge to take a bite out of her.

Marcus drew back and took a close look at Kristen. "You look rather familiar," he said to her. He stood there thinking for a second before it occurred to him. He looked over in Eddie's direction. "Ah, now I see. That is why you were having performance anxiety last night." Marcus snickered.

Kristen looked at Eddie. "What is he talking about Eddie?"

"Nothing," he replied. "I think perhaps maybe you should leave now Marcus."

Marcus stared at them tensely for a moment before tipping his cowboy hat. "Alright. But don't be a stranger Eddie. I'll be around. Maybe we could get together again tonight."

"Sure, maybe we will."

Marcus began to walk towards the door and opened it. But before leaving, he turned around and looked Eddie squarely in the eyes. "Just remember Eddie, if you do decide to feed solo, be discreet. I don't want to have to clean up one of your messes." And with that Marcus left and shut the door behind him.

Kristen looked over at Eddie. "Who was he Eddie?"

"An old friend. A very old friend."

She put her right hand on his. "You mean he was a vampire?"

Eddie nodded. "Yes, a very old vampire. Probably the oldest vampire I know."

"So I guess there are a lot of you around."

"I don't know if I would say a lot, but there are more than you would probably suspect. The majority of us don't last very long, so it is quite an achievement to be a very ancient vampire."

Kristen paused for a moment before asking Eddie the inevitable. "So where did you guys go last night?"

"Out."

"Out where?"

"Just out."

"Were you with another woman?"

The question sent Eddie into a rage. He lunged forward and grabbed Kristen's hands and squeezed them tight. He looked her directly in the eyes and told her, "And what business of that is yours?" At that, she drew back. Eddie continued."What I do in my own time is my business and my business alone. This isn't some kind of high school romance. We aren't 'going steady'and I'm not going to ask you to the prom. I am no Edward Cullen and I'm not going to vow eternal devotion to you. Do you understand?"

Kristen nodded and Eddie let go of her hands.

"Good," said Eddie, "I'm glad that you understand. But

since you have such a burning curiosity to know, Marcus and I had dinner last night."

"And by dinner you mean..."

"Yes, we fed on blood."

Kristen put her hands over her lips. "Was it another massacre?"

Eddie shook his head. "No, it was a light meal and very discreet. Word is getting around of my recent recklessness and Marcus felt it imperative to get me under control, for my own good, of course."

"Well, it sounds like he's a very good friend then."

"Well, we vampires have to look out for one another."

"So Eddie, what's on the agenda for today?"

"It's up to you, whatever you want to do."

Kristen rested her hand on her cheek and thought. "Well, maybe we could see a show. I have always wanted to see one of those live Vegas performers. Maybe see one of those shows where they train the tigers to do all of those tricks."

Eddie nodded. "Sure, if that is what you would like to do. I think that maybe I will just stay here and rest for the day."

"You don't want to come as well?"

Eddie shook his head. "I've seen these things before. I think I would just like to rest."

"I thought you said that vampires never sleep."

"We don't, but everyone likes to take it easy once in a while. Even if we don't sleep, we do need to rest."

Kristen nodded and began to get dressed. She didn't have much in her wardrobe.

"You know Eddie, I think I might do a little shopping today. Would that be okay?"

"Sure, go crazy, we aren't short on funds. But since you're planning on spending, I think that maybe I'll do a little more gambling, as I didn't get around to making the big wins that I had hoped last night."

Kristen nodded. "Can we meet back here later then and spend the evening together?"

Eddie nodded back. "Sounds like a plan."

"Good luck gambling."

"Thanks, but I don't rely on luck or believe in it. But then again, I didn't believe in vampires either, so I have been wrong about these matters before." Eddie smiled at Kristen and she smiled back. "So we'll meet back here at dinnertime."

Before Kristen could say goodbye Eddie had walked out the door.

Eddie decided that he would try his luck at the slots. Most of the poker tables were situated near mirrors and he didn't care to raise any more suspicions. There was a $25,000 jackpot that he could potentially win, although that would be more based on luck than anything. Oh well, maybe today would be his lucky day.

He sat down at a machine between an elderly woman and a fat man with bloodshot eyes. Eddie knew the signs of addiction when he saw it. That man had been at that machine without moving or even taking a bathroom break probably all night long. He was thoroughly unappealing and Eddie could smell the alcohol on him. But at least he wouldn't be a distraction and neither would the elderly woman. With no sex appeal and unappetizing blood, he could easily sit between these two without being overcome by a desire to feed.

Eddie began to play the slots. After the first five tries he had won nothing. Twenty tries later he had already gone through two handfuls of quarters without winning enough to break even. It seems that vampires did not have a supernatural ability of luck, just like he had thought.

After five more tries the stink of alcohol and the shallow breathing of the fat man proved to be too much for him. It was one thing to be unappealing enough to not be a distraction, but to someone with hyper keen senses a total lack of hygiene and poor health can be unappealing enough to be annoying. The old lady had left by then, probably equally turned off by the disgusting addict sitting so close to them.

Eddie got up and left. It seems that he wasn't having the most profitable day.

Kristin was having more fun shopping. She had bought five new dresses and was about to try on a sixth. That was when the woman in the fitting room noticed her necklace. She reached out and touched it with her right hand which caused Kristen to jump back.

"Sorry to have startled you," said the woman. "I just saw this lovely necklace on you and couldn't resist the urge to reach out and touch it. I realize that must seem extremely rude of me, but I have never seen a necklace so beautiful on such a young woman. I'm wondering where you have obtained it."

The question made Kristin nervous. Did this woman suspect something? Did she think that she stole it? She felt she'd better say something.

"My boyfriend got it for me," she said.

"You are very lucky woman to have a boyfriend willing to buy you something so exquisite. He must care very deeply about you."

"Yes," said Kristen, "he must."

"Do you mind if I ask where he purchased it?"

"Oh, well, he didn't exactly purchase it."The woman who gave her a puzzled look which increased her feeling of nervousness. She had better explain further. "By that I mean that it was a family heirloom that has been passed down for several generations."

"That is lovely. He must have known you for a very long time to give you something so precious and valuable."

"Well, actually, we just met recently."

"Oh." The woman looked surprised." Well, he must be quite smitten with you. You're a very lucky girl and I have to admit that I am jealous."

It looked as though the woman was finally about to back off when suddenly she noticed the puncture wounds on Kristen's neck. "What's that?" she asked.

"What's what?" responded Kristin.

"That mark on your neck!"

"Oh," she said as she covered the puncture marks with her hand. "Well, that's nothing, just a bug bite."

"That looks awfully big for a bug bite. Are you sure that it is not infected? Maybe you should get it checked out at a doctor."

"No, I'm sure it is fine. It's just a small bite."

"It looks like a rather large bite."

Kristen was beginning to feel even more nervous as these questions continued to grow more intrusive so she figured she'd better just lie. "I already got it checked out, the doctor said that it was fine."

That answer seem to satisfy the woman who nodded in approval. "I'm sorry for all the questions, I just couldn't help but notice. Would you like me to wrap that dress up for you?"

"Yes, please."

She was eager to get out of there.

"Will that be cash or credit?"

"Cash will be fine." Kristen handed her several hundred dollar bills. The woman wrapped up her purchases and gave her a nice bag to carry them in. As soon as she had finished paying she got out of there as fast as her legs would carry her.

As soon as she was outside, she went and sat down at the nearest bench. She sat there and gently rubbed where Eddie had bitten her. Although it had already mostly healed, for the first time she was genuinely nervous about it. She was still feeling a bit lightheaded from all the blood that Eddie had drained from her. Was it unhealthy for her to allow Eddie to be feeding off of her like that? Could she get some kind of disease from him? She had never dealt with vampires before and if she saw a doctor she wouldn't know what to tell them. She certainly wasn't going to tell them the truth as she didn't want to be locked up as mentally disturbed for believing she was having an affair with a vampire.

After resting on the bench for several more minutes, she decided it was probably best that she go back to the hotel and rest some more. In a few hours Eddie would be back and they could go out to dinner.

It was strange, but every time Eddie left she somehow felt less safe. When Eddie was around, despite the fact that he still scared her to some degree, she never felt more safe with anyone in her entire life. She couldn't help but laugh at the thought – the man she trusted most in the world and felt closer to than anyone she had never met before, was without question the most dangerous person she has ever encountered.

She sat there laughing until people started to stare and then made her way back to the hotel.

It was starting to get late and Eddie would have to meet Kristen for dinner soon. He had made reservations at a fancy restaurant, which he had to admit felt odd, because as a vampire he never actually ate anything other than blood. On the rare occasions he did eat in public it was solely for appearances. But now that he was with someone who is a pure human he would have to grow accustomed to spending more time pretending to eat.

He figured he still had a little more time left to gamble before it was time to meet Kristen, so he would play the slots for another half-hour.

He sat down at a machine that wasn't near any mirrors and was largely unoccupied and began playing. Maybe being a vampire would yet prove lucky. Having lost over $100 today, he wasn't feeling very lucky. But that was about to change. Just as he was getting ready to leave his machine to go meet Kristen, he put in one last quarter and pulled the lever on the machine. He was already getting up to walk away when suddenly the lights began flashing and balloons rained down from the ceiling.

Eddie looked up at the machine, which was flashing $25,000. He had won the jackpot!

Within a few seconds of winning the jackpot, the entire casino seem to be gathering around him. Several people began taking pictures with their cameras and cell phones.

Eddie covered his face and shouted, "No pictures!"

Through a series of flashes Eddie could see Kristen standing there in the crowd.

Before she could reach him a representative of the casino came over and shook Eddie's hand. "Well, congratulations!" said the man as he firmly grasped Eddie's hand. "It seems you have won our jackpot. How does it feel to have won $25,000?"

Eddie stood there in shock for a moment, not sure how to respond. That was when Kristen came running up to him and gave him a big hug. "Oh Eddie," she said, "I can't believe it, you've won the jackpot! And you said vampires weren't lucky!" She covered her mouth after she realized what she had said.

"Vampires?" asked the casino representative.

Eddie laughed nervously. "It's an inside joke. People have nicknamed me a vampire because of my pale appearance and the fact that I like my meat extra rare and juicy."

"Well it sounds like your lady friend there is right. You're a very lucky vampire to be $25,000 richer. Just come around later this evening to casino management and we will give you your check. But please don't stop gambling just because you have won the jackpot. Give the house a chance to win back some of that money!" He laughed heartily as he slapped Eddie on the back.

"Don't worry," said Eddie, "I think we'll be staying here for a while. But now it is time for us to have dinner. And I think that we will eat very well tonight."

The casino representative smiled. "Well, you don't exactly have to eat on a frugal budget, do you?"

"No," said Eddie, "I guess not."

With that the crowd began to disperse and Eddie and Kristen began to head towards the casino's diner. But before they could go more than a few feet they saw Marcus standing there in his cowboy hat, blocking their path.

"Well Eddie," said Marcus, "you are certainly keeping a low profile aren't you?"

"I won the jackpot, what was I supposed to do, run away?"

Marcus shook his head in a disapproving manner. "Several people took your photograph."

"So when they go to look at the picture later it will show nothing and they will have no proof that anything strange is going on. They will just write it off as a glitch and think nothing of it."

"And what about the security tapes?"

"What about them?"

"Are you really that stupid Eddie? They are going to review the security tapes before they give you your check. They are probably looking at them right now and wondering why you don't appear on the video. Don't you think that's going to make them a little bit suspicious?"

Eddie paused and put his fisted hand to his head. He hadn't thought about that. He had really never considered what would happen if he had won the jackpot. This is a situation that he didn't really anticipate.

"It's sinking in now, isn't it Eddie? So what are you going to do about it?"

Eddie lowered his glasses and stared directly at Marcus. "What I'm going to do, is I'm going to go and get my money."

"And what are you going to say when they question why you don't appear in the video?"

"I will just say that it is probably a glitch and that they witnessed things themselves, as did an entire casino full of people."

"And if they still don't believe you?"

Eddie lowered his glasses further before pushing them back up. "Then I will persuade them."

Marcus pounded his fist against the wall. "Dammit Eddie, if you needed money, you could've just asked me."

"I want the money that is rightfully mine."

"So now you're suddenly ready to play by the rules just because they're in your favor."

"I don't need to justify myself to anyone."

"Eddie," interrupted Kristen after having stood silently in the background during this entire confrontation, "maybe Marcus has a point."

Eddie was suddenly greatly annoyed. He shot an angry glance towards Kristen. "You are the one who is spending all the money. I wouldn't need money at all if I didn't have you tagging along. So maybe you should shut up and let me deal with this. Or would you rather go running back home to your worthless lowlife father? See if he will give you the same high life that I have been giving you."

Kristen suddenly got quiet. She fought back the desire to cry as she didn't want to seem weak and helpless in front of Eddie and Marcus. But she couldn't deny the truthfulness of Eddie's cruel words. She was just as much a part of this as Eddie was and certainly wasn't innocent of spending his blood money. That fact made her feel even more guilty.

"Well, that's no way to treat a lady," said Marcus as he shook his head. "Maybe you should just eat her." Marcus laughed sinisterly, which made Kristen even more uncomfortable.

"Unless you're going to help me," began Eddie, "you should stay out of this."

"I'd like to Eddie, but these matters concern all of our kind. If you don't learn to control yourself and take care of your own affairs someone's going to come and eliminate you."

"Are you going to help me or not?"

Marcus stood there silent for a moment before gradually nodding his head. "Fine. But you better not make me regret this."

Later that evening Eddie went to claim his winnings. Marcus decided to accompany him. They knocked on the door of management and were escorted in by two security guards.

"I'm here to collect my winnings," said Eddie. "I trust that won't be a problem."

"Ah, yes," said the casino representative, "the big jackpot winner from earlier in the day. Please sit down."

Eddie and Marcus sat down across from the representative.

"And who's your friend here?"

"This," said Eddie as he pointed to Marcus,"is my close friend Marcus. He is a big businessman from Texas and I like to have him with me when I am dealing with matters concerning money."

"I see," said the representative. "We were reviewing the security tapes, Mr. Edward."

"I prefer Eddie."

"Yes, well, Mr.Edw-Eddie, it is a very curious thing. We were reviewing the security footage of when you won the jackpot and it appears that you don't show up in any of the videos. Your little girlfriend appears, and I appear, but you are conspicuously absent. Don't you find that a bit strange?"

Eddie shrugged his shoulders. "It must be a glitch."

"For one person to not appear in a video when everyone else does. Have you ever heard of a glitch like that before?"

Eddie shook his head. "No, but then I'm not an expert on audiovisual problems in security cameras. Does it really matter? You were there, you know that I won. I'm just asking for what is rightfully mine. I am legally entitled to my winnings, am I not?"

"Well it's a very odd glitch wouldn't you say? How would you explain that?"

Eddie slowly smirked. "Would you believe that I really am a vampire?"

Both Eddie and the representative smiled and then began laughing and then Marcus slowly started laughing as well. Then the representative stopped laughing and looked straight ahead. "You have a funny sense of humor, Mr. Eddie."

That was when Marcus stood up, lowered his glasses and got right up into the representative's face, staring him directly into the eyes. "Look," he said, "my friend here is owed some money and I think you'd better just give it to him so that there isn't any trouble. And I think maybe it would be best if you give it to him in cash."

The representative stood there completely mesmerized by Marcus. He very slowly nodded his head and went around to a safe in the back and slowly counted out $25,000 in cash. He put the cash into a bag and handed it to Eddie still looking ahead with the vacant stare.

Marcus turned to Eddie. "You might want to count to make sure it is all there."

Eddie shook his head. "I think that it is all here."

"Good," said Marcus with the tip of his hat, "then I think it is best that we be on our way." Marcus then turned towards the representative staring him intensely in the eyes again. "None of this ever took place. I think that maybe tonight you are going to get drunk and swallow a bottle of pills." The representative simply nodded absentmindedly. "I'm glad we understand each other."

Eddie and Marcus got up and left with the money. Once they had gotten far away from the scene Eddie turned to Marcus and asked, "How did you do that? I thought we didn't really have the power to control people like that."

"You don't, but I do. With age comes increasing power. Only the most ancient of vampires have the ability to fully mesmerize people like that, and only for a limited amount of time. It took me many centuries to learn how to use this ability effectively. Perhaps if you can avoid getting yourself killed, you'll be able to do this by the 31st century." Marcus laughed heartily and slapped Eddie on the back. "You're okay Eddie. But take my advice, take your money and leave town."

"But I thought everything was taken care of."

"I did you a favor Eddie, one you probably didn't deserve and probably won't fully appreciate. So now I want you to do me a favor and get out of town before you cause more trouble. I would go far away from here and lay low for a while. Get what I mean Eddie?"

Eddie nodded and shook hands with Marcus. Marcus drew him close and whispered in his ear, "I mean it Eddie, don't make me have to clean up your messes ever again. I only do so many favors."

Eddie and Marcus parted ways and Eddie went back up to the hotel room, where Kristen was watching TV in bed. He tossed the bag with the money into her lap. "Get dressed," he told her. "It's time for us to be going."

"But we've only just got here!" exclaimed Kristen. "I was hoping we could stay for a while and really live it up."

"Well, our plans have suddenly changed."

"But Eddie –" she began.

"No buts, when I say we are leaving, we are leaving. Don't question me again."

Kristen nodded nervously. "Where are we going?"

Eddie smiled one of his big smiles. "I've got some place in mind."

Chapter 13

It was late the next afternoon that Eddie and Kristen arrived in the city of New Orleans. Eddie had been hoping that they would get there before sunset because he was eager to feed again. He wasn't used to feeding this frequently; it was becoming a compulsion. Vampires could get by with feeding only a couple of times a month, or even less for older vampires, but once you started feeding it was often difficult to stop and take a break. The more frequently that Eddie fed, the hungrier he would grow. That was why it was important to learn moderation; Eddie has not learned moderation just yet.

"We're here," said Eddie as he poked a sleeping Kristen, waking her.

"Where is here?" she asked as she rubbed her eyes.

"Well I said that I would surprise you. I know you were disappointed that we had to leave Vegas so soon, so I thought what would be the next best thing?"

Kristen looked up at him, still rubbing her eyes.

"Have you ever been to Mardi Gras?"

Kristen shook her head.

"Well, welcome to New Orleans!"

Kristen smiled at Eddie. "I always wanted to go to Mardi Gras. My friends went once, but my dad did not let me go."

"Well it's a good thing the worthless bastard isn't here to ruin your fun this time. I'll show you the time of your life. Mardi Gras starts tomorrow, so we have tonight to prepare."

"Where are we going to stay Eddie?"

"Don't worry, I know some people. New Orleans has a long and rich history of vampirism. It's not just horny teenagers who descend upon this city around this time of year; it is also a magnet for hordes of hungry vampires looking for an easy place to feed. To us large gatherings like these full of anonymous people are like our Thanksgiving. But don't worry, it's plenty of fun if you aren't a vampire, too."

"Eddie?"

"Yes?"

"How do you get used to it?"

"Get used to what?"

Kristen paused a moment before saying, "To the taste of blood."

Eddie laughed. "Well, it's an acquired taste. It comes with being a vampire. It changes your tastes."

Kristen looked puzzled. "In what way?"

Eddie pulled the car over to the side of the road and put the car into park. He then looked at Kristen very carefully and stared her directly in the eyes with his sunglasses down. "It is like a drug. You don't do the drug because you like the way it tastes, you do it because of the effect it has on your body. Vampires don't drink blood because of the taste, we drink it because of the effect. The first time you taste that blood is like a drug addict taking their first hit. Once you have had it in you crave it more and more and it takes more and more to satisfy your thirst. With age it becomes easier to control, but the desire for more blood will always remain. It is completely insatiable. And once you have become addicted to blood you don't want anything else, or need anything else for that matter. Do you understand?"

Kristen nodded. "I think so."

Eddie shook his head and began to laugh.

"What's so funny?"

"You don't know a fucking thing. No one can understand what it is like to have a craving you can never fully satisfy unless you also have had that craving."

Kristen gulped deeply before asking, "So do you crave blood all the time, nonstop?"

Eddie could hear that her heart was beating faster and faster with each passing second. He leaned down and got right into her face and told her, "Yes, every waking second of every day. It takes every ounce of self-control that I have to resist the urge to devour you. And being near you is like having your favorite drug dangling in front of you and not being able to consume it. Any other questions?"

Kristen took another big gulp and shook her head.

"Good. I'm glad we understand each other. Now let us continue, it is almost dark."

As the sun was beginning to set they pulled up in front of a large colonial townhouse. It looked like an old plantation or some kind of mansion. It was all white, with a large porch and surrounded by various hedge sculptures of different types of animals. One of them almost looked like a bat, although Kristen could not be sure.

"So it looks like you have a lot of friends in high places," said Kristen as she got out of the car with Eddie.

"When you live for several centuries, it is possible to accumulate a large amount of wealth. And when you live as long as we do, it pays to have friends in high places. We vampires look out for our own. Someday maybe I will have my own mansion, but I'm still young and lack a lot of the entrepreneurial spirit of my friends."

Eddie went up to the door and rang the bell. A few seconds later, the door opened and they were greeted by a tall and skinny African American woman with long black hair dressed in a red evening gown. Despite having dark skin, she had a pale complexion that seemed to be characteristic of all vampires. Her eyes glowed dark yellow with an intensity greater than Eddie's and seemed to stare right into Kristen's soul. She couldn't help but feel slightly mesmerized by her.

"Eddie," said the woman, "so glad that you could make it." She looked closely at Kristen. "And I see that you brought us an appetizer." She showed her fangs as she slowly approached Kristen.

"That's Kristen," said Eddie, "she isn't for feeding on."

The woman drew back away from Kristen and shook her head. "Well, that's just too bad. But it's okay, I have already prepared a first-class meal for us. Won't you please join us?" The woman gestured for them to come inside and they both followed her.

Inside the house was very dark, with most of the window shades drawn and dimly lit lamps provided the only available light. The woman led them to a long dining room table with a candelabra in the middle and several smaller candles elsewhere on the table. She gestured for them to sit down, so Kristen took a seat across from Eddie, who sat next to the mysterious woman.

"Well, now isn't this lovely," she said, "it's been ages since I've had any guests over. But where are my manners? My name is Lenora."

She reached out to shake Kristen's hand. Her hand was cold to the touch, icy, like Eddie's. She could feel her heart beating more rapidly.

"Don't be nervous," said Lenora, "you are my guest, and I never eat my guests. Although I must say it has been quite some time since I have had a human over for dinner without the intention of making them the main course." She licked her lips as she looked directly at Kristen. Kristen gulped and managed a faint laugh.

"Would you like anything to drink?" Lenora asked. "I take it you aren't a blood drinker. I have wine if you would like some. I have a very special bottle I have been saving for just such an occasion." She clapped her hands and a butler or some type of servant came out. "Charles, please get some wine for my lady guest and some blood for Eddie and I. By wine I mean the special bottle that I have been saving, you know the one I'm talking about."

Charles nodded and a moment later came out with a bottle of wine and three glasses, two of which were full of blood. Lenora took one glass of blood for herself and gave the other one to Eddie. She then popped the cork on wine and poured a glass for Kristen and pushed it slowly towards her.

"I hope you'll enjoy the wine," said Lenora, "it's almost as old as I am."

"How old are you?" asked Kristin

Lenora laughed. "Don't you know it's impolite to ask a southern lady how old she is?" She could sense that Kristin was very nervous as she could hear her heart beating ever faster. "Suffice it to say that this bottle of wine was from 1865, and I was well past the drinking age in that year. I have been saving a bunch of old wine bottles since that year. I had a good lot of it to celebrate liberation from slavery."

"You were a slave?" Kristen asked.

"I began life as a slave, but let's just say that the lifestyle didn't suit me very well."

"That must have been awful. I read about that in history class."

"Ha," snorted Lenora with contempt as she took another sip of her blood, "your history books aren't worth the paper that they are printed on. It isn't possible to capture in words what slavery was like. Most of it is watered down bulllshit, suited to minimize the guilt of middle-class white people whose ancestors were slave owners. But I was there, and there are few people left alive today, including few vampires, who have had the experiences that I have had."

"You should write a memoir!"

Lenora laughed heartily at that and Eddie joined in. "My dear, did I not just tell you that words cannot capture the experience. And do you think anyone is really going to believe an eyewitness account written by a current day person? You may not know it from traveling with this one," she pointed at Eddie, "but the majority of us vampires know that it is better not to draw attention to ourselves."

"Oh, right," said Kristin as she blushed. She paused for a moment before adding, "Maybe you could write it as historical fiction."

Lenora gave an angry look. "To fictionalize my actual true life experiences would be to trivialize them. And my life wasn't exactly typical."

Kristin looked puzzled.

"I'm a vampire Dearie," began Lenora, "I think that the historical accuracy of my story would come under question when I say how I escaped from slavery when I drained my master's family completely dry of their blood." Kristin's heart beat went up at that statement and Lenora noticed and got real close in her face and added, "And let me tell you, there is nothing more satisfying than watching the life drain from the face of the person who delighted in whipping you. He may have drawn blood from me on many occasions, but when it was my turn to draw blood I did not hold back. To this day I have never tasted blood so sweet as the blood of my oppressors."

Kristin drew back in fear. Eddie decided to break the tension and turned to Lenora and asked, "So what have you been up to more recently?"

Lenora took another sip of her blood and licked the remaining drops from her lips. "Nothing of great interest. The last time anything interesting happened around here was during Katrina. That was a feast I will not forget."

Kristin gulped back some wine and then slowly put her glass down on the table. "So, you fed on Katrina victims?"

Lenora finished the remaining blood in her glass. "I didn't just feed, I gorged myself. Most people were fleeing in terror, but for an immortal being, a hurricane isn't something to be feared, but is an opportunity to look forward to. In any situation where there is a disaster where large numbers of people go missing, I can guarantee to you, my dear, that there will be vampires not far behind. That," she turned to Eddie, "is a good way to feed discreetly. When lots of people go missing in such a large-scale event, no one is going to notice a few more go missing. All their deaths will be attributed to the storm and there isn't even a need to clean up. It was the most I fed at any one time since I slaughtered that group of Confederate soldiers shortly after I was first turned."

Eddie gulped down his entire glass of blood before slamming it down on the table. "Well, here's hoping that another disaster will present itself soon!" Eddie and Lenora both laughed sinisterly. All Kristin to do was manage to laugh feebly with them.

Lenora clapped her hands together and her butler came out. "Charles," she said as she motioned for him to come over, "I think it is time for the main course." He nodded and went into the other room. Lenora turned to Eddie. "I think that you will enjoy my selection for this evening."

A moment later Charles came through the door, pulling on the leash. Kristin looked up to see that at the end of the leash was a naked man with a black hood over his head, handcuffs behind his back and ankle cuffs around his feet. He sounded like he was trying to scream, although the sound came through muffled. Kristin couldn't help notice that he was fairly muscular and attractive. She instantly began to feel somewhat guilty feeling attracted to him, given the situation that he was in.

Charles forced the man to his knees and removed the hood from his head, revealing he had blonde hair and a ball gag in his mouth. He looked up with terrified eyes straight at Lenora and Eddie, before briefly glancing in Kristin's direction. He was breathing very heavily and trembling with fear.

Lenora slowly approached him, grabbed him around the throat with her right hand and removed the ball gag with her left hand.

"Who are you?!" the man shouted. "What are you going to do to me? Please let me go. I'll give you money."

Lenora and Eddie looked at each other and both laughed. Lenora looked the blonde man straight in the eyes and said, "Look around you. You do realize that you are in a mansion. This isn't a kidnapping for money."

"W-what do you want from me?" he pleaded.

Lenora smiled. "I suppose you would like me to say that I brought you here to fuck you." Lenora shook her head. "But that is not the case."

Eddie laughed. "A lot of guys would pay good money for this type of treatment."

The man looked up at them and then over at Kristin before looking back up at them.

Lenora shook her head some more. "You may be attractive, but you are rather dim. I hate having to explain myself to my food."

"You're cannibals!" he shouted.

Eddie grabbed him by the throat and picked him up to his feet. "No, you fucking moron, we are vampires!" Eddie threw him to the floor. "God, it isn't just blonde women who are stupid."

"V-vampires?" the man said as he tried to slink away.

Lenora shot an annoyed glance towards Eddie. "I am tired of playing these games. My food is getting cold. Shall we?"

Eddie smiled at Lenora, blood still leaving his lips a dark red. "Ladies first."

Before Kristin could even blink, Lenora ran over to where the man was trembling on the floor, picked him up and bit into his neck. He tried to scream but just began spitting up blood. A moment later Eddie came over and bit his right arm. Over the next few minutes Lenora and Eddie sucked the man dry until he was just a pale husk. They dropped him on the floor, which was covered in a puddle of his own blood. Lenora snapped her fingers, "Charles, be a dear and take care of this."

Charles nodded in her general direction and went to go get a body bag and a mop. Kristin just stared in shock. Lenora looked over at Kristin and smiled in her direction, her fangs still coated with blood. "Charles really is good help, and good help is very hard to come by these days. It pays to have a good cleanup crew."

"What is he going to do with the body?" Kristin asked, somewhat fearful of what the answer might be.

"I have an incinerator in the basement. Charles will cremate him and then sprinkle the ashes in the ocean, leaving no trace of him behind." She looked in Eddie's direction. "You know Eddie, it really does pay to have a good disposal system."

Eddie smirked. "Not all of us can afford one."

"You should think about settling down for a while. I know that you are trying to lay low. And I would so like the company." She smiled in Eddie's direction.

Kristin was beginning to feel that they had more than a platonic relationship and before she even gave it a minute's thought she blurted out, "So who was he?"

Lenora looked at her with her hands on her hips. "Who was who?"

"That guy you just killed!"

"He was nobody, just some random guy that no one will miss."

"Did he have a family?"

Lenora gave her a look of disgust. "Probably, I don't know, and I don't really care either." She looked over in Eddie's direction. "Your friend asks a lot of annoying questions, Eddie."

Eddie nodded. "Yeah, she does." Eddie gave her a cold look.

She was going to say something, but Eddie's tone made her decide that it was better not to say anything.

"I suppose you must be getting tired," said Lenora to Kristin. "You can stay in the guest bed upstairs."

Kristin nodded and then turned to Eddie. "Are you coming Eddie?"

Lenora looked at Kristin and then looked at Eddie. "She does know we don't sleep, right?"

"Yeah, she knows."

Kristin was beginning to feel awkward and decided it was best that she just go to sleep, even though she slept a lot earlier on the ride here. "Yeah, I knew that, I guess I just forgot. Good night Eddie."

"Good night," said Eddie in a dismissive manner.

Charles led Kristin upstairs to a fairly dark room with a canopy bed in it. The room was rather large and well furnished with numerous chairs and fancy looking pillows. Eddie was right, it was good to know people in high places, even though she didn't feel quite comfortable around Lenora. She went to sleep pretty quickly considering the fact that she wasn't all that tired, although with everything she witnessed tonight, she really could use a rest.

After several hours Kristen awoke with a start. She often didn't sleep well in unfamiliar places, although she was beginning to get used to it. More troubling was the fact that she was having an increasing number of nightmares. She never used to get nightmares before, but lately she has been waking up in a state of terror. But she supposed that, given the circumstances, who wouldn't be having nightmares.

Although she still loved Eddie, she realized that she was on a dangerous path. Since meeting Eddie she went from a normal girl working part-time at a McDonald's to the lover of a mass murderer. Just a few weeks ago she would not even have dreamed of hurting a fly. She was one of those girls who did not flinch at the sight of insects, and would often let them go without squashing them. She also used to volunteer at the animal shelter. And on top of all that, she used to be really squeamish around blood.

But now? Now she has witnessed more murder and carnage that a person living in a war zone normally would. She has become an accomplice to a killing spree and had blood soaked sex with a supernatural monster. And the truth is, although she still had bouts of conscience, she couldn't deny that she was enjoying the rush. With each fresh kill Eddie became more impassioned and more attractive to her. The terror of the situation was part of the excitement. She was beginning to get turned on by the sight of blood.

But why should she feel bad? She was living out her every fantasy. True, she never really fantasized about having sex with a murderous vampire, but she did enjoy paranormal romance, and she was attracted to bad boys. She had also always wanted to see the country and escape her boring life. Now she was doing all of those things and was one of the few people on this earth who was aware of a secret world of vampires. She was part of a very exclusive network, even if she was still something of an outsider to it.

She did wonder what her friend Kimberly would think. Kimberly had been her best friend and was always skeptical of anything spiritual or paranormal. She would so like to write to her and tell her all the things that have happened, but she would never believe it. Already her old life and her old friends seemed like something that happened a lifetime ago. It was like her life didn't even begin until she met Eddie. No, any communication with people from her old life would have to wait until she could think of a cover story.

It really is a shame that she couldn't tell anyone what was happening to her. She felt like she would like to tell someone, just to talk things out, but anyone she told would surely think that she was insane. And anyone who did believe her would be drawn into this dark world that she has become a part of. To know what she was involved with and to say nothing was to be an accomplice, and she did not want to involve anyone else in this, at least not for now.

She decided that she would go for a walk to try and take her mind off of it. She began to walk to the end of the hall when she saw one of the doors was open a crack and she could hear loud noises coming from within the room. She slowly tiptoed towards the door and discreetly looked through the crack. What she saw was not what she was expecting. There was Eddie, naked and covered in blood, and right on top of him was an equally naked and blood soaked Lenora riding him cowgirl style. Eddie took his blood soaked hands and caressed Lenora's breasts, finger painting them with the blood of their latest victim. Lenora threw her head back, her fangs dripping with blood and her shouting with pleasure.

Kristen quickly turned her head as she did not want to see anymore. She was right about Eddie and Lenora having more than a platonic relationship, and she shouldn't be surprised. She knew that Eddie was not monogamous, and for an immortal being it is understandable how monogamy probably would not work out. Until death do you part doesn't really apply to vampires.

She never really expected that Eddie was ever going to propose to her or anything like that, but she did wonder just how much she meant to him. Even if they were never going to be married or in any kind of monogamous relationship, circumstances have pretty much bound them together forever. She really couldn't go back home. This is not just a situation that you can easily walk away from. And, quite honestly, Eddie was still an unpredictable person. Truthfully, she was afraid; what would happen if she did try to leave? Surely Eddie wouldn't just let his partner in crime walk away and trust her to keep her mouth shut. But what would happen if he got tired of her? As safe as she felt with Eddie protecting her, she had no idea how long this would last. For all intents and purposes, Eddie could dispose of her at any moment. If she was just Eddie's latest plaything, then she was completely disposable. The thing that kept her awake at night was that she still didn't know just where she stood with Eddie. That was the scary thing.

Her thoughts were interrupted when she started to hear someone coming up the stairs. She ran back to her room and put the covers over her head. A minute later she heard a knock at her door.

"Ms. Kristin," said a male voice that she recognized as Charles, "is everything all right in there? I thought I heard you walking around."

"Yes, I just got up to go for a walk. Everything is perfectly fine here."

"Well, if you need anything, I'll be around."

"No, that's okay, I'm fine, really."

"Well, okay then. Sleep well."

"I will!" she shouted, but she knew that she would not get back to sleep, not after what she had seen. But she wasn't about to get up again, so she pulled the covers tightly over her head and closed her eyes.

Chapter 14

Kristen woke up late the next morning. She had managed to fall asleep in spite of herself, and the darkness of the room must've kept her from waking up even though it was already past 11 AM. The shades were all drawn and seemed to be specifically designed to keep as much light out as possible. Even if vampires did not burst into flames in the sunlight like in so many old movies she had seen, it was clear that they did not like it at all.

She walked downstairs to find Eddie and Lenora at the table, laughing and sipping what she assumed to be blood. It seems that Lenora had a fairly abundant supply. They both looked up as she came into the dining room and stopped laughing.

"So," said Eddie, "you are finally awake. Sleep well?"

Kristen nodded.

"Mortals," laughed Lenora, swirling her glass of blood,

"they waste so much time on things such as sleep. What a nuisance sleep is. There are so many better ways to spend the night." She smiled at Eddie as she said that. Eddie smiled back.

Kristen couldn't help but blush, which did not go unnoticed.

"What's the matter dearie?" asked Lenora.

"N-nothing," said Kristin as she blushed even more.

"Is it about last night?" Lenora asked causing Kristen's heart to begin to beat faster. "Don't be shy, I know you saw us. You don't think that we couldn't hear you? And smell you? I can smell and sense the presence of any creature whose blood is still flowing."

"Well I-" but she didn't know how to respond to that.

"Maybe she is jealous," said Lenora as she turned to Eddie and they both laughed.

"Maybe next time you could join us," said Eddie with a noticeable smirk. Lenora smiled back at him.

Kristen wasn't sure exactly how to respond and the situation was beginning to get really awkward. "So," she began, "Mardi Gras begins today, right?"

"Yes," said Eddie, "but for us the real festivities begin at night. It is much easier to dispose of your victims by the dark of the night. So there is really no rush to get there early."

"You could go early," said Lenora dismissively.

Kristen didn't really want to leave Lenora and Eddie alone together again, but she was getting the distinct feeling of not being welcome.

"Of course," continued Lenora, "you are free to stay here, if that's what you prefer."

The tone of the conversation suggested that she should probably leave, even though she didn't really want to.

"Well," said Kristin, "I do feel like getting something to eat in town. Would you like to come with me?"

Lenora turned to Eddie. "She does know that we don't eat regular food, right?"

"I just thought –" Kristen began, "I thought maybe you'd like to come along and pretend to eat!" She realized that she probably wasn't making the situation any less awkward.

"No," said Lenora, "that is quite all right Dearie, I gave up on pretending a long time ago. The only time I have pretend is when I am trying to convince someone that I am not a threat, just long enough to sink my fangs into them." She looked directly at Kristen when she said that and that sent a chill down her spine.

"Go ahead," said Eddie, "have fun. We will catch up with you. We will meet you at the big Mardi Gras ball at 8 PM."

"But it is a costume ball, how will you know it is me?"

"Trust us Dearie," said Lenora as she tapped her nose, "we've got your scent." She smiled rather ominously in Kristen's general direction. Eddie likewise tapped his nose and smiled at Kristen.

Kristin nodded. "So the Mardi Gras ball at 8 PM." And with that she put on her jacket, grabbed her wallet, and walked out the door.

As Kristen walked through the town and took in the sights, she began to feel a new sense of freedom, which was soon replaced by a feeling of foreboding. At first she felt the fact that Eddie let her leave meant that she was safe, but it was only in the last couple of hours that she had realized that they could identify her by scent. If it was that easy to track her, then she might not be safe anywhere. She wasn't so much afraid of Eddie as she was of Lenora. It was clear that Lenora did not think highly of her, and if Eddie wasn't there to protect her she might well have eaten Kristen without a second thought. She was not the type of person that Kristen felt comfortable with being able to find her all the time. If she is really that easy for vampires to track as their prey, then she technically wasn't safe anywhere. She almost felt like she should run and get help, but she still was in love with Eddie and did not want things to end.

While she was walking lost in thought, suddenly a man jumped out at her dressed in a black cape, like Dracula. All she could do was scream really loud and get ready to run.

"Whoa," said the man as he took off his mask to reveal himself as a young African-American man, probably in his late teens or early 20s, about Kristen's age. "I didn't mean to scare you that much. My name is Darrell." He held out his hand.

"I'm Kristin," she said as she caught her breath and shook his hand.

"I guess my costume must've been effective. That or you

must be really afraid of vampires!"

"Well, you never know when you're going to run into one." Although she meant that jokingly, it just occurred to her that what she said was technically true. She had never thought about it until now, but vampires didn't look all that different from normal everyday people. Anyone she meets on the street could well be a vampire. She has only known about their existence for a few weeks and already she has met four of them.

"Hey," said Darrell as he waved his hand in front of her face and interrupting her stream of thought, "are you there?"

"Yeah, sorry. I just got a lot on my mind."

"Maybe you should wear a crucifix and keep some garlic with you." Darrell laughed.

"That's only in the movies. It doesn't work on real vampires."

"So you're an expert on vampires are you?"

"Not until recently, but I'm learning a lot." Kristen laughed nervously.

"What's so funny?"

"Nothing, it's an inside joke."

"Oh, okay. So are you going to the Mardi Gras ball tonight?"

"Yes, I am actually."

"Are you going with anyone?"

"Yes, I'm meeting someone there."

"Oh." Darrell frowned a bit.

"But I don't have costume yet and I would love some company."

Darrell smiled at that. "Well, I would greatly enjoy keeping you company for the day. And I know where the costume shop is."

"That's great! Shall we?" Kristin extended her arm and Darrell took it.

Meanwhile, back at Lenora's mansion, Eddie and Lenora were lying naked together in bed, their bodies and the sheets covered completely in blood. Eddie turned to look at Lenora and between them was a young blood soaked blonde woman, drained to the point where she was pale as a ghost. She had so many puncture wounds all over her body that she could be easily mistaken for a pin cushion.

Lenora turned to look at Eddie, licking the blood from her lips. "You know, threesomes are really underrated. Maybe next time we can include that pale redheaded bitch of yours in our fun."

Eddie turned away from her and looked up at the ceiling.

Lenora turned towards Eddie and leaned on her elbows on top of the dead woman between them. "What has she got on you, Eddie?"

"What do you mean?" he asked as he continued to stare at the ceiling.

"I mean, why is it that you have grown so attached to your food. I know you are not monogamous, few vampires are, least of all you. Why would you want to spend so much time with a mortal? It's not exactly like she is anything impressive."

Eddie turned to look at Lenora and smiled, the blood still staining his lips and running down his cheeks. "Are you jealous?"

"Jealous?!" she said as she put one hand over her non-beating heart and began to laugh. "Jealous, of a mortal? Ha!"

"She sure seems to be jealous of you."

Lenora smiled a very wide smile. "Well, that I can understand, she should be jealous of someone like me. Any mortal woman should be envious."

"Well, it is good to see that you still have good healthy self-esteem and are just as modest as ever." Eddie smirked a little bit.

Lenora continued to smile leaning her elbow on her pillow and resting her face on the palm of her hand. "Really now Eddie, I am genuinely curious. What exactly are your long-term plans with this woman?"

Eddie leaned over to look Lenora more directly in the eyes. "What do you mean by that?"

"Well, Eddie, I know you're not a person who thinks of the long-term consequences of your actions, but you must have given this some thought. Are you honestly growing attached to this feeble mortal?"

"Attached?" Eddie gave her a puzzled look and shrugged his shoulders. "I just like having her around is all."

"I can't exactly see why. If I were you I would just eat her."

"You would," said Eddie with some degree of hostility and sarcasm.

Lenora shot him an annoyed glance. "What exactly do you mean by that?"

"I don't think that you have ever grown attached to anyone?"

Lenora raised her eyebrows. "That isn't exactly true. I was attached, to a mortal, to my husband."

"You were married?" Eddie was genuinely surprised that he had never heard this before.

"I didn't exactly choose it and I don't like to talk about it. But that was a relationship that ended the day that I became a vampire. Attachments are for mortals Eddie. Mortals have limited time in this world and to endure their short and pitiful existences they form all sorts of attachments that they believe will give their lives meaning. But they will all eventually die. When I became a vampire, I gave up needing to rely on other people. I will never allow myself to become attached to another person ever again. That is the scar that slavery leaves. Once you are free from bondage, you never want to go back to it, and I never intend to.

"Being a vampire is a solitary existence, Eddie. I know that you are young vampire, so you're not far removed from a mortal, but as you go on living, you will realize this. You especially do not want to become attached to mortals. You will only be all the sadder when they ultimately die. Trust me, Eddie, I am a person who speaks from experience. Mortals are good for one thing and only one thing – sustaining us. They are food, and any vampire forgets that fact is bound to bring unhappiness into their lives."

"What if I turned her?" Eddie looked at her dead seriously.

"You are seriously considering it? You want to turn her? You know what happened last time Eddie. I think that you have caused yourself enough trouble as it is. I really don't think you want to make your situation any worse. Quite frankly, Eddie, I am amazed that you're even still alive at this point. Creating another vampire, one even more inexperienced than you, that isn't exactly going to work out well Eddie."

"I guess, I guess I am just getting lonely." Eddie looked away from her.

"Lonely! You're feeling lonely! What, are you becoming one of these broody lovesick vampires now? Lonely, ha!" Lenora shook her head several times. "You are only in your 40s Eddie. If you are getting lonely now, how do you expect to endure eternity?"

.   Eddie stood up and stared at a mirror which showed no reflection except for the reflection of the blood soaked dead woman on the bed between them. "Maybe I am just having a midlife crisis."

"A midlife crisis!" Lenora shook her head even more. "For Christ's sake, Eddie, you're a vampire! There is no midlife point to eternity."

"But I would be having a midlife crisis if I were a mortal."

"But you are not a mortal, and I think that sometimes you forget that. Sometimes I think that you are not meant to live forever."

Eddie turned around and faced Lenora. He smiled and began to laugh a little.

"What's so funny Eddie?"

"When I was in the military I lived by the motto live fast and die young. I guess it's not exactly the best motto for a vampire."

"You may be immortal Eddie, but you can still be destroyed. And somehow, with your attitude, I don't think you are going to live for centuries."

Eddie shook his head. "Maybe I don't want to."

"Then it is probably not good that you're a vampire."

"No, it is good. Being a vampire is the greatest thing to happen to me. There is no more natural state of existence for killer then to be the top predator in the food chain. I wouldn't give up being a vampire for anything."

And with that, Eddie began to walk away.

"Where are you going Eddie?"

"It's almost time for the ball. We should get ready."

"I suppose so. Charles!" shouted Lenora.

Charles came running to the door. "Yes, Mistress?"

"Clean up this mess!" she yelled as she pointed to the dead woman on the bed. "And get my red dress ready, I don't want anything that's going to show bloodstains. Tonight I am going to feast on a meal fit for a queen."

Eddie smiled and nodded at Lenora and she got up throwing off the bloody sheet that was covering her.

Kristin and Darrell arrived at the costume shop shortly after sunset. She only had a few hours to select a costume for the ball and she was so hoping to make a good impression. She looked at several costumes before deciding on a green dress with a yellow facemask.

"How do I look?" she asked Darrell.

"You are looking mighty fine. But I think that outfit is a bit on the expensive side."

"That's okay, I have plenty of money. My boyfriend and I recently won a lot of money in Las Vegas."

"So you didn't have enough fun in Sodom so you decided you would come and see Gomorrah as well."

They both laughed.

Kristin had to admit that it felt good to spend time with Darrell. It was the first normal time she has had since meeting Eddie. She forgot just what it was like to interact with normal human beings and not to be constantly worried that someone was about to kill her or that she would have to flee immediately. And even though she couldn't quite tell Darrell about all of the things that had happened to her, it did feel good to get a lot of things off of her chest. Of course, if it were up to her she would prefer that he wasn't dressed as a vampire, as she could use a break from vampires. Not that vampires really dressed the way they did in the movies. Vampires were much more modernized than you would expect, as she was learning.

After they left the costume shop, Kristen and Darrell decided that they would stop at a café to have dinner. Kristen decided she would just have coffee, because she didn't really feel that hungry. Darrell decided to have a full spaghetti dinner.

"Are you sure you don't want anything more than just coffee?" asked Darrell as he sucked down a spaghetti noodle. "It'll be my treat."

"No, thanks, really it's okay."

"Are you planning on eating with your boyfriend later?" Darrell wiped some spaghetti sauce off of his mouth with a napkin.

"No, we agreed that we would get dinner on our own. He is probably already eating right now." As Kristen said that she couldn't help but think of last night, where she watched as Eddie and Lenora completely devoured that terrified man. For all she knew they were killing another person right this minute.

"Hey," said Darrell as he began waving his hand in front of Kristen's face again, "are you spacing out again?"

"Sorry, my mind tends to wander."

"What is it that you are thinking about?" Darrell continued to pile in the spaghetti.

"Oh, nothing in particular."

Darrell smiled. "Are you thinking about your boyfriend?"

Kristen frowned and blushed.

"Sorry, I didn't mean to make you uncomfortable. I understand that you don't want to talk about it. Are you worried that your boyfriend will be mad or jealous that you are having dinner with me?"

"It's not that it's just-" but that was when Kristen paused. Maybe that really was what was bothering her. Eddie was the unpredictable type and could well be very possessive. If vampires can identify humans by scent Darrell might very well be in danger just from being in contact with her. She began to feel very nervous.

"Are you okay?" Darrell looked at her with concern. "Was it something that I said?"

Kristen's heart began to beat very fast, and no doubt if Eddie and Lenora had been there they would have noticed the change. She turned to Darrell as she began to get up from her chair.

"What's the matter?"

"I'm sorry, I have to go. Thank you for taking me out today, but I have to be going."

"Wait," said Darrell as he stood up, "what's the matter?"

"Nothing. I just have to be going. I can't explain."

Kristen turned and started to walk away but Darrell grabbed her arm. "Wait, will I ever see you again?"

Kristen pulled back and pushed away Darrell's arm. "Let go!" she shouted so loud that several people at adjoining tables turned to look at her.

Darrell let go of her arm and drew back. "I'm sorry, I didn't mean to touch you like that."

"Please, go away! It's for your own good. You aren't safe around me."

"What do you mean? Is someone after you? Maybe I could help."

"No, you can't."

"If you would just explain to me, maybe I could help."

"I'm so sorry. I can't explain. You'll just have to believe me. I'm sorry, but I have to be going."

Darrell moved forward, but before he could grab Kristen again, she had bolted off and ran down the street. People turned and stared at Darrell and he began to feel awkward, so he just paid his bill and left. But by the time he had finished he had already lost sight of Kristen and didn't know where she went.

Kristin ran and ran until she was confident that Darrell was no longer following her. She stopped to catch her breath. She looked at her watch to see it was almost 8 o'clock and she didn't want to be late at meeting Eddie and Lenora at the ball. She fixed up her costume and slowly walked to her destination. All through the streets, people were celebrating and women were showing their breasts for shiny beads. When she had wanted to go to Mardi Gras's with her friends that was what she pictured she would be doing. But now it all seems so immature and trivial compared to all the other things that were happening in her life.

Kristen continued walking until she bumped into a group of guys in leather jackets who appeared to be drunk.

"I'm sorry," she said as she backed away from them.

The leader of the group of men looked at the other three men next to him and smiled. He then turned to Kristen and got up really close in her face. "Nothing to apologize for love," he said with a thick southern accent and the strong odor of alcohol on his breath, "I quite enjoy bumping into pretty ladies."

Kristen began to walk away, but then the man grabbed her shoulder and she turned around to find herself surrounded. "You know," said the leader, "if you really want to apologize, why don't you flash your titties."

"Excuse me," said Kristin with aggravation as she backed away even further only to bump into one of the three other men surrounding her.

"You know," said one of the other men, "I think that he had a good idea. If you're really sorry, why don't you show your sincerity by letting us see your tits."

"I bet you got nice ones," said a third man.

"We'll of course give you some beads," said the last man, "if that's really what you want."

"We'll give you two sets of beads if you let us cop a feel," said the leader as he slowly reached forward and touched Kristen's breast.

"Get away from me, you pervert!"screamed Kristin as she slapped his hand away.

The leader grabbed Kristen by her wrists as one of the other men grabbed her from behind and placed his hands on her breasts.

"You shouldn't have done that bitch," said the leader breathing his disgusting alcohol smelling breath right in her face, "I don't like being told no."

Kristen began to struggle and started screaming, but then she felt the man behind her let go and heard him fall to the floor. Two strong arms pulled her back and out of the grasp of the leader. She looked up and saw a man dressed in a cape and wearing a black face mask standing in front of her. Lying at his feet was the man that had been grabbing her lying dead on the floor.

"No," said the mysterious man in the Cape. And as soon as she heard his voice she knew it was Eddie.

"Who the fuck do you think you are?" asked the leader as he flicked out a switchblade. "No one tells me no, whether they be some stuck up bitch or some faggot wearing a cape and a face mask."

"How rude of me," said Eddie, "I suppose I should take my mask off."

Eddie took off his mask, revealing his glowing yellow eyes and his protruding fangs. The two men standing on each side of the leader drew back.

"What the hell is wrong with you?" said the leader as he held out his knife in Eddie's direction.

"There is no problem with me. You are the one with the problem. You are the one who is about to die."

The leader went to stab Eddie, but before he could even get his knife halfway to Eddie's chest Eddie had grabbed his arm and squeezed it hard until the switchblade dropped from the gang leader's hand. The two other men took off running.

"Now," said Eddie as he forced the leader to his knees and began crushing the bones in his arms, "I think you owe the lady an apology."

"I-I'm sorry," said the leader as he looked up at Kristen and Eddie.

"I'm sorry too," said Eddie, " because I'm still going to kill you."

With one pull Eddie tore the leader's arm off and tossed it aside like a piece of garbage. He then dove forward and began to devour the man, tearing his throat out. Kristen just stood there, too afraid to move until Eddie had finished off his latest victim. After what seemed like forever Eddie finally stood up and wiped the blood from his mouth with a hankerchief he pulled from his pocket.

"Are you okay?" Eddie asked as he threw away his handerchief.

Kristen just nodded feebly. Eddie could hear her heart beating 100 miles a minute.

"Luckily I arrived when I did."

"How did you find me?"

"I could smell you, and I could smell your fear. And I can smell you are still afraid right now. Was there anyone else bothering you today?"

Kristen shook her head. She couldn't deny that she was terrified, but whether she was more afraid of Eddie or the punks that attacked her she wasn't sure. Could Eddie have known about Darell? That was the question that frightened her the most.

"Well, " said Eddie as he put his facemask back on, "shall we be going? We don't want to be late for the ball." He offered Kristin his hand and she took it and held it tight.

Despite the fear that she had been feeling earlier, she did feel safer now that Eddie was around. It was strange. Even though she still couldn't deny she was afraid of Eddie, there was something about her fear of him that also drew her closer to him. She was beginning to think that maybe she was coming down with Stockholm syndrome. But that wouldn't apply in this situation. She wasn't exactly Eddie's prisoner, as a kidnapper would not let his kidnapped victims leave their site. But then this was an entirely different situation, because vampires seem to be able to find you anywhere. So even if she was technically free to leave, there was really no place that she could hide. But at the same time, that very same thing made her feel safe. She might have been afraid of what Eddie could do to her, but as her recent encounter with those punks demonstrated, she had more to fear from other people. As long as Eddie still wanted to be with her, she had a protector against any enemy, human or otherwise.

Kristin and Eddie soon arrived at the ball. It was being held at a fancy hotel called The Spirit of New Orleans. It was very crowded and that no doubt that was exactly what Eddie and Lenora preferred. In a large crowd it is easy for people to disappear without anyone noticing. But it still seemed like it was a very public place, and therefore any act of violence or murder would be hard to do discreetly. But they had been at this for longer than she had, so she had to assume they knew what they were doing. Speaking of Lenora, Kristin did not see her at the ball.

"Hey Eddie," she asked, "where is Lenora?"

"She's around, don't worry about her, she knows how to take care of herself."

That wasn't exactly why she was worried about Lenora. She could actually care less about Lenora, but she didn't feel fully safe by herself when she was around.

"I'm going to go scout around," said Eddie as he turned to Kristin, "do you think you'll be okay on your own for a while?"

That was the last thing that she wanted to hear, but she told Eddie that she would be fine. It was a lie, but one that he believed. She didn't want to show fear around Eddie, because she knew he could sense her fear. To show fear made her feel weak and she did not want to look weak around Eddie. She also did not want Eddie to think that she was afraid of Lenora, even though she was.

As soon as Eddie left, Kristin began to mingle among the other partygoers. Amid all of the music, good food and good company, she was actually starting to calm down and enjoy herself. She wanted to prove to herself that she could have fun on her own. And in such a public place she figured that Eddie and Lenora would be on their best behavior, and would not make a public scene. And as much a she disliked Lenora, the one positive affect she seemed to have on Eddie was controlling his recklessness. When he was around other vampires Eddie seemed to be more well behaved and less unpredictable.

As she munched down on some hors d'oeuvres, Kristin looked across the table and saw a familiar face. It was Darrell! She felt bad about what had happened earlier and she felt that maybe she should apologize. She really couldn't explain the real reason why she acted as she did, but she felt she owed him some kind of explanation. Although it was nothing more than a Platonic attraction, she had to admit that she really liked Darrell.

As she was trying to think of an explanation to give to Darrell that wouldn't come across sounding as though she were crazy, she lost sight of him. She looked around the room but did not see him. She pushed through the crowds and eventually saw him across the room, chatting with a dark skinned woman in a red dress. As she looked closer Kristin realize that she recognized the woman – it was Lenora! She felt that she had to warn Darrell, or to get Lenora away from him. Could Lenora smell her scent on Darrell? She didn't want to leave things to chance. She had to do something, even if Darrell ended up thinking she was crazy.

A man bumped into Kristen and spilled his drink on her dress. "I'm terribly sorry, Miss, let me help you clean that up," he said as he picked up a napkin.

"No, it's okay, I'm kind of in a rush."

The man shook his head. "No, no, no, it will only take a moment."

"I don't have a moment! Please get out of the way."

Kristin pushed past the man but had lost sight of Darrell and Lenora. She surveyed the room and saw Lenora leading Darrell towards the elevators. The elevator door closed, just as she approached it. Damn, she thought. Now what?

There were only five floors to the hotel, so she would just have to take a chance. She got in the elevator and pressed the button to go to the second floor. The elevator slowly moved at what seemed like a snail's pace. Finally, the door opened and she ran out. She didn't see them. She was beginning to panic. Then she saw Eddie and ran up to him.

"Eddie!" she shouted as she ran into his arms.

"Whoa," said Eddie, "what's the matter? I can hear your heart pounding in your chest."

"Eddie, do you know if Lenora has a room up here?"

"Yes, we had a room reserved specifically for us to take our victims to."

"Oh God," Kristen gasped as she put her hand over her mouth.

"What's the matter?" asked Eddie

"There's no time to explain! Just tell me which room you reserved."

"Room 226."

Kristin ran as fast as she could, and practically kicked open the door when she found it. It was locked. She started pounding her fists on the door, shouting "open up, open up!", but no one answered.

"Lenora! I know you're in there with Darrell. Let me in. Right now!"

Finally Eddie arrived and took out the key. He put the key in and opened the door. Kristin ran through the living room and over to the door to the bedroom and pushed the door open. As soon as she opened the door she saw Lenora kneeling on the bed completely naked. As soon as she heard Kristen, she turned around and looked directly at her with her glowing red eyes and her fangs dripping with blood. Lying on the bed underneath her was Darrell's body with a big hole torn in his throat. He was dead as a door nail.

Lenora smiled a big smile, blood still dripping from her mouth. She looked over at Eddie. "Sorry Eddie, but I couldn't wait for you."

Kristin stood there trembling and began to feel like she was going to faint.

"Are you okay?" asked Eddie.

But before she could answer Eddie she turned to Lenora and shouted, "You murderous bitch!"

Lenora smirked at Kristin as she walked over to her, her naked body glistening with the blood of her latest victim. "You and me both sister. This was a weak one, he never would've survived in my time. Or in this one it seems." Lenora laughed and licked her lips. "Not a bad body though, you should certainly try some Eddie."

Eddie smiled at Lenora and began to snicker.

"It's not funny! He didn't deserve this." Kristin could barely speak she was so angry.

"Are you having pangs of conscience again?" asked Eddie

with a snicker. "You didn't get this upset with the other ones."

"That was different!"

"Killing is killing honey," said Lenora snidely.

"But I knew him, he was a good person."

"Well, he certainly tasted pretty good," said Lenora with a big smile as she licked her lips again.

Kristin was fuming. Lenora must've killed him specifically to spite her.

"You see Eddie," began Lenora, "this is why you should never get involved with mortals. Look how easily and quickly they become attached to each other. They are we-" but before she could finish she saw the blade of a long knife coming out of her chest between her breasts. She let out an ear piercing shriek as her body began to convulse and blood began oozing out of every orifice in her body and gushing out of her chest. And within a few seconds her body turned completely pale and she turned into dust.

As the dust fell to the floor, Eddie saw Kristin there standing and holding the knife that killed Lenora. She dropped the knife and fell backwards onto the bed. She looked up at Eddie, closed her eyes and once more prepared for what she thought would be the end.

Chapter 15

But again it wasn't. She sat there trembling with her eyes closed for about a minute before opening them again to see Eddie standing there, the pile of dust that was Lenora on the floor by their feet. She expected him to be angry, she expected rage, she expected to be killed instantaneously. But Eddie just stood there staring at her. She looked him directly in his yellow eyes, too afraid to even blink, and that was when Eddie smiled and began to laugh. After a couple of seconds Kristen began laughing too, a nervous laughter more than anything else.

But then Eddie stopped laughing.

And so did Kristen.

"What were we laughing about?" Kristen asked nervously.

Eddie continued smiling and shook his head. "Now that," he said as he pointed to the pile of dust at his feet, "is how you kill a vampire!"

"I didn't-" she began. But she did. She knew it and Eddie knew it.

"Oh, but you did. And you did a pretty good job of it too. How did you know what to do?"

"I didn't. I didn't think at all. It was just instinct."

"This," said Eddie as he kicked the dust at Kristin, "is something that Hollywood got right. Sunlight won't cause us to burst into flames, but we decompose instantly when we are killed, and a stake through the heart will generally do the job pretty well. It needn't be a stake, the knife you used was just as effective. Any sharp object is. But it must be directly through the heart. Stabbing us anywhere else won't do much good, but a direct strike into the heart will destroy our ability to circulate the blood we have drank, and also make it impossible for us to heal. It is instant death. The good thing is, it doesn't leave any remains to be examined. A pile of dust is no more proof of the existence of vampires than a photograph, which we wouldn't appear in any way."

Kristen didn't know what to say in response to this so she just said the first thing that came to mind. "Is that the only way to kill a vampire?"

Eddie looked at her sinisterly, but then smiled. "Why do you want to know? Are you planning on killing anymore vampires?"

She immediately regretted what she had just said.

"Eddie, I would never-" she began, but he raised his hand to silence her.

"I know you wouldn't. And I think that now that you have dealt with a couple of my kind, it is natural and useful information to know how to vanquish us. It certainly is not easy, but anything destructive enough will generally do the trick. A stake through the heart, decapitation, burning – it all works just fine, and we dissolve as soon as our body ceases to function. But most vampires will not be distracted long enough for you to get in a kill shot. You got lucky. If Lenora had not been sufficiently distracted you would never have caught her off guard and she would've torn you limb from limb."

Kristin gulped. "You mean you aren't mad at what I did."

Eddie stood there for a moment, silent and unmoving before he slowly shook his head. "Lenora and I go back a long way, but I think that I was beginning to outgrow her. She told me something that I think is true. She said never get too attached to anyone, it only leads to disappointment and sorrow. The first lesson of being a vampire is to live for the moment. Before I was a vampire, I lived by the motto live fast and die young. I think that I have forgotten that. The prospect of an eternity is no fun if you must restrain yourself at every turn. I am tired of showing restraint, and I think you are too."

"What do you mean Eddie?"

"Exactly what I said. Up until now you have been a mere spectator to the carnage. But now you have reached a turning point. You have taken a life, and I think that you enjoyed it."

"I'm not a killer Eddie!"

Eddie kicked the dust at her. "I think that she would beg to differ. Don't deny that you hated Lenora. You hated her from pretty much the first moment. Don't deny that you were jealous of her. Now you have gotten a taste of killing. And I think you know that you enjoyed it."

"Eddie I-" she began, but Eddie put up his hand to silence her again.

Eddie shook his head. "It's okay, we've been together for a while now. Jealousy is only natural to crop up from time to time. Besides, you aren't entirely monogamous either." Eddie looked over at Darrell's mutilated body on the bed.

Kristen felt a sudden pang of guilt. It was her fault that Darrell was dead. Had he never met her, he would still be alive. She couldn't deny that she was fully complicit in his murder. She didn't want him to die, she tried to stop him from dying, but the fact remains that it is her fault that he is dead.

"There was nothing between us. He was just a friend, you have to believe that."

Kristin's heart rate was beginning to increase and Eddie noticed.

"I am not mad. We never agreed that this would be a monogamous union, and I never really expected things to last this long. I have never been in a relationship this long since I have become a vampire, and I still don't know why it is it lasted as long as it has."

Kristen's heart was now beating very rapidly.

"But," Eddie continued, "I like the way it feels. I don't want this to end and I want to continue with this, to whatever end it might lead to." Eddie offered Kristin his hand and she took it and Eddie helped her up from the floor and looked her directly in the eyes and smiled. "So the question is – where do we go from here?"

Kristin looked up at Eddie and smiled, her heartbeat normalizing. "I will follow you wherever you go, to death, undeath or wherever it may lead. "

Eddie continued to smile and nod his head. "We should be going."

Kristin nodded back but then looked over at Darrell's dead body on the bed. "But what about-"she began, but started to get emotional and could not finish.

Eddie shook his head and shrugged his shoulders. "Cleanup was Lenora's job, let her worry about it." Eddie began to laugh furiously and soon Kristin joined in. After a moment they regained their composure, left the bedroom and slowly closed the door.

"Where are we going to go now Eddie?" Kristin looked up at him with a puzzled glance.

"We're going to go get our car, get our money, eliminate all witnesses and get the hell out of here."

"Sounds like a plan." Kristin smiled up at Eddie, but as they walked out the door, she took one last glance at the bedroom door and wiped away a tear for Darrell. That was the last tear she ever intended to shed for anyone.

Within a short time, Eddie and Kristen had arrived at Lenora's mansion. They used her keys to open the door and saw Charles sitting on the couch watching television. He turned and looked at Eddie and Kristen.

"Home so soon?" asked Charles. He noticed that Lenora was not with them. "Where is the lady Lenora?"

Eddie smirked. "She is cleaning up. She might be home a little late. But Charles," said Eddie as he walked towards him,"there is one thing you can do for me."

Charles looked up at Eddie just as he approached him and put his arm on his shoulder. "Tell Lenora, I said hello." And before Charles knew what was happening, Eddie had bit into his jugular vein and he was dead before he could even scream.

Eddie just left Charles's body prostrate on the couch. He didn't even bother turning off the television.

Eddie then went down into the basement and Kristen followed him, not wanting to be left alone with Charles's dead body. Eddie turned on a light illuminating the basement. Chained against the wall were three naked men and one naked woman.

"Well," said Eddie, "I might as well eat before we run."

Kristin stood there and looked on as Eddie systematically devoured and drained the bodies of every last drop of blood. She did not turn away this time. The sight of so much blood no longer bothered her. And after Eddie was done devouring his victims, she helped him load their bodies into the incinerator. He then went back upstairs and dragged Charles's body down into the basement and shoved it into the incinerator as well. After that he went back upstairs and gathered as much money and valuables as he could from Lenora's room. He took one of her necklaces and put it around Kristen's neck.

"I hope you don't feel weird about wearing the jewelry of the woman that you murdered."

Kristen paused when she realize what it is she was doing, but somehow it didn't bother her anymore. She just shook her head and smiled at Eddie.

After getting everything that they wanted from Lenora's room and scouring the house for other valuables, they loaded up their car and got ready to leave. Eddie went back in the house one final time, lit a fire in the fireplace, and then sprayed some lighter fluid into it. The fire erupted and soon caught on to the curtains and the house began to burn.

Eddie ran out to the car where Kristen was waiting. They sat in the car, and watched as the house began to go up in flames. Eddie turned to Kristin, smiled and said, "Fuck subtlety. Burn baby burn!"

Kristin smiled at Eddie and the car pulled out of the driveway to set out for their next destination, come what may.

Chapter 16

Kristin and Eddie drove for several hours before Kristin started to get hungry. They decided to stop at a grocery store somewhere in

Arkansas. Kristen gathered up a bunch of groceries and was going to go to the checkout counter, but Eddie stopped her.

"Don't worry Kris," said Eddie to Kristin as he took the groceries, "I'll take care of that."

"What are you going to do Eddie?" she asked with some apprehension.

"I'll take these," said Eddie as he placed the groceries on the counter, "and one more thing." He turned to the clerk, an elderly woman. "Give me all the money in the cash register and that pearl necklace that you are wearing around your neck."

"Oh my God!" shouted the clerk as she began to tremble. "Do you have a gun?"

Eddie shook his head. "I don't need a gun, I prefer to kill people with my bare hands. Now give me the necklace and all of the money. As you can see my girlfriend here –" he pointed to Kristin "– looks good in necklaces and I have decided that yours would look good in her collection."

"Hey punk," said a large muscular man in a biker jacket as he began walking towards Eddie, "do you like picking on little old ladies."

Eddie turned around and faced the man. "As a matter of fact I do. But I don't discriminate, I also like picking on stupid biker douchebags as well. And I think I would like that jacket you are wearing. So why don't you be good and take it off."

The man rose his fist and went to strike Eddie but Eddie grabbed his hand and crushed it. The man started to bend at the knees and Eddie used the opportunity of his distraction to bite him directly in the jugular vein, tearing his throat out. Eddie picked up the man's jacket and put it on. He then turned around and wiped the blood from his mouth. The clerk took one look at him and fainted. Eddie shook his head. "My my my, people are dropping dead so young these days."

Eddie bent down, pulled the necklace off of the old woman's throat and tossed it to Kristin, who put it on without saying a word. She smiled at Eddie and he smiled back. He took all of the cash out of the cash register, picked up Kristin's groceries, looked over in her direction and nodded his head. Then they slowly walked out of the store together, arm in arm.

"Aren't you worried about cleanup?" asked Kristin as she

looked up at him.

Eddie just smirked and said, "Like I said, fuck subtlety."

Kristin just smiled back at him and they got into the car. Kristen began eating some cheese doodles as she opened the window and let the wind blow through her hair.

"I can see someone was hungry," said Eddie with a snicker.

"Would you like any?" asked Kristin as she offered the bag to Eddie.

"No thanks," he said, "I already ate."

They both laughed hysterically as Eddie sped up. Kristin turned to Eddie as she fingered her new pearl necklace and asked, "Why didn't you feed on the old lady?"

"I don't like the taste of old people. Their blood is thick with cholesterol and fainters generally don't make for good feeding."

"What if she tells someone?"

Eddie rested his hand under his chin as though he was deeply and thought before turning to Kristin and saying, "Personally I don't give a fuck. Whoever she tells will probably accuse her of suffering from senile dementia. 'I fainted because I saw a vampire bite some guys head off'. If your grandmother said that to you, what would you think?"

Kristin had to admit that he had a point. Even if people did witness their killing spree, the majority of people would not be believed when they said a vampire was the culprit. Kristen began to feel a bit of guilt. That woman was someone's grandmother, and now she was wearing her stolen necklace. But her pang of conscience faded just as soon as it came. For whatever reason, what they were doing no longer bothered her.

"Eddie," she began as she put down her cheese doodles.

"Yes?"

"I think that I want to get a gun."

Eddie shook his head a bit, mostly in bewilderment. "What do you need a gun for?"

"For protection."

"You're with me, you don't need protection."

"Well, what if you weren't around?"

"Afraid to be left alone now?"

Kristin shrugged and turned to look out the window away

from Eddie, before turning back and saying, "I want a gun, because what if I need to shoot someone."

Eddie looked at her and smiled one of his biggest smiles yet. "So you finally have come around. My little girl wants to play with guns."

"I'm serious Eddie," she shouted as she playfully hit his arm, hurting her hand in the process. She then shook out her hand to try and get feeling back.

Eddie began laughing. "Okay then, we'll get you a gun."

Kristin just smiled at Eddie and then turned her head to look out the window as Eddie sped up the car until they were speeding off into the setting sun.

The next day Eddie and Kristen stopped at a gun show and bought a couple of handguns. Eddie was just going to steal some guns for her, but he didn't want to make a scene at a place where people were heavily armed. He was more concerned for her safety than he was for himself. They then drove out into the woods where Eddie took out a bunch of old plates that they had taken from Lenora's kitchen and placed them wedged between the branches of several trees.

"These plates seemed like they might be valuable," said Eddie,"but who really gives a fuck. It's not like we are short on money."

Kristin aimed her pistol at the plates, and Eddie helped her steady her hand. She missed the first target, but then hit the second and third ones.

"Not bad for a first time," said Eddie,"but you aren't exactly ready for a killing spree just yet."

"Well," she said,"I wasn't planning on killing anyone anytime soon."

"Oh," said Eddie with a look of puzzlement,"why else do you think you would need to shoot somebody?"

She couldn't deny what she was really thinking when she wanted to get that gun. It wasn't for protection, Eddie was right about that, as she was always pretty safe when he was around. And a gun wouldn't do much damage if Eddie's vampire friends came after them. After killing Lenora something changed inside of her. She didn't feel weak anymore, she felt powerful. And she wanted to feel that rush again, the same rush that Eddie felt every time he killed someone. She was developing a sudden bloodlust, and any feelings of remorse that she had previously felt had now completely disappeared.

As the day went on Kristin's accuracy gradually improved. Even Eddie, the military veteran, seemed to be impressed.

"You had a pretty good first day," said Eddie as they walked back to the car. "You are practically a natural. Some people have good instincts for killing. It's something you develop over time. Once you have made your first kill everything changes. You know what I say is true."

Kristin nodded.

"And the more you kill without being killed yourself, the more invincible you begin to feel."

"Easy for you to say," said Kristin with a smile, "you're a vampire, nothing can hurt you."

"And you're a vampire killer, so you know that isn't true. You really should feel quite impressed with yourself. Few people are capable of encountering a vampire like Lenora and surviving."

Kristin had to admit she felt rather flattered and was feeling even more attracted to Eddie than she had been previously.

"Eddie?"

"Yes."

"I want to shoot someone!" She said that with such enthusiasm that even Eddie was taken aback. He said nothing in response.

"Did you hear me, Eddie? I want to shoot someone!"

"I heard you the first time."

"So what are you going to do about it?"

"What do you want me to do? There's no one-" but then he paused. He heard someone coming. He could hear talking – there were two people.

"What is it Eddie?"

"I heard something. Someone is coming."

"Who?"

"It sounds like two teenagers."

Kristin smiled wickedly. "I'll go hide in the bushes."

"Wait, what?" But before Eddie could stop her she had ran off and hid in the nearby bushes. A moment later a teenage boy and what seemed to be his girlfriend walked into the area and saw Eddie. They paused when they saw him and waved.

"Hi," said the boy. "I'm Jacob and this is my girlfriend Alice."

"Hi," said Eddie dispassionately.

"So what are you doing out here in the woods all alone?" asked Alice.

"I'm actually not alo-" began Eddie before Kristin walked out of the bushes behind Jacob and Alice holding a gun.

"Freeze," said Kristin.

Jacob and Alice turned around and walked backwards in fear when they saw Kristin was pointing a gun at them.

"Whoa," said Jacob, "we didn't mean any harm. Why are you pointing that gun at us?"

Kristin began to laugh fiendishly as she continued to point the gun in their direction.

"Please," said Alice, "we were just passing through. Please don't hurt us."

Kristin laughed loudly and looked them over and smiled. She then looked at Alice right in the eyes and told her, "That's a pretty nice jacket that you're wearing. Take it off."

Alice did as Kristen said and was visibly shaking.

Kristin nodded and Alice's direction and asked, "Are you shivering because you are cold, or because you are afraid?"

"Both," said Alice.

"Well then," began Kristin, "then I am afraid to inform you that I like your entire outfit. So take it off."

"Please," said Alice,"don't do this to me. It is freezing out. I'll catch pneumonia."

"Well, you probably shouldn't have been wearing something that looks so good on me."

Kristin smiled in Eddie's direction and he nodded his head in approval.

Alice slowly began to strip, first taking off her blue shirt, and then taking off her black jeans and black boots. Soon she was standing there in nothing but a white bra and panties. She hugged her body in an effort to keep from shivering. Something about seeing her there so vulnerable and helpless gave Kristin a rush. It felt good to have such power over another person.

"C-can, w-we, g-go n-now?" asked Alice with her teeth chattering.

Kristen shook her head. "Take off the rest too."

Alice began to cry as she slowly slipped off her bra and panties. She then tried feebly to cover herself up as Kristen continued to laugh and Eddie joined in.

"You," said Kristin to Jacob as she pointed a gun at him, "is this turning you on? To see your girlfriend naked and trembling."

"Not like this," said Jacob. "Please just let us go, we gave you what you wanted."

Kristen shook her head. "I'm not done with you yet. If you feel so bad for your girlfriend, then maybe we should even things up. I think what you're wearing would look pretty good on my boyfriend – so take it off." She aimed her gun directly at Jacob.

Jacob took off his heavy padded jacket, then took off his red shirt and his leather leggings. Finally he took off his boxer shorts and was standing there with his hands covering his genitals.

"Hands at your sides!" shouted Kristin as she raised her gun higher.

Kristin looked them over, standing there naked and trembling, their breath visible in the cold winter air.

"Not bad," said Kristin as she looked over Jacob and smirked before turning to Eddie, "but I've seen better."

Kristin stood there for a moment savoring the thrill that power over them was giving her. "You," she said pointing the gun at Alice," get down on all fours." Alice did as Kristen demanded. "Now, bark like a dog!"

Alice began barking like a dog, her breath being big white puffs and her whole body shaking with cold. Kristin could see the hair standing up on her body. She then pointed her gun at Jacob. "You, you see that bitch down there on the floor?" Jacob gave a glare of anger and did not respond. So Kristin repeated, "I said, you, do you see that bitch down there on the floor?" He still said nothing. Finally Kristin shot her gun at the floor in front of Jacob's feet, causing him to jump back. "Now I'll ask you one final time – do you see that bitch down there on the fucking floor? Or do I have to put a bullet in it to make my point!"

Jacob finally nodded, his angry visage beginning to tremble.

"Well, I would like you to get down on all fours and kiss her ass. Now!"

Jacob slowly bent down, got on all fours, leaned forward and kissed Alice right on the ass as she sobbed hysterically.

"That's a good doggie. Now I want you to both turn around, staying on all fours and face forward."

They did as Kristen demanded, both their asses facing her as they continued to huff and puff big white clouds out of their mouth.

"Now I'm going to fire my gun into the air. When you hear the signal, that means you have 10 second head start, then I am coming after you."

Kristin fired her gun into the air and Jacob and Alice both took off running. Just as they had ran until they were nearly out of sight, Kristin began firing. She hit Alice right in the back causing her to fall. She then ran over to Alice and shot her in the head to finish her off. She then fired several more shots into Alice's dead body, savoring every moment of it.

"You're letting Jacob get away!" shouted Eddie, the first sound he had made since Kristen began her little show.

Kristin waved her hand at him. "Let him."

"Are you sure that's a good idea?"

Kristin shrugged. "Who really cares? To be quite honest, I really like the idea of someone finding him running around naked and freezing shouting about how somebody shot his girlfriend. It's a shame that he didn't realize you're a vampire. Oh well, I think we scared him just as well by conventional means."

"Aren't you worried that he is going to identify you?"

Kristin grabbed Eddie's arm looked up at him and smiled. "What do I have to worry about. I've got a vampire protecting me and I'm a pretty good shot, wouldn't you say?"

"I have to say Kris, you've impressed me."

The big screen came over Kristen's face. "Let's get back to a motel and I'll really impress you!"

Eddie smiled back at her and they began to go back to the car. Kristen stopped briefly to pick up Alice's jacket, and Eddie picked up Jacob's jacket. They really did look good in them.

Chapter 17

Kristin and Eddie sat in bed in their motel. They turned to each other and smiled.

"That was great last night," said Kristin.

"It was," said Eddie as he put his hands behind his head and looked up at the ceiling. "Nothing is as great as a good fuck after killing."

"I'm not sure which is a bigger rush! But I do know that I want to experience it again. And I mean soon!"

Eddie looked at her and smiled and then looked back up at the ceiling.

"Eddie?"

"Yes?"

"I wanna kill again, now!" Kristin was so excited she was practically giddy.

"Whoa, calm down. You gotta pace yourself. You certainly have changed rather quickly. Just a week or two ago you were still nagging me to control myself, and now you can hardly wait to take another life."

Kristin got up from bed, throwing off the covers, and began to get dressed in Alice's clothing.

"You say that like it is a bad thing. Don't tell me that now you're going to develop a conscience all of the sudden."

Eddie began to laugh furiously. "I wouldn't quite worry about that. I think that that boat has sailed a long time ago. I can't remember the last time I ever felt guilty about taking a life. Actually, I don't remember ever feeling guilty about taking a life. And why should I? I'm at the top of the food chain. Morality is exclusively the concern of mortals. Nature only has one rule – survival of the fittest. And vampires are the most fit creature in all of nature."

"You know Eddie, technically I'm still mortal. "

"Maybe so, but you should know that you are rather impressive for a mortal."

Kristin smiled at Eddie as she finished getting dressed. "Well that is good to know, but I'm wondering, I would like to experience what it is like to be a vampire. Why won't you turn me?"

Eddie shook his head. "As much as I hate to admit it, one of the reasons why vampires are at the top of the food chain is that there are few of us. The only other major predator for a vampire is other vampires."

Kristin sat down on the bed and looked at Eddie. "Well has anyone ever considered making a vampire army? You could easily take over the world. Who's going to stop you?"

"Believe me, there have been vampires who have tried."

"What happened to them?"

"They were destroyed by other vampires."

"But why? If you combine your forces surely you could take over?"

Eddie laughed snidely and dismissively.

"What's so funny?!"

"That is precisely why I'm not going to turn you. You don't know the first thing about vampires."

"Oh, I think I know quite a bit about vampires, and I'm learning fast."

"Well, there is one thing you have yet to learn. Things aren't as easy as you think. Firstly, there are only a few thousand vampires and about 7 billion humans. No matter how much stronger and more powerful we might be, we are vastly outnumbered, and would eventually be overpowered. The successful predator knows its limits. The lion is the king of the jungle, but there can only be so many lions. For vampires to be successful, we must stay in the shadows. Humanity doesn't even acknowledge that we exist, which gives us the perfect means of hunting them. And did you ever consider what would happen if we started creating more vampires?"

Kristen shook her head and looked puzzled.

"The more vampires you create, the more competition that you create. A few thousand vampires pretty much have no competition, which is good, because most of us don't like to work together. We may keep in touch with other vampires, and we may assist each other from time to time, but we are never blind to the fact that we are all on our own. If we made ourselves visible and tried to take over, we would be quickly wiped out. Things are as they are for a reason, and nothing is going to change that."

Kristin turned away from Eddie, but then turned back around and whispered in Eddie's ear, "Well, I would sure like to see someone try."

Eddie simply smiled. "Well, first things first – where do we go from here?"

Kristin put her hand under her chin and thought. "Well," she began, "I've always kind of wanted to rob a bank."

"We've got plenty of money Kris."

She shook her head. "It's not even so much about the money. I just want to experience the thrill of it."

"Robbing a bank?" Eddie shook his head. "That is rather visible. As I have been trying to tell you, discretion is a vampire's greatest ally."

"If I recall correctly, you are also telling me how you are tired of showing restraint, and you are far from discrete. What do you have to fear from robbing a bank? It's not like you're going to appear on the security cameras or anything. Are you afraid?"

"Me, afraid, " said Eddie as he pointed to his chest and began laughing before looking straight at Kristin with very serious eyes glowing bright yellow, "never."

Kristin got up and began shaking her head before turning around and waving her finger at Eddie. "I think that you are. I think that you are afraid your vampire buddies will come after you?"

"They haven't so far, and I'm sure that Reggie and Thomas are aware I haven't stopped. They have probably also heard about what happened to Lenora. When a vampire is killed, it is big news in the vampire world. Word travels fast."

"So," said Kristin as she put her hands on her hips and began tapping her foot impatiently, "what exactly do you want to do about this?"

Eddie put his hands behind his head again, looked up at the ceiling, and then turned back to Kristin. "I think," he said, "I think it's time for us to go and rob a bank."

Kristin smiled wickedly and took out a pair of Eddie's sunglasses and put them on. She nodded her head. "Let's do this."

Kristin and Eddie packed up all of their belongings – they wouldn't be coming back to this motel. They probably wouldn't even be coming back to the state after this.

After a short drive, they arrived in a small town and came

across the First National Bank. It was the first bank that they came across, and it didn't look all that big or impressive. It was a small-town bank at best.

"This is it?" asked Kristin as she turned to Eddie.

"It's the first bank that we came to. Do you still want to do this?"

She nodded as she took out her gun and loaded it.

"How much do you think is in there?" she asked.

"Probably not a lot, but I guess we'll find out."

"Well you said you were doing this for the thrill more than the money."

Kristin nodded in approval and began to get out of the car, but Eddie grabbed her and stopped her.

"What's wrong Eddie?"

"Here," he said as he tossed her a bandanna. "Tie that around your face and put on your sunglasses. This way no one will recognize you."

"Is that really necessary?"

"You don't want to be identified, trust me."

"Okay, fine, whatever. If you're so insistent on it."

Kristin put on the bandanna and sunglasses and they both got out of the car. She kept her gun concealed under her shirt until they walked into the bank. There was hardly anyone in the bank, so Kristin went up to the teller – a small blonde woman with a big smile on her face who seemed excessively cheerful.

"How may help you miss?" asked the bank teller as she closed her eyes and grinned. When she opened them she saw a gun pointing in her face. She stopped smiling.

"I want all of the money in this bank, do you understand?" Kristen asked the teller as she pointed the gun at her forehead. "Just nod if you understand."

The teller nodded feebly and began to become pale and started gently sobbing. She then proceeded to slowly get up, walk to the safe in the back and take out as much money as she could carry. Kristin took out a bag and the teller dropped the money into it. That was when Kristen noticed a very large diamond ring on her finger.

"I want the ring too," said Kristin pressing the gun against the teller's breast.

The teller began to sob hysterically. "Oh please," she sobbed, "not the ring. It's my engagement ring. My fiancée just bought it for me last week."

"Well, you can't get married if you have a bullet in your head, can you? Now give me the ring?"

The teller took off the ring and tearfully placed it into the bag. Kristin then slowly backed out the door with Eddie, they got into their car and began to drive off at breakneck speeds.

"What a rush!" shouted Kristin as Eddie accelerated. "Did you see the look on that stupid bitch's face when she first saw I had a gun and when I demanded that she give me her engagement ring. "

"It was classic," laughed Eddie.

"Still," said Kristin as she slipped the ring onto her finger and pulled the bandanna off her face, "I feel like I should've just shot the bitch. Oh well, there is always next time."

Eddie turned to her and smiled. "Next time?"

"Of course," said Kristin as she held up her hand and stared at the ring, "next time. You didn't think I would be satisfied with just one bank, did you? Besides, you saw yourself that that was a small bank. It was a good enough start, don't get me wrong, but I think you'll agree we could probably do better."

"So then, where next?"

Kristin looked over at Eddie and smiled. "Well, to the next bank of course. We'll be just like Bonnie and Clyde."

"Whatever you say, Bonnie."

Eddie pressed his foot down on the accelerator and off they went to their next crime.

Chapter 18

"Police continue to be baffled," said a news reporter for the channel 6 news, "by a mysterious string of bank robberies occurring throughout Arkansas. Five banks have been robbed so far and over $3 million have been stolen. Witnesses described the assailants as a redheaded woman wearing a bandanna and sunglasses and a pale skinned man also wearing sunglasses and a black leather jacket. In a related case a teenager was found running nude across the highway half frozen to death. He claimed that he and his girlfriend were assaulted at gunpoint while walking through the woods and then hunted for sport like animals. He managed to escape, but his girlfriend was found in the woods with multiple gunshot wounds to her body. His description of his assailants matches the description of the bank robbers, one of whom was seen dressed in their stolen clothing.

"In an odd twist on this case, security camera footage of the bank robberies only captured the image of the redheaded girl, but not her boyfriend who was standing right next to her. Police and analysts do not know how to explain this bizarre anomaly. The suspects are also wanted in connection with a series of murders in Las Vegas and New Orleans. The media has dubbed them 'The Vampire Killers ' in reference to the fact that the victims have often been found drained of blood. If you see anyone matching their descriptions, you should call the authorities immediately and consider them armed and dangerous. Do not try to engage them. We might have a case of psychopathic thrill killers or cultists on our hands. More on the evening edition of the channel 6 news."

Thomas threw the remote into the TV screen shattering it and ending the news program. He turned angrily to Reggie. "You," he said as he pointed to him with a raised dagger, "you are the one responsible for this. He was your protégé and you didn't have the good common sense to kill him like I ordered you to do. Give me one good reason why I shouldn't stake you myself before going after Eddie."

"Calm down," said Reggie as he slowly stood up, holding his hands up defensively at his chest, "I'll admit that I made a mistake."

Thomas slammed his fist down on the table. "You made a mistake! You made a mistake! Is that all you have to say for yourself? You've made more than one mistake. Your first mistake was turning Eddie into a vampire in the first place. Your second mistake was not killing him the first time he screwed up. Do you remember that?"

How could he forget. It was shortly after he had turned Eddie in the spring time of 1992. They had been staying at this very mansion and Eddie brought up the very question that every vampire asked sooner or later.

"So," said Eddie as he sipped a glass of blood, "you said

that you wanted to talk to me about something?"

"Yes," said Reggie. "It has been brought to my attention that you have been turning more and more people into vampires. Do you deny this?"

"Yeah, so what?" asked Eddie as he sipped back another glass of blood and licked his lips. "The more the merrier, right?"

"Wrong," said Reggie as he pointed accusingly at Eddie, "that is not how this works. You can't just go around creating vampires willy-nilly. There are consequences to your actions Eddie."

"So big freaking deal, I created a couple of extra vampires."

"It is a big deal!" said Reggie, practically hissing as he bore his fangs at Eddie. "Thomas –"

"That blowhard again, I don't give a damn what the stupid fucker thinks."

"You should care what he thinks, Eddie. He isn't just some random vampire. He is a very influential vampire and he takes the rules that we have developed very seriously. The vampires that you have created have been running wild and that risks exposing us all. Did you think we wouldn't hear about the blood orgies, the very public mass killings, vampire sightings all around the area."

Eddie shrugged his shoulders. "So?"

"So..." began Reggie, "you didn't exactly think that this would go over well. Haven't you picked up anything I've been saying these past few months? About how we have to stay hidden in the shadows."

Eddie laughed dismissively. "I don't see why. We are more powerful than anyone who might encounter us. We could easily take over."

"Your arrogance will be your downfall. We aren't going to let a system that we have kept in place for thousands of years be exposed to to the recklessness of a single individual. Do you understand Eddie?"

Eddie chugged down the rest of his blood and leaned back smugly.

Reggie shook his head and motioned to the vampires guarding the entrance to the parlor. They opened the door and two more vampires dragged in a naked female vampire with long black hair who was completely chained up in unbreakable steel. She struggled to break free, but to no avail.

"Cindy!" shouted Eddie as he suddenly sat up before two more vampires came and held him down. "What is the meaning of this?"

"We have to set an example, Eddie," said Thomas as he entered the room. He walked over to Cindy, grabbed her by her hair and pulled her head back. "You turned this woman to join you in your reckless killing spree. And you have failed to control yourself or her. She has killed very visibly and publicly, as have many of the other women you have turned. And she has turned many people as well."

"What did you do to the others?!" demanded Eddie as he struggled to break free from the hold of the other vampires, who each grabbed him by the arm.

Thomas pulled out a stake and brought it to Cindy's bare chest, right between her breasts. "The same thing I am going to do to her." And, with one flick of his wrist, Thomas drove the stake into Cindy's heart and she promptly let out a shriek before turning to dust, causing the chains to fall on top of the pile of her remains.

"Cindy! No!" shouted Eddie as he continued to struggle.

"Let this be a warning to you," said Thomas as he poked Eddie in the chest with the stake, "if you try this again, you will share her fate, won't he Reggie?" Thomas turned to Reggie with his eyes glowing red and Reggie just nodded obediently.

Thomas left the room and the other vampires released Eddie and followed Thomas out. Eddie got up to run towards Thomas, but Reggie caught him. "No Eddie," he said, "eternal life is worthless if you choose to commit suicide so easily."

Eddie ran over to the pile of dust that was once his lover, picked it up in his hands, broke down and wept. Reggie patted him on the shoulder and left the room.

"So you understand," said Thomas as he got right up into Reggie's face, "what needs to be done? There are no second chances this time. Alert the other vampires in our network to be on the lookout. Eddie must be destroyed, and anyone else who happens to be associated with him. And you personally are not to leave my sight until he has been eliminated."

Reggie nodded in agreement. There was no denying the

truthfulness of Thomas's words. This time, Eddie had to die.

Chapter 19

Eddie and Kristen were camping out in the woods of Missouri. Now that they were nationally wanted criminals, they figured it wasn't safe to stay at motels anymore. In total they had stolen millions of dollars which they were now hiding in the trunk of the latest car that Eddie had stolen. In this case they had stolen an RV, which they felt was sufficient for the time being.

Kristin was cooking bacon for dinner on the stove.

"I must say," she began, "this really is a rather nice RV. There is something romantic about traveling along the country like this, don't you think?"

"Well, you did say you wanted to see the country," said Eddie as he reclined in an easy chair and put his feet up while he watched the news, "and this is the way to do it – in style."

"But I have been a little bit worried," said Kristin as she began making a bacon sandwich.

"About what?"

"About what?! Have you been watching the news? We're outlaws Eddie!"

"I thought you were enjoying that."

"I am," she said as she took a bite of her bacon sandwich, "but what about Reggie and Thomas?"

Eddie shrugged his shoulders. "What about them?"

"Well, should we be worried that they're going to come after us?"

Eddie laughed. "Yeah, probably."

"It's not funny Eddie!"

"Are you suddenly afraid to die?"

She put down her sandwich and looked angrily at Eddie. "I don't want to die Eddie!"

Eddie laughed some more.

"What's so funny?" she asked as she crossed her arms and began tapping her foot angrily.

"You want to be an outlaw, but you're still afraid to die." He shook his head. "But you shouldn't worry. Nobody knows where we are. Our crime spree is spanning several states, and is completely random and unpredictable."

"But can't the other vampires track us down?"

Eddie shook his head. "We can track our prey, but only so far. It will take them a while to find us. But I suppose that you are correct. By now the entire vampire community has probably heard of what we have done. People will be out there looking for us. We have both the human authorities and the vampire authorities on the lookout. I wouldn't worry about the humans though."

"What will we do if they find us?"

"Go down fighting, I suppose."

"Eddie," she said as she grabbed his arm and whispered in his ear, "I don't want to die."

Eddie nodded his head and kissed Kristin on her forehead as he pulled her close to him. "I know. We'll find someplace to hide, at least until the heat dies down. If we disappear for a couple of months we will go off the radar. People forget pretty quickly when they are not constantly reminded of the dangerous people and creatures out there. We have more to fear from the vampires, but even they will let their guard down if we don't make ourselves too visible."

"Where are we going to go Eddie?"

"I don't know yet, but I'll drive into town to pick up some supplies tomorrow. We'll find someplace remote, someplace where we can be comfortable for a couple of months without drawing any suspicion to us."

Kristin nodded and smiled. "Sounds like a plan." She leaned forward and kissed Eddie on the cheek.

After buying a large number of supplies in town, Eddie decided he would stop by a local bar to see if there were any easy victims lying about. The first bar that he came to was a dingy little dive called Moe's. He couldn't help but wonder if that bar was named after the bar on The Simpsons. He wouldn't be surprised if it was.

In surveying the room, which was thick with smoke, and whose alcohol drenched smell offended his hyper keen senses, he did not see that many people there, just a few rednecks playing pool and a couple of cops who looked like they were resting while they were off duty. He casually went off into the corner and decided it was probably best to leave. He didn't want to draw more attention to him, as he still had groceries with him that he wanted to get home. But just as he was about to leave, he began to hear the cops talking about him.

"Who you think is behind all these 'vampire' slayings?" asked the first officer to the second officer sitting next to him on the barstool.

"Maybe it's a real vampire." The second officer added a chuckle after saying that.

"I still think it is the work of cultists, possibly Satanists," said a third officer. "You know, kids today, they read all of these Twilight books and Stephen King and watch all of these brutal gruesome horror movies and then they get all involved in the occult and that eventually leads them to committing all of these copycat killings. When I was a kid we read the Bible."

"They say they found puncture wounds on the victims," said the first officer. "So if these are some kind of cultists, they are certainly taking things very literally. Maybe they are mentally ill and really do believe they are vampires."

"Or maybe," said the second officer," like I was saying, maybe they are real vampires!" He laughed heartily at that and smacked the first officer hard on the back causing him to spill his beer.

"Did you ever consider that maybe vampires actually are real?" asked the bartender as he cleaned up the spilled beer.

"Real vampires," said the second officer with a sniff of contempt.

"Well officers," began the bartender, "how do you explain how the blood was drained from the bodies. In several of these killings the arms and legs were ripped right out of the sockets. What actual human being would have the strength to do something like that? And why doesn't this mysterious individual appear on any cameras? Even you have to admit that these killings have a lot of features that are mysterious and bizarre, but consistent with the legend of vampires, real vampires."

The second officer rolled his eyes.

"He does have a point," said the third officer. "I have been a police officer for over 20 years, and I don't recall any previous case that was anything like this. There really is no explanation for these bizarre anomalies. And being a God-fearing Christian, even I have to admit that the good book doesn't deny the existence of supernatural evil. Whoever or whatever we are dealing with here, it certainly doesn't seem to be your run-of-the-mill killings. My worry is that people are going to hear about these killings and want to copy them."

"You're right," said the first officer. "If they do catch this guy and his girlfriend, they will probably become celebrities. There are a lot of sick people out there who view people like Ted Bundy and Charles Manson as people to be idolized. I almost think that in today's atmosphere they could even get their own reality show. And mark my words, I am not exaggerating when I say that these two psychopaths are in the same league as those two."

Eddie continued eavesdropping from across the room, not even noticed, by the very people who were tasked with catching someone like him. He couldn't help but laugh.

"What do you think is so funny?" asked a fat bearded man approaching Eddie.

"Nothing," said Eddie.

"Well," said the bearded man as he poked Eddie in the chest as he held the pool cue in the other hand, "you are obviously laughing at something."

"You might want to think about not poking me," said Eddie as he slapped away his hand.

"And you might not want to slap me," said the bearded man.

Eddie laughed derisively. "I think," he said as he grabbed the man's hand, "that if you know what is good for you, you won't pick a fight with a person that you don't know."

"And who the hell are you to grab my hand like that?" asked the bearded man.

"I don't think you want to know just who it is you are talking to, because if you did, I don't think you would be a stupid as to want to start something with me."

"You look like some stupid little faggot!" said the bearded man as he spit into Eddie's face.

"What did you call me?" asked Eddie as he began to crush the bearded man's hand until he could hear bone cracking.

The bearded man began to whimper as Eddie continued to

crush his hand. "Hey, lemme me go," he said with a strained breath, "I didn't mean anything by it."

"Isn't it funny," Eddie began saying, "that is soon as the victimizers become the victim they become so weak and pathetic. They play the tough guy and then break down, whimpering and begging for mercy like a little girl as soon as the tides turn against them. It never ceases to amaze me and the result is never different."

"Come on Mister," begged the bearded man, "you know I was just joking around. Can't you take a little joke?"

Eddie began to laugh. "Here is a joke. Knock knock."

"Who's there?" said the bearded man as he began to cry.

"Fuck."

"F-fuck who?"

"What I was going to say that I was going to fuck your wife, but I don't think an ugly piece of shit like you could get a wife." Eddie paused as he continued crushing the man's hand. "Aren't you going to laugh?"

The bearded man simply whimpered and Eddie pressed down and crushed his hand even more causing him to scream out in pain and fall to his knees grabbing his mangled hand.

"I'll admit," said Eddie, "I was never that great with punchlines."

Eddie began to walk away when the three officers came over.

"What seems to be the problem here?" asked the first officer.

"Nothing," said Eddie, "just a friendly little handshake."

"That son of a bitch broke my fucking hand!" wailed the bearded man as he continued clutching his hand.

Eddie pointed to himself with both hands. "Me? Crush your hand? I guess I don't know my own strength." Eddie laughed and began walking away but the three officers blocked his path.

"Excuse me officers," said Eddie,"but I really must be going."

"I'm afraid we can't let you do that," said the second officer. "This is a clear case of assault. You have injured this man and you will have to come in for questioning so that we can sort this out down at the station."

"I'm afraid I've made other plans for the evening," said Eddie as he began to push the officers aside.

"Maybe you don't understand how this works," said the third officer as he stood in Eddie's path. "I'm afraid I'm going to have to place you under arrest."

"Like I said," said Eddie, pushing the officer aside, "I've got other plans."

"All right freeze!" shouted the first officer as he pointed his gun at Eddie. "Now come along peacefully and there will be no trouble."

The second officer came towards Eddie with handcuffs and he began to laugh maniacally.

"What the fuck is so funny?" asked the second officer.

"The man is crazy!" shouted the bearded man, still kneeling on the floor rubbing his injured hand.

"The funny thing is, "said Eddie, "that you think those weak little things are going to hold me."

"I'm warning you, Mister," said the first officer as he raised his gun towards Eddie's face.

Eddie shook his head. "I so tire of this. It's always the same. Stop or I'll shoot. Come along quietly. Etc. etc."

"Put your hands up over your head right now!" shouted the first officer.

Eddie smirked as he put his hands behind his head. "Okay, I'll humor you. You can see my handcuff escape trick."

"Don't try anything funny," said the second officer as he placed the handcuffs on Eddie's wrists behind his back. At that point Eddie broke into a wild fit of laughter.

"The guy is completely fucking nuts!" exclaimed the third officer.

"I don't deny that I am completely insane," said Eddie, "but what I was laughing at was the whole irony of the situation."

"Irony?"asked the first officer as he began to frisk Eddie. "What is ironic about all of this."

"Well, I couldn't help but overhear your conversation a few minutes ago. You were talking about and scoffing at the idea of a real vampire killer being out there."

"So," asked the first officer as he continued to frisk Eddie, "what is ironic about that?"

"Well," said Eddie, "you are about to be killed by a vampire."

"What?" asked the first officer. But before he could process what Eddie had just said, Eddie snapped the handcuffs apart, swung around and bit into the officer's jugular vein. He let out a garbled scream before falling to the floor grabbing his neck and trying to stop the bleeding.

The other two officers turned around to see Eddie standing over the first officer bleeding at his feet. They fired two shots into Eddie's chest and he pretended to fall to the floor dead. The second officer kneeled down to try and help the first officer, while the third officer approached Eddie's body.

"It looks like I got him," said the third officer as he stood over Eddie's body. He turned to look over at the other two officers and as soon as his head was turned Eddie leapt up from the ground, grabbed him by the neck and threw over his shoulders and smashed him down onto the pool table. Before the second officer could get up, Eddie kicked him in the stomach, causing him to drop his gun. He then grabbed the officer's head and pulled it straight out of his neck, splattering blood all over.

Seeing all of this the bearded man and his two friends got up and started running towards the door, as did the bartender. But before they could get there, Eddie blocked the entrance. They started to slowly walk back in fear.

"What the hell are you?" asked the bearded man as he was trembling and holding his hand.

"You never pay attention. Do you?" said Eddie as he was shaking his head. "That is the most annoying thing – always having to explain everything to the ignorant people you come across. So you know what, I don't have time for explanations. I am just going to kill you and be done with it."

The two men with the bearded man picked up pool cues and swung them at Eddie. He grabbed them both and snapped them in two. He then turned the pointed ends towards the two men and stabbed them both in their stomachs. The bartender attempted to run but Eddie hit him in the face, knocking him unconscious.

As Eddie slowly approached the bearded man, the bearded man moved back and fell backwards onto the floor near the bodies of the first two officers. He covered his face up with his good hand

and prepared for death. But after a moment he looked up to see Eddie still standing there.

"W-what are you waiting for?" asked the bearded man looking up at Eddie and trembling.

"You know what," said Eddie as he crossed his arms over his blood covered chest," you're so pathetic, it isn't even worth my time for me to finish you off. So you know what I'm going to do?"

The bearded man shook his head and continued trembling.

Eddie picked up the gun of one of the dead officers and pointed it at the bearded man. "Take off your clothes and turn around."

The bearded man slowly took off his clothes and threw them on the floor beside him and then turned around. Eddie picked up a pair of handcuffs and cuffed the bearded man's hands behind his back. He then pushed the bearded man to the ground.

"Now originally," began Eddie, "I was going to kill you. Then I thought I would be a complete asshole and sodomize you with the pool cue. But then I thought that might kill you, but I really want someone alive to spread the story of what happened here. So I'm going to leave you alive. It will be a funny story you can tell people when they find you lying here naked on the floor amongst the pile of dead bodies. Tell them you are one of the few survivors of the vampire killers. But also, don't forget to add that I am not normally this merciful. Do you understand me?"

"Uh-huh," muttered the bearded man as he broke into tears.

"Good," said Eddie as he began to walk away before pausing and turning around to him one last time. "And forgive my poor manners – have a nice day!"

Eddie picked up his groceries and started laughing as he walked out of the bar.

Within a short time, Eddie had arrived back at the RV covered in blood and carrying the groceries. Kristin looked up at him with a shocked expression. "Let me guess," she started,"we have to be leaving in a hurry again, don't we?" And right after that she burst out laughing and Eddie joined in.

"Let's be getting out of here now," said Eddie as he started up the RV,"and on to our next adventure."

Kristin just smiled as she sat up front next to Eddie and

they began to drive away.

Chapter 20

"It is a sensation!" shouted the newscaster into his microphone as he stood in front of Moe's bar. "We are here at the scene of the latest victim of the vampire killer slayings where six men were slaughtered just a few hours ago. This time he acted alone and left one survivor – a man who was handcuffed nude with a completely crushed hand. It was nearly an hour before anyone came into the bar to be confronted with another scene of horror. The walls were splattered with blood, and the victims were heavily mutilated. According to the one survivor, the assailant killed them all using just his bare hands and a couple of pool cues. He allegedly tore an officer's head right out of its socket. He alleges that this was after, mind you, after he took two bullets directly to the chest and did not die."

The newscaster put his microphone up to the face of one of the investigators at the scene. "What do you make of the story as related by the lone survivor?"

The investigators shook his head. "Well, we have to keep in mind, he was found in a state of extreme shock, and we know that when you are an extreme shock, the mind sometimes plays tricks on you and that can distort the memory."

The newscaster looked at him with a puzzled look. "But isn't it true that all of the injuries on the bodies that have been recovered are consistent with the story that he related?"

"Well," began the investigator, "our preliminary report –"

"Are you calling the witness a liar?" asked the newscaster, interrupting the investigator as he thrust the microphone right into his face.

"I didn't say that exactly. What I am saying is that we haven't got all the facts in yet and are still investigating. It is possible that the lone witness could be a suspect."

The newscaster gave him an exasperated look. "Are you honestly trying to suggest that a man with a broken hand who was handcuffed and left naked in the bar had committed the crimes, crushed his own hand and handcuffed himself?"

"I didn't say that, I am just saying that the facts aren't all in yet."

The newscaster turned away from him and towards the camera. "You've heard from the investigators, but now let's hear from the public. Earlier we interviewed some people on the street about their feelings on this whole vampire killing spree story. Let's roll the footage."

"Excuse me miss," the newscaster said as he put the microphone to the face of an elderly woman, "but what are your feelings on these vampire slayings?"

"Well," she began to say in a scratchy voice that showed its age as she smoked a cigarette, "I think it's just awful. This is what happens when society's morals decline. You have all of these Satanists abusing children and converting people to devil worship, it's only natural that things like this would happen. In my day we would never hear of it. People have to start fearing God once again, and then they will have nothing else to fear. We need to bring back prayer in schools and beat the little brats. A good couple of lashings across the wrist with a ruler will set them straight."

"What are your feelings on this whole affair," the newscaster asked, putting the microphone in the face of a morbidly obese middle-aged man wearing a hat with a Confederate flag on it.

"If I see this damn vampire man, you know what I'm gonna do – I'm gonna kick his ass. That will teach him to mess with anyone. He's probably a queer." The obese man let out a belch at the end of that sentence.

The newscaster cut to another clip. "But not everyone has an entirely negative view of the killers," he began, "there are some who see these mysterious killers as heroes."

"Well," said a teenage girl as she was jumping up and down with excitement, "I think vampires are totally sexy and this guy sounds like a total bad ass."

"What about the girl that has been spotted with him," asked the newscaster as he brought the microphone closer to her lips.

"Well, she is one lucky woman. I'd give anything to be in her place."

The newscaster turned to another teenage girl. "And what do you think of all this vampire stuff?"

"I think it's totally cool. I always knew that vampires existed and this proves it."

"And why are vampires cool?"

"Well, because they are immortal, and deep and romantic. Vampires are totally sexy." And with that she couldn't suppress a fit of the giggles.

"If there was any one thing that you could say to this mysterious man, should he be listening, what would that be?"

"Will you be the Edward to my Bella?!" And with that she couldn't help but burst out laughing before adding, "I love you!" And she ended by blowing a kiss at the camera, before giggling some more.

The newscaster turned to the camera. "And for our final input I interviewed a group of 'real'vampires."

"I understand that not everyone is happy with the characterization of vampires as ruthless killers. Is that correct?" The newscaster put the microphone up to the face of a pale skinned teenager with spiky hair, black lipstick and dressed completely in black. Next to him was a pale skinned girl with long black hair dressed in the same exact manner.

"We vampires are not killers. We don't murder people and our lifestyle is one of peace."

"But what about these vampire killers? They have murdered dozens of people so far, as well as robbed and assaulted many others."

The pale skinned teenager put up his hand and shook his head." These vampire killers do not represent us. We completely condemn their actions. They are not true to the vampire lifestyle."

"But doesn't your lifestyle involve the consumption of human blood."

"We don't take blood from unwilling victims. We will sometimes allow each other to bite one another and consume each other's blood, but it is strictly voluntary and we consider it to be a spiritual act that is not to be taken lightly."

"What about the critics who say that it is people like you who inspire these types of killings."

He shook his head. "We are misunderstood. People take one single case like this and try to characterize our entire lifestyle by people who do not share it. These people are common run-of-the-mill killers who are shaming our peaceful community."

"What do you make of all the strange anomalies that accompanied this case – the drained blood, the thoroughly mutilated bodies, the fact that the assailant does not appear on camera. Do you believe yourselves to have real supernatural powers?"

"I don't know how to explain those, but I will say one final time – the vampire community is not violent and these people are not one of us." The girl next to him was nodding in agreement.

"Do you have any last words you would like to add?"

He shook his head. "I think that we have explained ourselves and made things perfectly clear. I hope that whoever these people are, they will abandon their course of destruction and that they will be brought to justice."

The newscaster turned back to the camera. "You have heard it, straight from a real-life vampire. What are your thoughts on this? Go to our website and share your thoughts on the strange and inexplicable killings. For the channel 6 news, I am Harold Glock."

Thomas turned off the television. "Stupid goth vampire wannabes teens. They give us all a bad name."

Thomas turned to address a circle of about two dozen vampires seated around him. "We face an unprecedented crisis. This is something we have feared for years. Until recently it was easy enough for us to hide in the shadows, but this day was probably long in coming and I have dreaded it. I knew it was only a matter of time, with all this modern media, that someone would discover our existence. And I am sad to say, I'm not surprised that Eddie is the one who risks exposing us. The question is what are we going to do about it?"

A vampire in a black cloak stood up to address the Council. "We have already alerted all vampires in our networks to be on the lookout for Eddie and to kill him and his lover on site. But we really don't know where he is or when he will strike next. There does not seem to be any pattern to his attacks and every new attack is in a new state. All we can say is that he appears to be moving north."

Another vampire stood up, this one dressed in a red cloak. "Do you think that he is intentionally trying to expose us?"

Reggie stood up raising his hand to silence the other vampires. "No. Eddie has always been an uncontrolled menace, one I am sad to admit responsibility for. Having known him longer than anyone else here I can say that he has very little restraint. That he has managed to last this long is amazing. I can't say with any certainty where he might go, but he has already killed one vampire and doesn't seem to be concerned about being caught."

The vampire in the black cloak stood up again. "Do you think he will intentionally try to go public?"

Reggie put his hands to his face and then looked up. "I honestly cannot say. I know that in the past, Eddie has expressed desire to come out and try and take over. I think he realizes the implausibility of that, but I also think that he is reckless and does not care either way. He is completely unpredictable and I really don't know what he's going to do next. It is possible that his new lover convinced him to do all of this, he never did have much restraint when it came to listening to women."

Another vampire rose to address the Council and pushed Reggie aside. He was dressed in a brown robe. "There is one possibility that we must consider. It is possible that Eddie is on a suicidal rampage, but it is also true that he might not want to die. This raises the disturbing possibility that he will do one last thing to protect himself – he will give himself up."

Reggie rose to address the Council. "But why would you want to give himself up? What purpose would it serve?"

Thomas came over and placed his hand on Reggie's shoulders and then turned towards the other vampires. "Surely by now Eddie knows that we must be looking for him. However insane he might be, he still must know that he cannot take on the entire vampire community. Eventually one of us will find him and overpower him. Perhaps his best chance at survival is to turn himself in, expose himself as a vampire, and then be taken into protective custody. Once people realize that he possesses the secret of immortality, it's all over for us. All we need is for one vampire to be proven real and then we will be hunted down and destroyed. Those of us who survive will most likely end up imprisoned in a lab and experimented upon until people find out what it is that makes us tick."

Reggie turned to Thomas. "What do you suggest we do?"

"I think that we might have to try the most unorthodox solution of all. We might have to enlist the help of humans and their own authorities in order to catch Eddie. They want to catch Eddie just as much as we do, and we know that they are unlikely to do so without help. We also don't want to risk them capturing Eddie alive. What we need to do is enlist the trust of the human authorities. We have friends in law enforcement that we can trust, and they are the ones who we must use to help lead us to Eddie. Unless there are any objections, I suggest we do so immediately. Are there any opposed?" Thomas looked around the room and saw no one rise to challenge him. "Good, so it is decided then, we enlist the help of the humans. And any of them that betray us, we eliminate. This Council is hereby adjourned."

Chapter 21

Kristin and Eddie had been driving for nearly a day and were now somewhere in Nebraska. They were driving down a mostly abandoned road, with Kristen enjoying the feeling of the wind blowing in her hair. They were playing the radio loudly.

"There are many who say," said the voice on the radio,"that the witnesses to all of these vampire slayings are all part of some kind of network. Skeptics contend that they are making up the story and they are the ones behind the killing. Still others think that the witnesses were hallucinating. But police continue to be baffled by the unusual nature of these killings and are wondering when these killers will strike next."

Kristin turned off the radio. "Doesn't it bug you?"

"Doesn't what bug me?" asked Eddie.

"The fact that people are trying to think of all these alternate explanations for your killings. People just can't accept the fact that there is a real vampire out there. We're celebrities now Eddie. Have you ever considered just going public and proving all of those skeptics wrong. Just imagine the look on everyone's faces. It would be awesome."

Eddie shook his head. "You still don't get this. If I went public, do you think that they would ever let me go, let us go? You'd probably go to jail for the rest of your mortal life, while I could be subjected to an eternity in some kind of science lab. I'm sure that you don't want that. Once people realize that vampires exist we won't exist for very long. We can only keep up our current lifestyle so long as no one knows about us."

Kristin folded her arms across her chest and made a huff.

"What's the matter?" asked Eddie.

"What about all of that talk of to hell with restraint, live fast and die young and all of that stuff?"

Eddie shook his head. "I wasn't thinking clearly. You said that you don't want to die. If we don't keep a low profile for a while, we will be killed. And I don't want that, at least not yet, do you?"

Kristen shook her head. "I guess not." She turned to look out the window.

"We don't want the fun to end just yet, now do we?"

"No," said Kristin as she continued to look out the window. "But Eddie?"

"Yes?"

"Where are we going to go and where we going to strike next?"

"I have to admit, I am starting to get hungry again. All of this excitement sure works up an appetite."

"Too bad we're in the middle of nowhere," Kristin sighed. But then, up ahead, she caught sight of a barn in the distance. "What about there?"

"Where?"

"Right there, right up ahead," said Kristin as she pointed ahead to the barn.

Eddie shrugged his shoulders. "I suppose it's as good a place as any."

Eddie drove off the road and up to the barn. He and Kristin then walked to the house right next to it and knocked on the door. They were greeted by an elderly man and an elderly woman that Eddie assumed was her wife.

"Hello," said the man, "what can I do for you?"

"Well," said Eddie, "my girlfriend and I have been driving for many hours and we don't quite know where we are. Would it be okay if we came in and talked to you?"

"I don't normally let strangers in," said the man.

"Don't be rude," said the woman before turning to Eddie

and Kristen, and adding, "don't mind my husband. He isn't used to visitors. Of course you can come in. Please sit down." She motioned for them to come in and the man nodded in acknowledgment.

"Thank you for your hospitality," said Eddie as he and Kristin sat down on the couch, "it is good to know that we can always rely on the kindness of strangers."

"Dear me," said the woman, "forgive my manners. Earl, turn off that damn TV."

"Yes, Ethel," he said as he turned the TV off.

"Anything good on," asked Eddie.

"Oh, just the news," said Ethel as she and Earl sat down across from them.

"Anything good on the news," asked Eddie.

"Oh, it's all awful news," shouted Ethel. "All they are talking about is those horrible vampire killings."

"It's just awful, isn't it," asked Eddie secretly smiling at Kristin, who smiled back.

"It never would've happened in our day," said Earl. "Back when I was growing up, young people had common courtesy and morals. Young people today are all violent punks."

"Oh, I agree," said Eddie, "people today are just awful. But do you think that vampires really exist?"

"Hogwash!" exclaimed Earl

"Well I certainly hope not," said Ethel.

"But how could you possibly know?" asked Eddie

"Because if vampires were real, the good book would've said something about it," said Earl as he shook his head.

"Well, certainly there are things that exist that aren't mentioned in the Bible," said Eddie.

"Well, I'll believe it when I see it," said Earl with a laugh of contempt.

"Well," said Eddie, "you did request it." And before Earl could say a word Eddie bore his fangs and took off his glasses, staring Earl directly in the face with his glowing yellow eyes.

"Dear sweet Jesus!" shouted Earl. "What the hell is that?"

"This," said Eddie as he pointed to himself,"is what a vampire looks like. Believe in them now?"

Earl started to stand up in his chair and move backwards, as did Ethel.

"What the hell are you?" asked Earl.

Eddie shook his head and turned to Kristin. "See what I mean. I tell people I'm a vampire, and then they ask the same questions that I have already answered. It is really rather annoying."

"You look here," said Earl as he pointed his finger at Eddie, "I don't know what you are, but I want you out of my house right this minute or I'm calling the police."

Kristin took out her gun and pointed it at them. "I don't think you want to do that. I suggest you sit down because the police weren't going to be much help to you in this situation."

Ethel fainted and Earl fell backwards into his seat with a look of terror on his face.

"What do you want from me?" asked Earl as he began to tremble. "I've got money. Whatever you want, just take as much is you need, but just leave us alone."

Eddie shook his head as Kristin smiled and raised her gun.

"I'm afraid I can't do that," said Eddie. "We aren't short on cash, and I certainly can't let you go, as I doubt you would keep quiet about this. Besides which, I am hungry and the only thing I want to do right now is to satiate my hunger with your blood."

Earl began to run, but as soon as he did Kristin shot him in the back causing him to fall on top of Ethel. Eddie then dived on top of him and began to tear him apart. Kristin sat there smiling and twirling her gun in her hand. Finally Eddie had finished, got up and wiped the blood from his mouth. He looked at Kristin, his eyes glowing bright, and she gave him a very big smile, and together they walked off upstairs.

Kristin and Eddie awoke the next morning, naked and covered in the blood of their latest victims, just as the sun was coming in through the windows. Kristin got up to close the shades. Eddie watched as she slowly walked, covered in blood stains.

"You know Eddie," she said as she turned around and put her hands on her hips, "this place actually isn't that bad. Did you ever consider that we might just stay here?"

"You have a point. It is decidedly remote, probably gets few visitors and we could easily hold up here for a couple of months. We can survive by picking up people driving along the road. And with so many wide open spaces, there's plenty of places to burn and bury the bodies."

"So we can stay?!" she asked with excitement.

"Yes," said Eddie as he was nodding, "we can stay."

"Oh Eddie, " she said as she kissed him, "I really do love you."

Eddie smiled and Kristin got back into bed. He turned to her and said, "I think I'm going to need more blood, because I could do this all day long."

Chapter 22

Several months passed and the farmhouse where they had taken up residence proved to be the perfect place to hide for the winter. It was remote enough that no one ever came by, except on rare occasions. The elderly couple that they had killed had no friends or relatives, so there was no inquiry about the fact that they hadn't been seen or heard from by anyone. They would only occasionally go into town for supplies, but they would be discrete about it, and it would usually be Kristin who would go into town. Fortunately there were no incidents over the next four months, and the media frenzy gradually died down.

"So Eddie," began Kristin as she cooked a breakfast of bacon and eggs, "are we going to stay here forever?"

Eddie scratched his head. "I don't know about forever, as forever is a very long time, but when you literally do have forever there is no rush to do anything. We are lucky that no one has come to investigate. We haven't heard any mention of us in the news for months and so far Thomas, Reggie and any other vampires have failed to track us down. Aren't you happy here?"

"It's not that Eddie," she said over the loud sizzling of her bacon, "but I was enjoying our constant traveling. How long do you think we have to stay here before anyone stops looking for us?"

"Reggie and Thomas will probably never stop looking for us. Odds are that they have vampires watching all the crime bureaus throughout the country to investigate anything that seems unusual. The only way that they will ever stop looking for us is if someone kills them. But even then, we wouldn't be forgotten that easily. After everything that we have done we are probably number one on the vampire council's most wanted list. We are pretty much permanently shunned from the community of immortals."

"But we haven't made ourselves very visible lately, maybe they have forgiven us."

"Not a chance. Trust me, these guys mean business and they never forgive. Exposing myself in a very visible manner like that is pretty much committing the unforgiveable cardinal sin for vampires."

"But if they are scouring the country looking for us, wouldn't it make more sense for us to keep on the move? Maybe you could throw them off the trail."

"How do you propose that I do that?"

"Well," she said before pausing and resting her fisted hand on her face in contemplation, "maybe you could go commit a series of very visible massacres up in Canada and then return here. This will make them think that you were in Canada and they might stop looking around in America."

"So you think we should make our crime spree international now?" Eddie scratched his head again. "Not that I haven't thought of it myself."

"Well I'm still happy just seeing this country, but I'm getting kind of bored spending all my time out here in the middle of nowhere. We have millions of dollars Eddie, and here we are living like a bunch of dumb rednecks on some farm in the most boring area of the country."

"You might have a point, but for now I think it is time for me to feed again."

Kristen began to show a sign of excitement and was practically jumping up and down. "Let me go with you, I need some excitement. Just let me finish my breakfast first."

Eddie nodded in agreement.

Soon Eddie and Kristen had walked down to the path leading up to the barn to go wait by the road for potential victims. Not many cars came by on any given day, but they could always count on at least a few people driving by. After about an hour of waiting, Eddie could hear a car coming off in the distance.

"Are you ready?" asked Eddie.

Kristin nodded with a big smile on her face.

Eddie picked up a large log and threw it on the road. They both went and hid not far off and waited for the car to come by. As expected, the car was speeding by very quickly and did not see the log. The car hit the log and rapidly crashed into the ditch along the road. As soon as they saw that, Eddie and Kristen started running over to the car to be of assistance, i.e. to go get Eddie's breakfast.

Once they got to the car, it appeared that the two travelers inside – a man and a woman – were seemingly okay. Eddie ran over to the car and knocked on the window. The driver rolled it down.

"Are you okay?" asked Eddie.

"I think so," said the man. "I'm just a little bit shaken up is all." He turned to the woman beside him and asked her if she was okay and she nodded.

"If there is anything we can do," began Eddie.

"Thank you, but I think we'll be okay. I will just call for help on my cell phone."

As the man reached for his cell phone, Eddie grabbed it and crushed it in his hand.

"What the hell do you think you're doing?!" shouted the man.

"I don't think you'll be needing that," said Eddie as he tore the door off of his car and picked the man up by his plaid shirt.

"Get out of the car," said Kristin to the woman as she pointed a gun at her.

The woman got out of the car slowly and Kristin led her over to where Eddie was holding the man. Eddie put the man down next to the woman and Kristin pointed her gun at both of them.

"What do you want?" asked the man as he put his arm up defensively in front of the woman next to him. She was visibly trembling. "We'll give you anything that you want," she said,"just don't hurt us."

"Follow me back to the barn," said Eddie as he waved them forward. Kristen followed behind them, putting a gun to the woman's back.

They led them to the barn, where Eddie instructed them to undress. They slowly got undressed and threw their clothing on the floor in front of them. They both tried covering up, and the woman was visually blushing, while the man looked more angry. No doubt if he hadn't had a gun trained on him at the moment he probably would've done something violent.

Eddie smiled in Kristin's direction and she smiled back as she pointed the gun straight at the couple.

"What should we make them do?" asked Eddie.

Kristin rested her free hand on her cheek in contemplation. "I have an idea," she finally said. "Let us have them do 100 jumping jacks!"

"100 jumping jacks?" asked Eddie. "Why do you want them to do 100 jumping jacks?"

Kristin put her finger in her mouth and smiled a very large smile. "Because we can of course!"

Eddie laughed heartily as he grabbed his stomach. "I have to admit, blood tastes better when the heart is beating more quickly. Okay, so 100 jumping jacks it is. Get started."

The man and the woman looked at each other in confusion.

"Are you fucking deaf?!" shouted Kristin. "The man said to get started. So get started!" Kristin shot a bullet at the ground, inches from their feet and a split second later they began doing jumping jacks.

"That's 10," said Kristin. "Let's pick up the pace a bit." She fired another shot at their feet.

As they began jumping faster and faster Eddie and Kristen both burst out laughing.

"What's so funny?!" demanded the woman as she stopped jumping.

Kristin fired another shot at their feet. "Hey, did I say to fucking stop? Well, did I?!"

They both resumed doing their jumping jacks and began huffing and puffing as they started running out of breath.

"Since you asked, "said Kristin, "I was just laughing seeing your flabby naked bodies with your junk and your boobies all flopping about."

Eddie and Kristin looked at each other and both burst out laughing again. They could barely restrain themselves. The woman began to cry and the man gave a look of rage. It looked like the vein on his forehead was going to explode. At that moment, after just 37 jumping jacks, they both stopped.

"I didn't say to stop," said Kristin as she raised her gun. "That wasn't 100 jumping jacks."

"We aren't going to do anymore," said the man. "If you're going to kill us, just go ahead and do it, but we won't give into your demands anymore."

Kristin shrugged her shoulders. "Whatever you say." Without so much as a moment's hesitation, she rasised her gun, and she shot the man straight in the head, and he fell down dead. The woman screamed and began to run, but Kristin shot her in the leg and she fell down in the mud. Eddie began devouring the man, tearing him limb from limb as Kristin stood over the woman, pointing the gun at her face. Tears streamed down her face and she closed her eyes. But after a moment she opened them to see Kristin was still there.

"Just do it already!" she she shouted as she sobbed hysterically, her dirty blonde hair covering up most of her face.

Kristen shook her head. "I don't think so. I haven't had my fun yet."

Eddie came over drenched in blood. He looked at Kristin and asked, "What are you waiting for?"

"You know Eddie," she said, "remember that thing we were discussing the other day?"

"What thing?" asked Eddie.

"You know," said Kristin with a big smile as she started shaking with excitement with her finger in her mouth, "the thing."

Eddie looked at her, blood running down his lips, and smiled a big bloody smile at her. She nodded and closed her eyes briefly before looking back up at him, her eyes wide with excitement.

"What the fuck are you talking about?!" shouted the woman as she pounded her fist into the mud.

"Oh, you'll find out," said Eddie as he grabbed her under her armpits. She began kicking and screaming, but Kristin shot her in her uninjured leg. She let out a wail of pain that was deafening.

"God," said Kristin, "will you shut the fuck up already! I hate how victims always carry on and on. Now, are you going to be quiet, or do I have to torture you first?"

The woman continued sobbing, but she nodded at Kristin.

Eddie dragged the woman by her arms through the mud and into the house while Kristen followed behind pointing the gun at her. They began to drag her up the stairs to the bedroom, leaving a trail of blood from her injured legs. Eddie picked her up and threw her onto the bed, took some handcuffs out of the dresser drawer and handcuffed each of the woman's hands to the bedpost. She began to scream some more and tried to kick her legs around as blood gushed all over the bed.

"God dammit!" shouted Kristin. "Will you put a fucking cork in it!"

"How about a ball gag?" asked Eddie as he shoved the gag into the woman's mouth.

Kristin smiled. "That's better. It's a good thing that we're millionaires, because we wreck our sheets with human blood more than anyone else I know."

Eddie couldn't help bursting out laughing, as did Kristin. They were practically in hysterics again.

"And how many people," said Eddie between fits of laughter, "do you know who have a problem washing human blood out of their sheets?"

"Just you baby," said Kristin, "just you."

"Shall we?" asked Eddie as he pointed at the muddy, blood covered woman squirming on the bed.

Kristin nodded, put her gun down on the dresser, and both of them began to get undressed. The woman looked at them in total confusion. Here she was, chained naked and bleeding to a bed, and now her kidnappers were undressing in front of her.

"Look at the crazy bitch," said Kristin, "she has no idea what we're doing."

"Not a fucking clue," said Eddie, "but she's going to find out in just a minute."

Eddie and Kristen both sat down on the bed on either side of the woman. They both looked at each other and then looked the woman in the eyes and smiled at each other. The woman continued sobbing hysterically as Kristin and Eddie began making out on top of her. The blood of her dead boyfriend was dripping off of Eddie and onto her body.

After a few minutes of making out and wiping blood on the naked woman between them, Kristin grabbed a knife from the nightstand and began making deep cut wounds on the woman. She began screaming, but her screams were muffled by the gag in her mouth. Kristen began to lick the bloody wounds on her body and then made out more with Eddie. She then started dipping her fingers into the bloody wounds on the woman's leg and sticking her fingers into Eddie's mouth.

"Taste good?" asked Kristin as Eddie licked the blood from her fingers.

"Exquisite," said Eddie as he sucked on her finger.

The woman's muffled screams grew louder and louder as she struggled to try and break free, but to no avail. Struggle as she might, she could not break free. As she slowly lost her blood, she began turning pale and struggling less and less.

"I think that she is almost dead," said Kristin.

"Almost," said Eddie,"but as long as her heart is beating, she can still feel pain."

Kristen began to finger the woman's nipple. She looked up at Eddie, who was fondling her other breast. "Shall we finish her off," Kristen asked.

"Well I hate to end such an exciting and good thing, but I think it is time."

Kristin nodded, took the knife and plunged it into the woman's right breast. She then withdrew the knife and stabbed her in the left breast. She writhed and wiggled around, her muffled screams being extremely loud in spite of the ball gag. Eddie began to drink the blood from her breasts, lapping it up like a dog laps up water from it's bowl after not having drank all day. Then, Kristin looked up at Eddie and he nodded once more. Kristin plunged the knife into the woman's heart and blood gushed out all over her body. Eddie continued to lick the blood off of her like a starving animal. Then once he had consumed his fill, he laid on top of the woman's mutilated body and Kristin jumped on top of Eddie and mounted him. Eddie caressed Kristin's naked body and breasts with the blood of the dead woman as she moaned in ecstasy. Then the blond woman's screaming finally stopped.

Chapter 23

The phone was ringing and Thomas was quick to pick it up.

"Hello," he said, "have you heard anything?"

"There is one thing that we have found that looks rather suspicious," said the voice on the phone. "It seems there have been an unusual amount of disappearances along this road in Nebraska. It might be nothing, but then again..."

"I understand," said Thomas, "thank you for your assistance."

"Mind if I ask you something?" asked the man on the phone.

"What?" asked Thomas.

"Well," the man began, "I am just curious, but how many people do you vampires tend to kill each year?"

Thomas tried to conceal a laugh, but he couldn't help himself. "Let's just say that a substantial number of the unsolved murders and disappearances in this country and around the world are due to vampires."

"How many precisely?"

"I'm afraid we don't keep statistics. Most of us work alone and try to be discrete."

"But not this Eddie guy?"

"No, not Eddie. Eddie is a fucking moron and will pay dearly for his ignorance. Any other questions?"

The man could detect a tone of disdain and aggravation in Thomas's voice so he figured it was probably better to end this. "No," he said, "that is all for now."

Thomas put down the phone and turned to Reggie.

"So," said Reggie, "have we got anything?"

"Possibly. There has been some suspicious disappearances along this road in Nebraska."

"I think I remember hearing something about that. And these mysterious disappearances only began recently, at around the same time that Eddie disappeared and went off our radar."

"We'll send one of our contacts in that area."

Reggie leaned back against the wall and crossed his arms. "Do you really think that we can trust the human authorities?"

"I don't fully trust any humans. Would you trust your food to help you?"

"But this guy you talk to, your contact, what was his name again?"

"Sgt. Whitaker."

"Do you think this Sgt. Whitaker character can be trusted to keep our secret?"

"Like I just said, I don't trust the food. As soon as Eddie is taken care of, I think the Sgt. will have to be eliminated. But for now, it helps to have extra eyes and ears."

Reggie nodded in agreement. "Let's just hope that our people find Eddie before the human authorities do. Although I don't see Eddie easily giving himself up, and while humans are generally no match for us, Eddie is also careless and reckless, so if enough people overpowered him, who knows what could happen."

"We won't let that happen. And you had better hope, for your sake, that Eddie doesn't screw up again. I hold you personally responsible for anything that he does. You created him, it is your duty to see that he is destroyed."

"I understand, completely. Eddie is certainly the worst regret of my long life."

Sgt. Whitaker put the phone down, stood up and looked at a large map of the country. There were pins in all of the places where the vampire killers had struck. That was when he heard a knock at his door. "Come in," he said.

Another officer walked in the door. "I hope I'm not disturbing you," he said.

"No, no, no, come in."

"Who were you talking to on the phone just now?"

"No one in particular."

"Was it related to the vampire killers again?"

"If you must know, yes, it was."

"I'm beginning to worry about you Sgt. You haven't rested since these 'vampire' killings have started. You don't really still think that these people are actual vampires."

The sergeant turned his back to the officer and looked at his map.

"Dammit Sarge," said the officer as he slammed down some papers on to the Sgt.'s desk."You're beginning to get a reputation. People are beginning to talk."

"Oh," he said, still looking at his map with his back turned to the officer, "and what exactly are they saying?"

"People are saying that you are a man obsessed. People are questioning your rationality. Do you honestly still believe that it was vampires that killed your sister?"

The sergeant turned around and faced the officer as he slammed his fists down on his desk. "Do you think I am crazy?"

"Sir, I-"but then he stopped as the sergeant raised his hand to silence the officer.

"It is okay officer. I understand your skepticism, and I understand that you must think me a rather silly person. But you didn't come home one day to find your sister dead and drained all of blood with bite marks on her neck."

"I didn't intend any disrespect to your sister. I just think that there is some other explanation."

The sergeant shook his head. "Like I said, I understand your skepticism. I was skeptical too, at first. But then I did some research. People have reported these things for centuries. The more and more I researched it, the more and more I felt that there might be something to it. Have I considered the possibility that I am wrong, that I might be jumping to conclusions or letting my grief get in the way of logical and clear thinking? Of course I have. But what if I am right? If you had the chance to possibly prove that your darkest fears are true and that you could bring the killers of your loved ones to justice and save thousands of people from being brutally murdered by some unholy monster, what would you do?"

The officer was going to say something, but he didn't know quite how to respond to that.

The sergeant turned his back to the officer. "You are dismissed."

"Sir, I-"

"You are dismissed," said the sergeant more forcefully. And the officer left.

The sergeant walked over to his map and stared at Nebraska. He clutched a crucifix that he wore around his neck and opened a locket with a picture of him with his sister, which he then closed and stuffed into his pocket. "I'll avenge you," he said as he made the sign of the cross,"with God as my witness. I will catch the servants of the devil, expose them and vanquish them from this world. I swear it."

Chapter 24

Kristin and Eddie laid in bed, covered in blood, with the dead woman still between them. They turned to each other, staring and smiling.

"I take it back, Eddie," said Kristin as she turned her head on her blood soaked pillow, "this place isn't so bad after all."

"Indeed. But I suppose I had better clean this up, before she starts to smell too much. I should also take care of the car, as it looks suspicious to leave the car in a ditch. We don't want to draw too much attention to ourselves. As much as I enjoy it here, I do think you had a point before. We have stayed here for far too long, and it is getting time to move on."

"Yes," sighed Kristin, "I suppose you are correct about that. I think that I will take a shower and wash off all of this blood." Kristin threw the sheets off and walked naked and covered in blood to the door.

"But I have to admit," said Eddie, "you do look sexy all covered in blood like that."

Kristin couldn't help but laugh. "I never thought I would hear a guy tell me that. My old boyfriend wouldn't even have sex with me when I was having my period."

"Do you know where he lives? Maybe we should pay him a visit."

"I'm not sure, but he might still be living in town. I have to admit I am getting a little bit homesick. But not for the reason that you might suspect."

"Oh," said Eddie with a look of surprise, "and what reason would that be?"

"Well, to be honest, there's a lot of people back home that I would like to kill!" She grinned with excitement as she said that.

"Sounds like a plan. Well, I suppose I'd better be disposing of the trash. Enjoy your shower."

Eddie began to get dressed as Kristen headed down the hall to the bathroom.

Officer Steiner had just pulled over at the side of the road when he noticed the car in the side of the ditch. He checked the license plate. He then started to look around to see if there were any survivors when he noticed the crushed cell phone on the floor. He also saw the log in the road. This was no accident, he thought. He had remembered reading a report about a series of mysterious disappearances around this region. Not far up ahead was a farm. He thought it was best to investigate.

"I am going up ahead," he said to officer Carlson. "I will only be a couple of minutes. You stay here in case something happens."

Officer Steiner approached the barn. He saw a pile of clothes sitting in the mud. He reached down and looked in the pocket of the pants. He saw that the wallets were left inside, which was most unusual. He then went behind the barn where he saw what looked like freshly dug graves. There was definitely something up here.

"Carlson," said Steiner into his walkie-talkie, "I have found possible evidence that something fishy is going on here. I would call for backup. I'm going to enter the house. I think we have probable cause here."

Officer Steiner saw that the door to the house was open. He took out his gun and slowly walked inside. Nothing seemed to be out of place. After checking the downstairs he proceeded to go up the stairs. He saw that the bedroom door was left open and he looked inside. Sitting there on the bed was the mutilated body of the blond woman and a trail of blood leading out the door.

Steiner took out his walkie-talkie. "Carlson, I have found the mutilated remains of a woman in the bedroom. Do you copy?" There was no answer. "Carlson, are you there? Pick up." Still no answer. "Dammit Carlson."

That was when he heard walking. He ran out into the hall and coming out of the bathroom, he saw Kristin standing there naked with a towel wrapped around her hair. Her eyes were closed.

"Is that you, Eddie dear?" she asked as she rubbed her eyes. "Did you dispose of the bodies yet?" That was when she opened her eyes to see the officer standing there. She let out a scream and immediately tried to cover herself up with the towel. "Who the fuck are you and what are you doing in our house?"

Steiner raised his gun at Kristin. "Freeze. Put your hands up! You are under arrest on suspicion of murder."

Kristin dropped her towel and Steiner couldn't help but be

distracted by her naked body. Seeing her standing there completely naked took him off guard. He stood there staring for a moment without saying anything when he suddenly heard someone coming up the stairs. Before he could turn around completely, Eddie had knocked him to the ground and began biting his face-off. Eddie did not linger though. As soon as the officer was dead, he got up and wiped the blood from his face.

"We have to go now!" said Eddie. "I just killed the other officer and immediately came back. It won't be long before a million police officers descend on this place."

"But what about all the bodies?"

"There's no time. People already are going to know that something's up when these officers don't return. They may already be on their way now with reinforcements. Just get dressed and meet me at the RV. I'll get the money. As soon as you get to the RV, I'm going to light the house on fire to try and cover up our trail."

Kristin ran and quickly started to get dressed and packed a small bag of things. She started to run down the stairs and was running towards the door when she stopped. Standing there in the doorway was a man she had never seen before who was dressed completely in black.

"Who the hell are you?!" shouted Kristin.

"My name is Paul and I am here to kill you." Paul took off his glasses revealing glowing yellow eyes and he bore his fangs.

"You're a vampire!"

"Nothing gets by you, does it?"

Kristin began to walk backwards, her heart beating noticeably fast, and she didn't doubt that Paul could sense her nervousness.

"I've killed vampires before."

Paul snorted with contempt. "Well, you won't be killing any today. But maybe I will let you live for a little while longer if you tell me where Eddie is."

Kristen decided it was better to play dumb to buy herself some time. "Who is Eddie?"

"Don't play games with me you lying bitch. I can smell Eddie's stink all over you. I bet you just fucked him, didn't you, you cheap little whore. Now tell me where Eddie is."

"I'm right here you worthless piece of shit," said Eddie as he walked into the door.

Paul turned around and Eddie splashed gasoline all over him. Seeing that Paul was momentarily blinded Kristen pulled out her gun and shot him in the head. Paul fell right to the floor, motionless.

"Nice shot," said Eddie smiling at her. She smiled right back and blew smoke from her gun.

"Did I kill him?"

"No, you just stunned him. So long as we have enough blood in us a vampire can survive a headshot, but it does send us into a temporary coma, and gives us one bitching headache. I'll make sure to finish him off. It is necessary to completely destroy the body, and fire always does the job and leaves no remains. His ashes will mix in with the ashes of the rest of the house."

Eddie splashed the rest of the gasoline all through the living room and got as much as possible on Paul. As soon as Kristin had run out of the house, Eddie took his lighter and lit Paul on fire. The house rapidly went up in flames as Kristen and Eddie drove away in the RV.

"Burn baby burn!" said Eddie as he put his sunglasses back on.

Kristin smiled a wicked smile. She was taking fiendish delight in such destruction. "You know Eddie, I always thought of fire as a major turn on. Still, I think I'm going to miss that place."

"So where to next? Do you still want to go back to California?"

Kristin nodded as she took her own sunglasses out of the glove compartment and put them on. "Yeah, I do. I got a couple of old scores to settle."

"I know the feeling. But right now we just have to put as much space between us and this place as possible. Luckily vampires don't need to sleep, so I think it's best that we just drive straight to California without stopping."

"Do you think they will be following us?"

"I don't know. But it is best that we get as far away from here as possible. I don't doubt that there may be more vampires on their way and the human authorities will be there just as soon, if not sooner."

"Did you know that Paul guy?"

"Yeah, and I've always hated the bastard."

"Who was he?"

"He was one of Thomas's right-hand men. They fought together in the Crusades. Trust me, even before they were vampires they had a reputation for ruthlessness. They won't stop until they know we are dead."

"Well, it is a good thing that you took care of him."

Eddie grinned. "You didn't do so bad yourself. It's not too many people that can claim they have killed two vampires."

Kristin nodded in acknowledgment. "I'm not such a bad shot. You are right Eddie."

"About what?"

"Killing definitely is addictive. I can't believe it took me this long to start enjoying it."

"I knew you'd come around. I could tell there was something special about you, even if I didn't know right away what it was. I was always looking for a partner in crime. You are the first person that I am glad that I did not eat."

Kristen laughed. "I'll take that as a compliment."

"Then I guess it's off to California, and our next kill."

Eddie sped up and the rising smoke from their burning home of the last few months was no longer visible.

Chapter 25

A throng of cops and detectives immediately descended upon the burning farmhouse. The firefighters had managed to put out the fire, but not before the house had mostly burned down. Picking through the burnt rubble of the house, they found few clues as to what had happened. All they found inside the house was the charred remains of officer Steiner and the blond woman and a bunch of burned clothes.

Sgt. Whitaker had arrived on the scene. "Did you find anything?" he asked the detective on the scene.

The detective nodded. "We didn't find the suspects, but we found the remains of several bodies, not just in the house, but buried in mass graves all around the property. Our preliminary investigation suggests that maybe dozens of people have been killed here. Identifying these bodies is going to be a big task. I don't doubt that a large number of those who have disappeared in this area will be found in these graves. We'll have to do a lot of DNA testing to identify the remains. But at least the families of the victims will finally have some sense of closure."

Sgt. Whitaker made a fist. "Closure," he said, spitting contemptuously on the floor as he lit up a cigar and put it in his mouth, "you consider this closure?" He shook his head and took a puff on his cigar. "There will never be closure, not until the killers are brought to justice." He turned to the detective. "Did you find anything else at the scene that would be considered mysterious?"

"Mysterious how?"

"You know," he said as he blew smoke out of his mouth, "mysterious. As in, not usual, something you wouldn't expect to find it a crime scene. Something unexplained."

"Hey," said the detective as he raised his finger to Sgt. Whitaker, "I know who you are. You're that guy who believes that the vampire killers are real vampires." The detective couldn't help but laugh. "Vampires, it's amazing what people will still believe in these days."

"Actually," began Whitaker, "it is only one of them that is a vampire. The other one is just some random murderous bitch that's been tagging along with him for the ride."

"You don't say?" said the detective with a note of scorn and contemptuous laugh. "Do you know something that you're not telling us?"

"Let's just say that I have a source that wishes to remain anonymous who might have a lead."

"Is that so? And are they vampires too?" The detective laughed heartily as he began to light a cigarette of his own.

"Never mind that. Now just answer my question."

"Actually, there was something a bit unusual. Although we found the burnt clothing and personal effects of three people in the house, we only found the remains of two bodies. One body seemed to have been entirely turned to ash, while the other two left behind bone. The third body shouldn't have burned quite so completely."

A vampire, Whitaker thought. Thomas must have sent him. But even he did not seem to be able to stop Eddie.

"I think that I need to make a call," said Whitaker as he walked away from the scene. He quickly dialed up Thomas on his cell phone.

"Hello," answered Thomas. "I guess by now you have heard what has happened?"

"Unfortunately, yes."

"According to the report one of the bodies left behind nothing but ash, while the other two only burned down to the bone. You sent one of your own kind to investigate, didn't you?"

"Yes, I did. But that idiot Paul didn't follow orders. I sent him specifically to scout the area but not to engage Eddie in combat alone. Had he just waited, instead of being arrogant and assuming he could've taken on Eddie himself, I would have had an entire vampire army on the scene to make sure that he was eliminated. Now he has escaped again."

"So now what do we do?"

"All we can do now is wait for Eddie to strike again."

"Just wait for him to claim more victims? To take more innocent life?"

"I should remind you, lest you should forget, that I am not concerned about the loss of human life. I am concerned only with eliminating Eddie before he exposes us all. If you think I have any other purposes beyond that or that you're going to stop all vampires from killing, well then you are sadly mistaken. Just keep that in mind. We have a mutual enemy and that is as far as our relationship goes. Is that clear?"

"Crystal."

"Good. Keep me informed if anything new comes up."

Thomas hung up the phone. To Whitaker's great frustration he appeared to have an untraceable phone. It was dawning on him that capturing Eddie alive was the most important thing. If they catch him alive, then he will have proof of the existence of vampires. Dead he is just a pile of ashes and the vampire menace will continue operating in the shadows where the majority don't even realize the threat exists. And if he captures Eddie alive, maybe Eddie will lead him to Thomas. But first he must find Eddie.

Eddie pulled up onto the beach. There was a full moon that night, and he decided to wake Kristin up with a gentle nudge. She awoke with a yawn. "Are we there yet Eddie," she asked as she rubbed her eyes.

"We are at the beach."

"It's the middle of the night Eddie."

"In case you haven't noticed by now, I prefer the night. Fancy going for a stroll?"

Kristin smiled and nodded and they both got out of the car.

"Look at the beautiful moon Eddie," she said, staring up. "That is one of the brightest I have ever seen it. You don't by any chance sparkle in the moonlight. Do you?"

"Don't even joke about that!"

Kristin pushed him playfully. "And are you sure that there aren't any werewolves out there?"

"Positive. And if I happen to be wrong about that, I'll tear the fucking werewolf's head off!"

Kristin smiled at him and began to undress.

"What are you doing?"

"It's a nude Beach Eddie. Aren't you going to get undressed?"

"I'm not sure if I should expose myself so visibly in public."

"Are you getting prude all of a sudden Eddie?"

"No, it's not that. It's just-"

"Or maybe you really do sparkle and you just don't want me to see." She giggled.

"That's it," said Eddie as he began to take his shirt off, "I'll show you that real vampires don't sparkle."

"That's the spirit," said Kristin as she ran her fingers through her hair.

They began to walk up and down the beach, enjoying the fresh summer air and the bright light of the moon.

"Isn't this romantic Eddie?"

Eddie paused and started looking around.

"What is it Eddie?" She looked up at him with concern.

"I think I heard someone," said Eddie as he put his arm in front of Kristen to stop her.

"Hey, nice ass," said a male voice from behind them.

They turned around to see a naked man and woman standing before them. Both were skinny and pale and had blond hair. They looked like they were in their late teens or early 20s.

"I'm Mike and this is my girlfriend Michelle," said the man as he pointed to the woman.

"I'm Eddie, and this is Kristin." Kristin put her hand up and did a small wave.

"So what brings you to the beach?" asked Michelle. "Would you like to go skinny-dipping with us?"

Eddie and Kristen looked at each other and then looked at Mike and Michelle.

"Sure," said Kristin, "race you to the water!"

Mike and Michelle ran on ahead as Eddie and Kristen staggered on behind, giving each other sinister nods and grins, their unspoken signal that they were about to have some fun with their newest friends.

"Looks like we beat you," said Mike as he playfully splashed at them.

Eddie and Kristen looked at each other and began laughing.

"What's so funny?" Michelle asked with a little bit of nervousness in her voice.

"Nothing," said Eddie as he shook his head.

"We were just wondering," said Kristin, "if maybe you would like a rematch. How about a swimming contest?"

"Sounds good," said Mike. "How about we swim out as far as we can go and the first one to turn back loses."

"Sounds like a plan," said Eddie.

Kristin and Eddie let Mike and Michelle swim on ahead and slowly tread just behind them. Kristin was holding on to Eddie until they got pretty far out.

"Getting tired yet?!" Mike shouted.

Eddie and Kristen looked at each other and snickered slightly.

"I don't know," said Eddie, "we are getting pretty far away from shore."

"Give up then?" asked Mike.

Eddie and Kristen suddenly swam forward at a much more rapid pace until Eddie was right behind Mike and Kristin was right next to Michelle.

"Wow," said Michelle,"you sure caught up fast. How did you do that?"

Eddie smirked and looked at Kristin, who smiled back and began laughing.

Mike and Michelle looked at each other before Michelle asked, "What's so funny?"

"Nothing," said Eddie. "I was just going to say that something like that is easy to accomplish when you are a vampire."

"A what?" Michelle asked.

"I guess a demonstration is in order," said Eddie as he grabbed Mike by the arms.

"Hey buddy," said Mike, "what are you doing? I don't have a problem with skinny-dipping, but I don't go out for any of that gay stuff."

Eddie gave a look of anger as his eyes began to glow. "What did you say about me?"

"Whoa, whoa, calm down buddy," said Mike. "I wasn't judging you or anything, I just don't swing that way. Hey, what's with your eyes? Are you high or something?"

Eddie began to crush the bones in Mike's arms and before he could react, Eddie lunged forward and bit him hard in the neck, causing blood to splatter out in all directions, turning the water around them completely bright red, which was reflecting in the moonlight.

Michelle screamed, but Kristin came around behind her and grabbed her under her armpits and held her still. She struggled to try and break free from Kristen's grasp but Eddie saw that she was going to get away so he flung aside Mike's body and let it sink beneath the waves as he grabbed onto Michelle. She continued to scream, but Eddie moved forward and took a bite of her right breast. She screamed louder as the blood gushed out. Eddie rose from the water and finished her off with a bite to the neck that finally silenced her screaming.

Pushing aside the two dead bodies Eddie and Kristen embraced in the bloodstained water and Kristin could feel Eddie entering her and caressing her breasts. They began to kiss and Kristin could still taste the fresh blood on Eddie's lips which she lapped up with her tongue. As they continued there floating in the moonlight in the newly illuminated bloodbath they had created, Kristin knew this would be a night that she would never forget.

"I told you I didn't sparkle," said Eddie.

Chapter 26

"Is this it?" asked Eddie the next morning as they pulled up to a dilapidated looking house. "Did you really live in that shithole?"

"Unfortunately, yes." Kristin couldn't help but sigh as she looked at the house and remembered all the unpleasant memories she had of the place.

"Are you sure you want to just go in?"

Kristen shook her head. "Maybe I should wait."

"I could go ahead and check to see if anyone is there."

"I guess that would be okay. I don't think I want to go inside if my father is there. This is what he looks like." Kristin handed Eddie a family photograph showing her with her parents and her little brother.

"Your dad kind of looks like my dad. I bet he's a big bastard too."

Kristin nodded in acknowledgment. "I wouldn't have ran away if it was otherwise."

Eddie snickered.

"What are you laughing at Eddie?"

"I suppose I should thank this fat ugly bastard. Because if it wasn't for him I never would've met you."

Kristen managed a faint smile and kissed Eddie on the cheek.

Eddie nodded. "Okay then, I'll check to see if anyone's at home."

Eddie began to get up but Kristin grabbed his arm. "Wait!"

"Yes?" Eddie gave her a puzzled look as he raised his glasses.

"Don't hurt my little brother Timmy." She looked up at him with pleading eyes and he nodded in acknowledgment as he lowered his sunglasses.

"I will just be a minute."

Eddie walked up to the door and rang the doorbell. Timmy answered the door, but kept the glass front door locked. "Excuse me, little boy," he said, "but is your father home?"

"I'm not supposed to talk to strangers," said Timmy.

"Well, do you know when your father will be getting home?"

Timmy shook his head.

"Okay then, I guess I will just have to come back later."

Timmy closed the door and Eddie returned to the RV.

"So?" Kristen asked.

Eddie shook his head. "The only one there was your little brother. What do you want to do?"

Kristin put her fingers in her mouth and thought for a moment. "I think I want to go home."

Kristin and Eddie went back to her house and Kristin used her key to open the door. As soon as she walked in Timmy saw her standing there with Eddie.

"Kristin!" Timmy shouted as he ran up to her and hugged her leg.

"Hey there tiny Tim, how have you been?" Kristin hugged him.

"Where have you been?" Timmy asked.

"I ran away from home."

"Why did you want to do that? I missed you." Timmy began to cry.

"Don't cry little Tim. Big boys don't cry, remember?"

"Where have you been all this time?"

"I have been traveling across the country. Kind of like a vacation."

"A vacation?" Timmy looked up at her wide-eyed with confusion."Why didn't you take me with you?"

"I'm an adult now. Sometimes adults go on vacation by themselves."

"All alone?"

"Well, not completely alone. I've been traveling around with Eddie here." Kristin pointed at Eddie and he waved at Timmy.

"He was a stranger who just came to the door." Timmy walked backwards slowly as Eddie approached him. "Dad says I'm not supposed to talk to strangers."

"He's not a stranger. I have been traveling with him for many months."

"But why is he so pale?"

"Cute kid," said Eddie as he patted Timmy on the head, causing him to draw back and hide behind Kristen's leg.

Kristen shook her head. "That's not important now. The important thing is, do you know when dad is getting home?"

Timmy shook his head. "No, but he said he would be home for dinner and if he's not that I could just eat whatever is in the refrigerator."

Typical, Kristin thought. Dad obviously hasn't changed much while she was gone. He was still just as negligent as ever and the house was a total mess. But she really didn't care, as she wouldn't be staying very long.

"Are you going to be coming back home now?" Timmy asked, looking up at Kristen with pleading eyes.

"I don't know. But it is important that you don't tell anyone that I am home. Can you do that for me, Tim?"

"I guess so."

"That's a good boy." Kristin patted him on the head.

"So what do you want to do?" Eddie asked.

"I just want to get some things and bring them out to the RV."

Eddie nodded and they began going up to Kristen's room. When she opened the door, she found that the room had been left intact. Surprisingly most of her things were still there, although she noticed that a couple of her more valuable things had been taken. No doubt her father had sold a lot of her things in order to buy booze and drugs. That he left this much as he did didn't really speak in his favor. Most of her things were pretty worthless, although she did have a few things that she would like to reclaim such as old pictures and other things of sentimental value. She and Eddie packed these things up and brought them out to the RV.

Once they had finished packing up her valuables, they decided they would just wait around until her father gets home. They decided to just sit on the couch and watch TV until he returned. Kristen went into the kitchen to make dinner for Timmy when she heard the door open.

Kristen's father walked in the door and slammed it behind him. He was a fat, bearded man dressed in torn up clothing and Eddie could smell the stink of booze on him from a mile away. His hyper keen nose always found the smell of alcohol offensive, which is ironic considering that before he became a vampire Eddie could drink himself unconscious several days a week.

When Eddie saw her father approaching he dropped the remote on the floor and began to get up.

"Hey punk," said Kristin's father, "who the hell are you and what are you doing in my house watching my TV?"

"Dad it's okay," said Kristin as she ran into the room from the kitchen.

"Kristin!" Her father shouted as he froze and dropped the beer can he was carrying in shock at seeing her. "Where the hell have you been? You've got a lot of nerve coming back here after stealing my money."

"Your money," Kristen scoffed. "That was money you stole from me, and no doubt used to get high."

"You disrespectful little bitch," her father said, "I ought to slap you for talking that way to your father."

"I don't think so," Kristin said as she took out her gun and pointed it at her father.

"What the fuck are you doing, pointing a gun at your father."

"Shut up dad," she said as she pointed the gun towards his head. "I didn't come back here out of love. I got tired of taking your shit all of the time. I left for the same reason that mom did, because you're a fat, worthless abusive old drunk who only cares about himself and steals from others. That's probably why I'm so messed up. Have you been watching the news lately?"

"What the hell are you talking about?"

"Have you heard about the vampire killers?"

"What does that have to do with anything?"

"Remember the girl that had been seen. That was me dad. And the vampire who has killed all those people, he's the guy standing right in front of you."

"What?!"

"Exactly as she said," said Eddie as he turned to face Kristen's father.

"And who the fuck are you, you faggy little punk?"

Eddie grabbed Kristen's father's arm and began to crush it. "I believe she just told you who I am. I am the guy who has been fucking your daughter. And I can tell that she gets her good looks and her intelligence from her mother."

"Why you little-"began her father before Eddie pushed him to the ground, causing him to fall over and into the TV shattering it.

"Son of a bitch!" Her father shouted as he wiped away the blood from his forehead. Seeing all of that blood gushing out of Kristen's father's forehead, Eddie began to feel intoxicated with bloodlust. As her father looked up at Eddie, he took off his glasses and bore his fangs.

"Eddie, wait!" shouted Kristin. "Not yet."

Eddie nodded and lowered his sunglasses. Kristen's father sat there shaking and pissed his pants.

"Dignified to the very end, eh dad?"

"Kristin, come on," her father pleaded, "I'm your father. Don't do this. I raised you better than this."

"Stop reminding me that you're my father and you didn't raise me better than this."

"I'll admit I'm not perfect."

Kristin couldn't help but snort. "If that's not the understatement of the century."

It was then that Timmy walked out of the kitchen and saw his father sitting there while his sister pointed a gun at him. He screamed and went running off.

Kristin turned in the direction that Timmy was running. "Timmy, wait!"

Kristen's father began to get up but fell backwards and Kristin turned back around and pointed the gun back at her father.

"Now look what you've done to your brother," grumbled her father.

"Shut up!"

"You murderous little whore, I knew I should've aborted you. You're worthless ungrateful little cunt just like that bitch of a mother of yours."

"Shut up! Shut up! Shut up!" Kristin was shouting and holding her head in frustration.

"That's no way to talk to your own daughter," Eddie chimed in.

"And who the fuck are you telling me how to talk to my daughter?"

"He's more of a father to me than you ever could be!"

"The man that you are fucking?! Now, what does that say about you?"

"Shut the hell up right now! If you say another word I'm going to put a bullet in you."

"Come on, Kris, you know you're too much of a pussy to do it. I bet you've never fired that damn thing in your whole worthless li-", but before he could complete his sentence, Kristin had fired the gun, shooting him in the right arm.

"Son of a bitch!" her father shouted as he clutched his wounded arm with his hand. He began rubbing his wound as Eddie began to lick his lips with hunger. Kristin's hand was shaking and Eddie could hear her heart beating rapidly.

"I take it back," her father said, "you know how to shoot. How about you let me go now?"

"Get up," Kristen said, the gun shaking in her hand.

"I could use a little help."

Eddie grabbed Kristen's father by the throat and picked him up and placed him down, standing.

"Now move," said Kristin still pointing the gun at him. "And don't try anything. You know that I am willing to use this and that I know how. Just nod if you understand."

Kristen's father nodded and gulped down his saliva. Eddie could hear both of their hearts beating rapidly and the scent of her wounded father's blood was driving him crazy.

Kristin led her father upstairs focusing the gun on his back the entire time. When she got to the top of the stairs, she saw Timmy there crying.

"Go to your room Timmy," her father said.

"Do as he says Tim," said Kristin as she nodded in his direction, "and don't come out until I tell you to. Understand?"

Timmy nodded as he continued to sob.

Kristin led her father into her room and Eddie shortly followed them in. She closed the door and locked it.

"Kneel down in front of the mirror," she said still training the gun on her father's back. He did as she said. "Notice anything interesting?"

"I-interesting?" he asked as he continued to rub his arm with his lips trembling.

"Tell me what you see in the mirror."

"I see my daughter pointing a gun at her father." He began to sob.

"Yes. Now tell me what you don't see?"

"W-what do you mean, d-don't see?"

"Is there anything missing in the mirror?"

"What are you doing, Kris," he pleaded as he began to sob some more.

She raised the gun to his head. "It's a simple fucking question dad. Now, answer me."

"I-I don't know," he said between sobs.

"You are so pathetic. Dry your eyes for a moment, look into the mirror and tell me what is missing."

Kristen's father looked up into the mirror, but all he saw was her pointing a gun at the back of his head.

"All I see is my daughter, the person who I gave life to, about to put a bullet in my brain."

"I think that he needs a hint," said Eddie. Eddie grabbed her father's hair, pulled his face up and put his face right next to his. "Do you notice anything now?"

"I don't see you in the mirror."

Eddie stood up and began to clap. "Very good, we have a winner! And do you know why that is?"

Kristen's father shook his head as the tears rolled down his cheeks.

Eddie leaned forward and whispered into Kristen's father's ear. "Because I am a vampire. And do you know what vampires do?"

"D-drink blood?" he sobbed.

"Very good," said Eddie as he clapped some more. "You're not as dumb as you look. But you're still pretty fucking stupid. And do you know what you win?"

He shook his head.

"Well, Kris, tell your father what he has won."

She looked him directly in the eye. "You win a first-class ticket to hell."

"Kris, please. I'm your father."

Kristin looked him close in the eye and then looked up at Eddie and nodded. "Do it."

"Kris, wait!" shouted her father.

"Goodbye dad," she said as Eddie bit into her father's throat.

As Eddie tore her father apart, Kristin slowly got undressed and let the blood of her father splatter all over her naked body. She stood looking at herself in the mirror, put her hands on her hips and began laughing maniacally. Then, when Eddie had finished dismembering her father, she walked over, squatted over his head and took aa piss right in his lifeless face.

"That's more than you deserve, you worthless piece of shit."

"Wow," said Eddie, "and I thought that I had father issues."

Kristin turned to Eddie. "Get undressed, I need a good fuck after that."

Eddie smiled wickedly. "Yes, ma'am."

As soon as Eddie was undressed Kristin dived on top of him and began straddling him. She threw back her head and screamed with ecstasy as Eddie caressed her body with the blood of her murdered father.

In the next room Timmy sat on his bed weeping as he listened to the sounds from the next room.

Finally Kristin and Eddie finished and got dressed. She walked down to Timmy's room and knocked on the door. "It's okay to come out now Timmy," she said. "But now I'm afraid you're going to have to leave."

"Leave," he sobbed. "Where am I going to go?"

"Just leave the house and go over to a friends house."

"What happened to daddy?"

"It's okay Timmy, he's not going to hurt you anymore. You're free now."

As soon as Timmy was out of the house, Eddie took his lighter and lit the curtains on fire.

"Where are you going?"

"I don't know yet."

"Can I come with you?"

Kristen shook her head. "I'm sorry Timmy, but you can't."

By now Timmy was sobbing hysterically. "B- but, w-why, n-not?"

"It's not safe for you to come with me."

"W-will, I e-ever s-see you again?"

"I don't know."

Kristin and Timmy stood and stared at each other, neither of them able to hold back tears anymore. Kristin hugged Timmy until Eddie came out as the house began to go up in flames and with it all the bad memories that she had of it.

"We've got to get going," said Eddie as he began to walk to the RV.

Kristin patted Timmy on the head one last time. "Goodbye, kiddo, be good."

"I'll miss you big sis."

"I'll miss you too."

Fighting the urge to do otherwise, Kristin then turned and walked to the RV. They waved at Timmy and he waved back and they drove off as the smoke from her house rose into the night sky.

"Burn baby burn," said Eddie as they pulled away.

"Burn baby burn," said Kristin in a whisper as she wiped away a tear.

Chapter 27

"Tragedy has struck in the small California town of Sunny Valley," began the news report. "On a nearby beach two skinny dippers were found torn apart, and their bodies completely drained of blood in what is believed to be a shark attack."

"Shark attack," snorted Thomas, "this was no shark attack, it must have been Eddie."

"In other news," continued the news report, "a house was burned down in the same town. There was one survivor – a six-year-old boy named Timmy."

The news report switched to a scene of Timmy sobbing hysterically as he was being comforted by a social worker.

"Can you tell us what happened little boy?" asked the news reporter as he put the microphone up to Timmy's face.

"Count Dracula killed my daddy," sobbed Timmy. "And then he lit the house on fire and ran off with my sister."

The news reporter turned to the television camera. "According to this young boy a vampire killed his father. The vampire and the girl seen with him matched the description of the alleged vampire killers. We now have a positive ID on the girl – 18-year-old Kristin McDonald. She is believed to be the accomplice of the vampire killer, and if you see her you should not engage her and should call police immediately. She should be considered armed and highly dangerous."

Thomas crushed the TV remote control in his hand with anger. That was when his phone rang and he answered it.

"Are you watching the news?" Sgt. Whitaker's voice asked.

"Yes, I am."

"So we finally have a positive ID on Eddie's girlfriend. It seems she has decided to come back to her hometown."

"I will dispatch my people right away."

"Good. Call me if you have any new info."

"Don't worry, I will."

Thomas hung up the phone and turned to Reggie. "We have to get to Eddie, before Whitaker does. The human authorities are going to be looking all over for these people and anyone close to them. We only have a limited amount of time before they are caught and it is vital that we are the ones who catch them and not the humans."

"I wouldn't worry, Eddie will mess up soon enough, and then we've got him. Now all we have to do is wait."

Eddie and Kristen drove over to the next nearest town. Kristin had managed to look up the address of her old friend Kimberly.

"So, do you think we can trust this girl?"

"She's my oldest friend."

"But that was over six months ago. A lot has changed since then. You've been identified. This is going to complicate things. We need a place that we can hide and we have to be absolutely sure we can trust whoever it is we are hiding with."

"I'm sure that we can trust her."

"You'd better be sure. Because if you are wrong, she will have to die."

A chill went up Kristin's spine, but she nodded in agreement.

"We're here," said Eddie as they pulled up in front of a nice-looking house. "This is a pretty nice place. How does your friend manage to afford this?"

"Her parents are pretty well off."

"Oh," said Eddie with a sneer.

"What's with the attitude Eddie?"

"Back when I was in school all of the rich kids were snobs who looked down on me."

Kristen shook her head dismissively. "Kimberly isn't like that at all. She used to work at soup kitchens and always gave to charity. She's pretty much your typical California hippie."

"Well, we'll see."

Kristin ran up and rang the doorbell. A brunette haired woman with a ponytail and headphones in her ears answered the door and almost fainted.

"Oh my God," said the woman, "Kristin, it's you!" She hugged Kristen. "Where have you been? I've seen your picture on the news, they're claiming you are a murderer."

"I promise I will explain everything, but can I please come in?"

"Of course. Come in right away, before someone sees you."

Kristin motion for Eddie to come over.

"Kimberly, this is Eddie."

Eddie smiled and waved at her.

"Well, please, come in, the both of you. We obviously have a lot of catching up to do."

Kristin slowly but surely explained everything to Kimberly as they sipped lattes.

"So that's the story," said Kristin. "We are on the run and we need someplace where we can hide out until things die down a bit."

"Well, Kris, of course you are welcome to stay here, but do you really expect me to believe your story?"

"Well, you've seen the news reports, haven't you?"

"Well, yes, but c'mon. You have to realize how absurd this whole thing sounds. I mean really, Kris, you tell me you are dating a vampire named Edward. Haven't we heard that somewhere before?"

"What are you saying?"

"Well, I know a lot of people like Twilight, but my God, Kris. You are telling me that you have a vampire lover and you're going around the country killing people. You must've gone completely insane. I know you've been attracted to some strange guys in the past, but this one takes the cake. It sounds like you are in an unhealthy relationship and I'm worried about you. As a women's studies major I'm aware of all the signs of an abusive relationship. This guy doesn't respect you as a woman and is taking advantage of you and your belief in vampires."

"I guess I'm going to have to show you then. Eddie!"

Eddie came in. "So Kris, it seems like your friend is skeptical."

Kristin nodded and smiled. "Indeed she does. I think a demonstration is in order. Got a mirror?"

Kimberly led them to the bathroom. As soon as they were all standing in front of the mirror they could see that Eddie had no reflection.

"Nice trick," said Kimberly, "how'd you do it?"

Eddie shook his head. "It is no trick. If you do not believe me still, listen to my heart beat, or lack of one."

Kimberly put her ear directly over where Eddie's heart should be and she could hear nothing. She felt for his pulse and did not detect one. She felt his chest and could see that he was not breathing. He looked her directly in the eyes, his glowing bright yellow. He let her feel his fangs and pull on them to see that they weren't fake.

"So," said Eddie, "do you believe me now?"

Kimberly stared at him in astonishment. "I'll admit," she began, "I really have no idea how you have managed to do any of this. But there has to be some kind of logical explanation. Vampires are fantasy."

"I can see that she is going to need more convincing," he said as he looked at Kristin. He then turned to Kimberly. "Do you still have that weight room?"

Kimberly nodded and lead them to the gym that she had set up in the basement. Eddie walked over and put up 500 pounds on the barbells and then lifted it with his pinky. He then went over to the pull up bar, and lifted his whole body with his pinky. He jumped on her exercise bike and put it up to full power. And he managed to do it without breaking any kind of a sweat or even huffing and puffing as he did not need to breathe.

"Convinced now?" Kristen asked as she turned to Kimberly. Kimberly just gave her a blank stare in response.

Eddie walked over to her carrying a 100 pound weight, which he then brought up to her face and crushed it in his hands. He then took out a knife, cut his arm and put it right in Kimberly's face so she could watch it heal almost instantaneously.

Kimberly fell back into her easy chair and looked up at the both of them standing there, smiling. "So," said Kimberly, "do you have any other superpowers?"

Eddie came up to her and looked her right in the eye. "I think that you have seen them all. But I can also run extremely fast, I can hear your heart beating from across the room, and I could track you by scent over the course of many miles. And no, I don't sparkle, and don't even think about asking."

"Well," said Kimberly, "this has certainly been an interesting day. It is not every day that you learn of the existence of an entire new species of humanity. I would love to study you, scientifically. In college I took a course in anthropology."

"Well," said Eddie with a laugh, "with your degree in women's studies and your minor in anthropology I can say that you are very lucky that you have wealthy parents."

Kimberly frowned. "You know it's not very respectful to mock someone in their own home."

Kristin shot Eddie an angry look.

"Sorry," said Eddie, "I have been told that my social skills need work. It is not too often I talk to people for an extended amount of time."

"Why not?" Kimberly asked.

Eddie laughed again. "Because eventually I will get hungry and will usually end up eating the people that I am talking to."

Kimberly's heart began racing. She didn't really feel comfortable around Eddie, and Eddie could sense it.

"Don't worry," said Eddie, "I promise I won't eat you. Just so long as you keep my secret."

Kimberly gulped then nodded. "Your secret is safe with me. Besides, I don't think anyone else would believe this, unless they saw it themselves." Kimberly turned to leave, but then turned back to Eddie. "But why are vampires always hiding in the shadows all the time? Why don't you come out and let people study you?"

"So basically, you are asking me why don't I want to be a lab rat? What do your anthropologist's senses tell you?"

Kristin leaned over and whispered in Kimberly's ear. "Eddie doesn't exactly like to be questioned."

"You know," said Eddie, "I can hear whatever you are saying from a mile away, so there really is no need to whisper when you are in my presence."

"Come on Kim," said Kristin, "I think we still have a lot more catching up to do."

"Don't mind me," said Eddie, "I could use some alone time. You girls have a good time now."

Kristin and Kimberly left the room, but Kimberly looked back briefly to see Eddie staring at her, which made her uncomfortable.

Later that night Kimberly had gotten up to go to the bathroom and saw Eddie watching Dracula on TV. She tried to sneak past Eddie without him seeing her, but of course he was able to hear her coming from the second she got up. He turned around and looked at her.

"Sorry," she said, "I didn't mean to disturb you. I guess you can't sleep either."

"Vampires don't sleep."

"Ever?"

"Never. On the plus side, it gives us a lot of added free time. That and the fact that we live forever."

Kimberly left feebly and looked at the television. "So, vampires watch vampire movies then. Are any of them accurate?"

Eddie shook his head. "It is mostly Hollywood. But it is entertaining to watch."

"I took a film studies class where we analyzed how the vampire has changed in cinema in the last century. You've gone from monsters to heroes and romantic brooding loners."

Eddie snorted. "Drivel. I can tell you that now or in any other era the majority of us vampires are complete and total assholes, and I'm a bigger asshole than most of them."

"It doesn't sound like you think too highly of your own kind. Are you some kind of self hating vampire?"

"My own kind doesn't think very highly of me. But I don't hate myself, hating oneself is what weak people do."

"So you're sort of an outsider?"

"All vampires are outsiders. But I was an outsider even before I came a vampire."

"I understand."

"Why, did you take a course in psychology as well. All that Freudian bullshit." Eddie laughed and this time she laughed with him, although not fully sincerely. "But trust me, you'll never understand vampires, not unless you are one."

"Well," she said as she sat down next to Eddie, "I would be interested to learn."

Eddie could hear her heart beating faster and faster, but not out of nervousness, but rather, excitement. He started to look more closely at her – she wasn't all that bad looking and she was in better physical shape than Kristin was.

"So," said Eddie as he moved closer to her, "you find me fascinating."

Kimberly blushed a little bit and tried to move back, but she couldn't help but find Eddie attractive. "Well," she said, "of course I am fascinated. I mean, from a purely scientific perspective, who wouldn't be fascinated."

Eddie smiled and with a hint of sarcasm added, "Yes, purely scientific."

Kimberly blushed some more, and was beginning to feel awkward, but she was very attracted to Eddie.

Eddie leaned in closer to her. "Are you sure that your interest in me doesn't extend beyond that?" Eddie began to stroke her hair a little bit and stared down her chest.

Kimberly got up and moved away from Eddie. "I can't do this Eddie, it's wrong. What would Kristin think?"

"It doesn't matter. She knows that I am not monogamous."

"But still," said Kimberly as she drew back.

"But what? You can't hide your secrets from me. I can tell

when someone is turned on. I don't have telepathy like a lot of these 'literary' vampires, but I know what question has been on your mind since you first heard about me – what is it like to fuck a vampire? "Eddie began to undress. "So why don't I show you."

She was about to leave the room, but then when she saw Eddie standing there naked before her, something overcame her. She stood there, her heart beating with desire, her blood visibly pulsating through her body and driving Eddie wild. Eddie walked over to her and began taking off her shirt and pulling down her pajama pants. Soon they were both standing there completely naked. Eddie pushed her down on the couch and climbed on top of her. Overcome with desire she submitted to Eddie and felt him entering her as he began to lick her breasts with his thick tongue. Eddie began kissing her body all over and caressing her. He looked her right in the eyes, slightly mesmerizing her and then, feeling the blood coursing through her veins, he could not control himself. Just as Kimberly began to arch her back with desire, Eddie lunged forward and bit her in the neck. She didn't even have a chance to scream before she was dead.

Just at that moment, Kristin came running into the room and turned the light on. Eddie jumped up suddenly, blood dripping from his mouth and down his naked body. Kristin froze and put her hand over her mouth. "Oh my God," she whispered under her breath before shouting, "Eddie, what the hell did you just do!"

Eddie began running towards her with his arms spread wide. "I'm sorry, I couldn't control myself."

Kristin ran over to the couch, looked at Kimberly's lifeless body, leaned over and began to vomit.

"I'm sorry Kris, but I just couldn't control myself."

"Dammit, Eddie, she was my only friend!"

"I'm the only friend you need now."

Kristin turned her back to Eddie, but he turned her around and looked her in the eye. "Kris, I-" but then he paused.

"You what?"

"I thought I heard something."

"Don't try to change the subject!"

"No, really, I thought I heard some-"as Eddie was about to complete his sentence, the door came flying loose and another man dived on top of Eddie. Kristin screamed. As Kristen looked closer she realized that the man on top of Eddie was a vampire and he was trying to kill him.

Eddie flipped the vampire onto his back and got on top of him. Eddie began to grab him by the throat and pushed his face to the side. He continued pushing down on the vampire's head until he managed to turn it completely around, snapping it off. The vampire's body turn to dust beneath Eddie. He got up and dusted himself off. "Are you okay," he asked Kristin. She nodded. "I think so," she said.

That was when Eddie paused again.

"What is it Eddie?"

Eddie slowly turned around as another vampire came charging at him through the door. Just as the vampire was about to dive on Eddie, he grabbed one of the barbells sitting on the floor and smashed the other vampire in the face, knocking his fangs right out of his mouth. Eddie then dived on top of him, smashed his face again with the barbell and tore his head off, turning him into dust.

Eddie turned his head and listened for more. "I think that's all of them," he said. "But we have to get out of here right away. No doubt there are more vampires on their way. Go warm up the RV while I get dressed."

Kristin nodded and began to run towards the RV. Eddie joined her a few minutes later, and sped off.

"Where are we going to go now Eddie? Shouldn't we go back and dispose of the bodies?"

"There's no time. With any luck, no one will discover what had gone on there for at least a couple of days, and by then we could be out of here. We'll cover our tracks better by not burning her house down." Eddie looked at her with a feeling of apprehension. "Kris, I'm sorry about everything that has happened tonight. But I have to level with you now. Things aren't looking good for us. It won't be long before the vampires manage to find us. We might not have much time left. So if there is anything that you would like to do, now is the time to do it."

Kristen wasn't sure how to respond. Her heart was racing a mile a minute and Eddie could sense her fear. After a few minutes she managed to calm down. "Eddie," she said as she turned to him.

"Yes?"

"Remember when you told me your motto – live fast and die young."

"Yeah. So?"

"I think I understand what you mean now and I know what I want to do."

"Oh, and what's that?"

Kristin just smiled and shook her head. "It's a surprise. Just take us to this address." She handed him a piece of paper.

"Well, I always have liked surprises."

Eddie smiled at Kristen and she began to laugh as they drove on to their next destination.

Chapter 28

Kristin and Eddie pulled up in front of what looked like a Palace, but was actually just a mansion, albeit a rather exquisite one. It was an even nicer mansion than the one that Lenora had. It had numerous hedge sculptures, a giant lawn and in the back a built-in swimming pool. It was surrounded by a gate.

"What is this place, Kris? I have always hated gated communities."

"So have I. But I figure since we are millionaires, we deserve a mansion of our own. And we deserve it much more than the stupid stuck up Bible thumping bitch that lives here. You weren't the only one that the rich kids looked down on. And this woman gave me shit every single day for being poor."

"I can't stand those type of people."

"And she's also one of those Jesus freaks. Somehow that part of the Bible where Jesus said to give all your money to the poor was a part that she missed. She once told me that if Jesus had wanted me to be rich I would've been born rich like she was. She even spat on me once. Her and her rich stuck up friends."

"What do you want to do here?"

"I want her to suffer. I want her to suffer slowly and I want her friends to suffer with her. So when we get in there, don't kill her right away."

"Okay, I'm guessing you have some detailed plan."

Kristin nodded and smiled very wide. "You better believe that I do."

They got out of the RV and Eddie pushed the gate open with his super strength. They drove inside and Eddie closed the gates. They parked the RV and walked up to the door and rang the bell. The door was answered by what appeared to be a Butler.

"Hello," said the Butler, "and who might you be? Do you have an appointment?"

Kristin took out her gun and pointed it at the Butler. "This is all the appointment that I need, Jeeves."

Kristin led the Butler into the kitchen where she saw her worst enemy, Madeleine, eating with what she assumed were her parents. They went to get up.

"Sit the fuck down," said Kristin as she pointed the gun in their direction. They did as she said.

"Kristin?" asked Madeleine with a look of shock.

"So nice of you to recognize me without your spit all over my face."

"Why are you doing this?" Madeleine asked.

"Gee, do you really wonder that or you just asking out of instinct? Take a guess, Sherlock."

"Look, "said Madeleine's father, "if it is money you want-"

"It's not," said Kristin pointing the gun directly at his face. "Now, answer me this. Is there anyone else in the house?"

Madeleine's father shook his head.

"Good. And no one else is coming over? There's no one who's expecting you all who will wonder where you are if you don't show up."

Madeleine's father shook his head again.

"Good. And I want you all to line up against the wall, take off your clothes and kneel down with your hands behind your head."

"What?!" shouted Madeleine's mother. "I will do no such thing. It's indecent!"

"Indecent," scoffed Kristin. "You know what's indecent? People like you living in a place like this who raise their daughter to spit on those who are less fortunate."

"I'm sorry," sobbed Madeleine, "just please don't hurt us."

"Everyone is sorry when there's a gun pointed at them." Kristin pointed the gun directly at Madeleine. "Now, do as I say, or I'm going to put a bullet in you."

Madeleine started sobbing hysterically as she slowly took off her shirt.

"You'll go to hell for this," said Madeleine's mother.

"Good," said Kristin, "tell the devil that I am on my way." Kristin pointed the gun at Madeleine's mother and then shot her straight in the head. Madeleine screamed as she, her father and the Butler backed up against the wall. "Now," continued Kristin, "everyone get undressed and no one else mouth off unless I ask them something."

They all did as Kristen said, throwing their clothes in a pile on the floor. Madeleine covered her breasts with her arms and the two men both put their hands over their genitals.

Eddie and Kristen started pointing at them and laughing hysterically.

"You know," said Eddie, "no matter how many times we do this it never gets old."

"You're right," said Kristin, "it's just as fun every time we do it as it was the first time. Look how pathetic they look, trying hard to cover up what God gave them. Bunch of prudes." Kristin pointed the gun straight at them again moving it back and forth and training it on each of them individually one by one. "Now, hands at your sides."

They all stopped covering themselves up and Madeleine was sobbing hysterically.

"Okay," said Kristin, "now who here wants to survive to see the next sunrise?"

They all raised their hands.

"That's good," said Kristin, "very good." She pointed the gun at Madeleine. "Now get down on all fours like an animal, like the stupid bitch that you are."

Madeleine slowly got down on her knees as she continued to sob hysterically.

Kristin pointed the gun at Madeleine's father. "Now, you get down there and fuck her like the filthy disgusting animal you are."

"What?!" exclaimed Madeleine's father.

Kristin sighed in exasperation and continued to point the gun at Madeleine's father. "It's not rocket science. It's a simple instruction. If you want to live get down on your knees and fuck your daughter like an animal."

Madeleine's father made his hands into fists. "Why you sick, depraved little bitch. I will do no such thing."

Kristin sighed more deeply. "Okay," she said, "suit yourself." Kristin raised her gun and shot Madeleine's father directly in the head and his bloody body fell down right next to Madeleine, who started screaming.

"Shut up!" shouted Kristin as she pointed the gun at Madeleine. Madeleine stopped screaming, but she continued to sob. Kristin then turned her gun in the direction of the Butler. "You," she said to the Butler, "you want to have a go at her or should I put a bullet in your head too?"

The Butler slowly kneeled down and began having sex with Madeleine doggy style. Madeleine sobbed and sobbed and Kristin and Eddie both laughed. Kristin took out her camera phone and started recording.

"Don't cry," said Kristin, "you're about to become famous on the Internet."

"I always wanted to make my own porno," said Eddie, "but of course I don't appear on film, so this is the next best thing."

They both laughed hysterically as they continued videotaping. Finally, after several minutes of this, they decided that they had had enough. "Okay," said Kristin, "that's enough. We had our fun."

The Butler withdrew from Madeleine and stood up against the wall. "Are you going to let me live now?" asked the Butler.

Kristen shook her head. "No," she said. "On top of everything else I guess you can say I'm a liar." Kristen pulled back the trigger and shot the Butler right in the chest and he fell down dead on top of Madeleine, who continued sobbing.

"Just shoot me already," shouted Madeleine between sobs.

"No," said Kristin, "I have something else in mind for you. I don't think I'm going to kill you, at least not yet. Now get up and come upstairs. I'm assuming you have the Internet."

Madeleine got up and nodded as she continued sobbing and sniffling.

"That's good," said Kristin as she looked at Eddie and smiled and he smiled back, "because you're about to throw the party of a lifetime and you're going to invite all of your rich friends who made fun of me and spat on me back when we were in high school together."

Chapter 29

A group four vampires soon arrived on the scene. They immediately ran through Kimberly's door that was torn off of its hinges. They searched the house and found the ash pile that was their comrades. One of the vampires walked over to Kimberly's lifeless body and licked up the remaining amounts of blood that were splattered all over.

"They were here," said the lead vampire, "but it seems that we have missed them." He turned on his phone and dialed up Thomas.

"Have you found anything?" Thomas asked.

"We have found the remains of one human and two vampires."

"Dammit. I told those two bastards to wait until reinforcements arrived. Whatever you do if you find Eddie do not engage him. Just report back to me immediately once you have found him or Kristin."

Thomas hung up his phone and slammed it down on the table. "Idiots!" he shouted.

"Did they find anything?" asked Reggie.

"They found him, but the two people who were sent ahead decided to foolishly engage Eddie before the reinforcements arrived and he managed to escape yet again. But he couldn't have gotten far. As far as we know he is probably still in the town somewhere not far away. We've got people looking for him and it is only a matter of time before we capture him."

"Are you going to contact Whitaker?"

"No. There is no help that he can give us in this situation. Our best bet is to just find Eddie ourselves, eliminate him as quickly as possible and then eliminate Whitaker."

"What we do in the meantime?"

"Unfortunately all we can do is wait and be patient. Fortunately, that Eddie is such a worthless fuck up that I doubt we will have to wait very long."

Kristin and Eddie had done his best a job as they could, disposing of the bodies of Madeleine's parents and the butler. They had forced Madeleine to send out an e-mail and Facebook invite to all of her friends that had made fun of Kristen to come to her house tonight at 7 PM for the party of a lifetime.

"Oh, Eddie," said Kristin, "I have always wanted to have a party in a mansion."

"See, I am making your dreams come true. This will be a party that none of them ever forget, at least in the few minutes that it will take for them to die."

They both laughed wickedly at that.

"So is everything all ready?" said Kristin as she patted Eddie on the shoulder.

"Yep, and the guests should be arriving any moment now. I almost wish we had let that butler live to help out, but I suppose we couldn't really trust him."

That was when they heard the doorbell ring.

"It seems that our first guests are arriving," said Kristin.

"Well, it is best that we not be rude and keep them waiting."

They both smiled at each other and went to let the guests in.

The first guest was Kristin's old boyfriend Jeremy, who dumped her for Madeleine because she had more money than Kristin did. He was your traditional preppy who thought that someone like Kristin was beneath him. He never officially broke up with her until she caught him making out with Madeleine. All he told Kristin was that someone such as him deserved to be with a girl with better standing than Kristin. He would get what he deserved tonight, she thought with growing excitement.

"Jeremy," said Kristin as she opened the door to let him in, "how nice it is that you could make it."

"Kristin," said Jeremy with shock, "I didn't expect to be seeing you here."

"What's that supposed to mean?"

"I just thought that you and Madeleine hated each other."

Kristen laughed and waved her hand dismissively in his face. "That's water under the bridge. We've made up a long time ago. She even asked me to host her party tonight."

"So there are no hard feelings? I mean about how we left off."

"Not at all, that was ages ago. Now I have a marvelous boyfriend named Eddie."

"Hi," said Eddie as he waved to Jeremy.

"Hi," said Jeremy as he waved back to Eddie. Then he turned back to Kristin. "So, where is Madeleine?"

"Oh, well, she's waiting for everyone to arrive before she makes an appearance. She has a big surprise planned for tonight. Why don't you wait in the dining room area."

Kristin led him to the dining room area where he noticed there were lots of red stains on the carpet in the living room. Kristin noticed that he was staring at the blood stains on the carpet.

"You're probably wondering about the red stains on the carpet. Unfortunately, when we were setting up the punch bowl before we spilled it all over the place. We didn't have time to clean it up fully before everyone arrived."

"Those stains look awfully bright for some punch."

Kristen laughed nervously. "Well, you know punch stains can be a total bitch to get out."

Fortunately their conversation was interrupted when they heard the doorbell again.

"Excuse me, Jeremy, but it seems like some other guests have arrived. You just wait here."

Within a half-hour all of the guests had arrived. While they waited for the festivities to begin, they all waited in the ballroom area. Kristin couldn't stand the fact that Madeleine was so rich that her house had a ballroom in it, but it was great for hosting parties, and this would be the greatest party she had ever seen. Once everyone was in the ballroom, Kristen decided to make an announcement.

"It seems that everyone is here. I will be your host for this evening. Many of you know me as Kristin. But you might not recognize me without your spit in my face. But I bet you are all wondering where Madeleine is. Well, here she is!"

Kristen pulled back a giant sheet revealing Madeleine completely naked and nailed to a giant crucifix, but still alive and with a ball gag in her mouth. Everyone drew back and started gasping.

"What the hell is this all about?" asked a woman in the audience.

"Is this some kind of a sick joke," shouted another woman.

Kristin took out her gun and Eddie took off his glasses and bore his fangs. "This is no joke," said Kristin," but it sure as hell is funny. Now I want you all to strip naked and and get on your knees. And if anyone tries anything, they're going to get a bullet in them."

"I bet that thing's not even loaded," shouted some guy in the audience. Kristin raised a gun and shot him in the chest. He fell down dead and everyone started screaming.

"Shut up!" shouted Kristin. "Now everyone strip naked, get on your knees and no one else try anything funny."

Everyone quickly complied with Kristen's wishes. She took out a video camera and began pointing it towards them. "Don't frown," she said, "smile. You're all about to be famous – the latest victims of the vampire killers! Now we're going to play a little game. It's called what degrading things would you do in order to save your own worthless pathetic lives. What should we do for round one?" She turned over to Madeleine, still hanging up their crucified on the cross and trying to scream through her ball gag. "Well, let's see if Madeleine has any suggestions." Kristin took the ball gag out of her mouth and she began screaming.

"You'll burn in hell for this," shouted Madeleine as she sobbed hysterically. "I always knew that you were a worthless piece of trash. Why don't you just kill me and get it all over with?"

Kristin squeezed her cheek. "But where would be the fun in that? If I killed you now you would miss all the fun. Now, do you have any suggestions for your guests? This is your party after all."

"Burn in hell you worthless whore!" sobbed Madeleine

Kristen shook her head. "My, my, my. That is very rude of you Madeleine. I guess I will just have to think of the game for us to play. Let us play Simon says. Let's begin. I'm assuming everyone knows how to play. Okay, Simon says stand on 1 foot."

Everyone began hopping on 1 foot and Eddie and Kristen laughed hysterically at them.

"That's very good," Kristen said with a smile, "very, very good. But I think we could make this a little more interesting for those watching at home, don't you, Eddie?"

"Absolutely."

"Okay, round two. Well, it seems we have an even number of men and women here. That works out good – 10 men and 10 women. Okay, Simon says for all the women to bend down on all fours."

All the women kneeled down on all fours like Kristin said.

"Very good. Now all of the guys get down on the floor and lick the women's assholes."

"Fuck that," said one man as he began to walk away. But Eddie stopped him. "Out of my way," he said pushing Eddie.

Eddie shook his head. "I'm afraid that would be against the rules."

"Well then, go ahead and shoot me."

Eddie grabbed him by the hands and began crushing them. "I'm afraid that that would be too good for you." Eddie pulled down and yanked his arms straight out of their sockets, then grabbed him by the head and ripped his head right off of his body and threw it over by the party guests. All of the guys immediately got down and started doing as Kristen said.

"Very, very good," said Kristin. "Give yourself a round of applause."

Everyone began to clap very faintly at first.

"Come on," said Kristin, "you can do better than that. Now clap motherfuckers!"

Everyone immediately began clapping very loudly.

"That's better," said Kristin. "You should all be very proud of yourselves. I almost feel like letting you live. But of course I don't think you would keep quiet about this. But I'm getting bored and I think that Eddie is getting hungry, so I'm going to be merciful and I'm just gonna kill you all right now."

Some people started getting up but Kristen began shooting them. As some scrambled for the door, Eddie ran after them and started tearing them apart. Blood was flying everywhere and between Eddie tearing everyone apart and Kristin shooting people it was hard to tell who was dead and who was alive.

After several minutes the ballroom floor was a puddle of blood with various dismembered organs and bleeding bodies.

"Did we get everyone?" asked Kristin.

"There's one left," said Eddie as he dragged Jeremy across

the floor.

"Wait," said Kristin, "don't kill him yet."

Eddie held up Jeremy's body, which had a bullet wound in the chest, but a nonfatal one. Kristin came up close to his face. "Well," said Kristin, "first to arrive, last to leave."

"Please," said Jeremy, "just make it quick."

"You mean you're not going to beg for me to spare you?"

Jeremy shook his head as he began to cry. "No. I'm not afraid to die. Just do it. But first, can I just say one last thing."

Kristin shrugged her shoulders. "Well, no one's got a gun to your head." She started to break into laughter as she said that, and Eddie couldn't help but join in.

"I just want to say," said Jeremy, "that I'm sorry for what I did."

Kristin laughed derisively and put her hands on her hips. "Ha, everyone is sorry when they're about to die. Your apology is a little bit late."

"I mean it," said Jeremy as he struggled to breathe with blood coming out of his mouth. "I always felt bad about the way I treated you. I know there is no excuse for it, but I'm sorry."

"Do you think I'm going to spare your life now?"

"No. I probably deserve this. I just want you to know, that whatever happens, I hope you find happiness."

"Happiness," said Kristin as she began to fight back tears, "I torture you and shoot you and am about to kill you and you want to wish me happiness."

"With all my heart."

"Shut up! Shut up! Shut up!" shouted Kristin as she stomped her feet and began to cry. "Damn you, damn you, damn you!" She leaned forward and kissed Jeremy on the lips. She then turned to Eddie. "Do it!"

Eddie nodded and bit into Jeremy's throat and then tossed his lifeless body on the pile. Kristin turned her back to the entire scene and stood there holding her gun at her side. Eddie came up behind her and put his hand on her shoulder.

"Are you okay?" Eddie asked.

"No," sobbed Kristin, "I'm not okay."

Eddie turned Kristin around and looked directly into her eyes and kissed her. He then drew back, and got down on one knee.

"W-what are you doing?" sniffled Kristin.

"Just calm down and be quiet for a minute. I know this probably isn't the best time, but I hope the moment isn't ruined. It's just I knew this would be a special night for you and I wanted it to end perfectly. And Jeremy was right about one thing – you do deserve happiness. So I'm going to ask you the question that I should have asked you a long time ago." Eddie took a ring out of his pocket and placed it on Kristin's finger. "Kristin McDonald, will you marry me and be mine forever, for as long as we both may live and however long after?"

Kristin started choking back her tears and smiled. She lifted Eddie up from the floor, pulled him towards her and kissed him on the lips. She could taste the fresh blood on them.

"You monsters!" shouted Madeleine from across the room. "You're both going to burn in hell!"

Kristin lifted her gun up without turning away from Eddie and shot Madeleine in the leg. She then walked over to Madeleine, slapped her in the face and said, "That's for ruining my special moment you stuck up bitch. I was going to kill you, but now I think I'm going to just let you hang up there until you die a slow, agonizing death. You always said everyone has their crosses to bear, so I hope you appreciate the irony of your current situation. Also, I read your diary this afternoon. I hope that heaven has a liberal attitude towards giving blow jobs to married men at fancy dinner parties. So when you get to hell, I hope you appreciate that irony as well. Let your mother know that I'll be there shortly."

Kristin turned back to Eddie. "We're all covered in blood. Want to go for a swim?"

"It sounds like the perfect end to the perfect evening."

"Oh, Eddie," she said as she started to undress, "you've made me the happiest woman in the world!"

Chapter 30

After washing off in the pool, Kristen and Eddie wasted no time in packing up their things and hitting the road again. They knew that the vampires were still pursuing them and it was only a matter of time before they found them if they remained in that town.

Kristin was using her iPhone to upload the video she took of the party and the slaughter. All the video showed was a a group of naked people being torn apart by an invisible assailant.

"What are you doing?" asked Eddie.

"Just uploading last night's fun to the Internet. If we're going to go down, we might as well go down famous."

"You'd better chuck that phone when you're done uploading the video. We don't want to be traced. But I would give anything to see the look on Thomas's face when he sees this video."

"Okay, done uploading. Bye-bye phone!" And with that, Kristen chucked her phone out the window. It shattered to pieces the moment it hit the ground. "That was a nice phone. But I guess if I need another one we can always steal it. That was actually Madeleine's phone."

They both had a good laugh at that.

"Eddie, where we going now?"

"There is something that I want to show you."

"What is it?"

Eddie turned to her and smiled. "It's a surprise."

Kristin smiled back at him. "I hope it's a good one."

"Trust me, it is."

Thomas and Reggie arrived at Madeleine's house, as soon as his cohorts had tracked Eddie to that place. There were five other vampires there. Thomas approached Madeleine's body, still just barely alive on the crucifix and grabbed her cheeks with his hand.

"Help me," muttered Madeleine.

"I will," said Thomas, "but first I need help from you."

"I'm dying," Madeleine choked out.

"I need to know where Kristin and Eddie are. If you tell me that I will help you."

"I don't know. They slaughtered everyone – all my family and friends are dead. You've got to call the police and an ambulance."

"Don't worry, they are on their way now. But if you want us to catch these killers, you have to tell us everything you can about where they went."

"I don't know," she said in a very faint voice as her breathing became labored. "T-they s-said, s-something, about mmarriage."

"Do you know any more details?"

Madeleine shook her head.

"Okay then. Then you are no longer any use to me."

Madeleine raised her head up about to say something, but Thomas grabbed her by the neck and snapped it. Madeleine's head fell forward completely lifeless.

"Dammit! Where could Eddie have gone now?"

Thomas's phone began to ring and he answered it. "Hello?"

"This is Whitaker. Someone just uploaded a video to the Internet that I think you should see."

Thomas began to watch the video and after just a few seconds have it he had crushed the screen of his iPhone. Eddie wasn't trying to hide anymore.

A few hours later Eddie and Kristen arrived at the cemetery.

"What are we doing in the cemetery, Eddie?"

"Follow me," he said as he waved Kristin on.

After a few minutes they arrived at a gravestone. The gravestone said Edward, along with his birthdate, his alleged death date and a record of his military service.

"This is my grave," said Eddie as he touched the top of his tombstone. "I just thought you should see it. I haven't visited my own grave in many years. I used to visit it every year on the anniversary of my 'death' or more accurately my rebirth. I'm sentimental that way. I even attended my own funeral."

"What was that like?"

"It was surprisingly very satisfying. I remember it like it were only yesterday, even though it was more than 20 years ago."

Eddie had arrived at his own funeral incognito. He dressed in all black, wore a black hat, his dark sunglasses and most of his body was covered. No one even recognized him and it wasn't a very impressive turnout as he had few friends and wasn't close to his family. But he recognized one of the people at his funeral – his father. He was actually rather surprised to see him there, but he figured it would look strange if he didn't. Him being there was all about keeping up appearances. After the service had concluded Eddie had followed his father home. He knocked on the door and as soon as his father answered, he pushed his way inside and closed the door behind him.

"Who the fuck are you?!" shouted Eddie's father. "I've got a gun."

Eddie took off his disguise and his father stood back in shock. "Eddie? Is that you? You're alive?!"

Eddie shook his head very slowly. "Not exactly. Didn't you read the suicide note that I left?"

"Well that obviously must've been fake. They never found your body when you said that you went to drown yourself."

"Indeed. I did not kill myself. But nor would you say I am still alive."

"What the hell are you talking about? Your eyes look strange. Are you high again?"

"Actually I am on a permanent high. And as I said I am not alive, but I am not dead either. I have transcended the boundaries of life and death and achieved a higher form of existence."

"You aren't making any sense."

"I am a vampire."

"A vampire! You mean that you are one of those faggy goth kids. Or are you just plain insane? Either way, I wish you had killed yourself. What the hell did you come back for?"

"Originally I was just coming to collect some things of mine. But now that I have actually seen you again, I am reminded how much I deeply hate you and I have decided that I want revenge for all of the abuse and neglect."

"Abuse and neglect? You ungrateful little bastard. I put a roof over your head and this is the way you repay me. I ought to knock your block off."

"You're welcome to try it."

Eddie's father came running towards him and took a swing at him, but Eddie grabbed his fist in his hand and crushed it. He let go and his father drew back.

"You son of a bitch, you broke my fucking hand! I guess that military training really did toughen you up."

"Indeed it did. Because before all of that I wouldn't be able to so easily take a life without feeling any guilt over it."

"Easy there boy," said Eddie's father as he raised his uninjured hand up at Eddie, "we can work this all out."

Eddie started shaking his head and walking towards his

father. "That is what I intend to do." Eddie ran towards his father and grabbed him by the neck and began choking him. "Who is the weakling now."

"You God damned faggot," Eddie's father managed to choke out. Eddie looked him directly in the eye and then leaned forward and bit his face off.

Kristin stood there staring at Eddie not saying anything.

"I'll tell you," said Eddie, "I have never taken more satisfaction from a kill than that day I killed my own father. Though killing your father was a close second, and the entire time I was killing him I thought back to my own father. But enough about killing. I believe that we have a wedding to arrange." Eddie held out his hand and Kristen took it. "Soulmates," he said.

"Until death do us part," replied Kristin.

Chapter 31

In a short time, Eddie and Kristen had arrived at the tent of a traveling preacher.

"Does this place even perform weddings?" Kristen asked.

"It was the nearest place I found that was advertised. We could go somewhere different if you prefer."

Kristen shook her head. "I don't need a big fancy wedding. Besides, under the circumstances, I don't think that we would be able to do that without someone taking notice."

Eddie laughed. "I suppose you have a point there. Well, after you." Eddie pulled back the flap of the tent and they walked inside. What they saw was a bunch of people sitting on fold up chairs all listening to a preacher who was up on a podium preaching about God's forgiving nature.

"So who wants to be saved?" The preacher asked.

"How about a wedding," said Eddie, interrupting him.

"Well now," he said, "which one of you wants to get married?"

"We do," said Kristin. "And we are kind of in a hurry. So if you could do it fast, that would be the best."

"Well well well now," said the preacher as he began walking off the stage towards them. "It seems like we have a bunch of young lovers who are in a rush to get married."

"I look younger than I am," said Eddie as he began to laugh. "But all we need to know is can you do it right now in front of all these people as witnesses?"

"Well," said the preacher, "I reckon I can. Providing, of course, that you believe in the Holy Spirit. Do you believe in the Holy Spirit?"

"Lordy Lordy Lordy," shouted Eddie as he held up the cross that he wore around his neck, "I do believe."

"And do you believe young lady?"

Kristin nodded as they walked up to the stage.

"Well then," said the preacher, "let's get started."

"Can we skip the preliminaries and just get down to the basics," said Eddie, "as I said we have a constraint on time."

"Okay then," said the preacher, "I wouldn't want to people in love to be denied the Lord's blessing, if that is their hearts desire. And what are your names?"

"Eddie and Kristen," said Eddie.

"Well then Kristen," said the preacher as he helped Kristin and Eddie on to the stage, "do you take Eddie to be your lawfully wedded husband for as long as you both shall live until death do you part?"

"I do," said Kristin as she looked lovingly into Eddie's eyes.

"And do you Eddie," said the preacher, "do you take Kristin to be your lawfully wedded wife for as long as you both shall live until death do you part?"

"I do," said Eddie.

"Then, by the power invested in me by Almighty God, I now pronounce you man and wife. You may kiss the bride."

Eddie and Kristen kissed and then began to laugh.

"And what exactly are you laughing about?" asked the preacher.

"Nothing," said Eddie, "just that line about till death do you part."

"And what may I ask, is so funny about that?"

"I have been dead for over 20 years!"

"What's that?"

"Just like he said," said Kristin, "he died 20 years ago. He showed me his grave. It was kind of romantic."

The preacher and the audience began to look at them a bit

oddly.

"Is that so?" asked the preacher.

"Yes, it is," said Kristin, "Eddie is a vampire."

"Really now," said the preacher as he turned to his audience with a skeptical look.

"If you don't believe her," said Eddie, "why don't you take our picture."

"Everyone should have a wedding photo," said the preacher as he took out his camera and many others in the audience took out their phone cameras. "Say cheese."

Within a minute, a million flashes were going off as everyone in the audience took a picture of Kristin and Eddie standing there on the stage.

"Now everyone take a look at your cameras, "said Eddie.

Everyone in the audience did as Eddie commanded, and they all started gasping in shock.

"It has been said," began Eddie, "that the reason that vampires cast no reflection is because they have no soul. What are your thoughts on that Reverend?"

"Well, I was never taught to believe in vampires. The good book doesn't say anything about vampires."

Eddie looked over to see a snake in a glass cage sitting up on the stage. "What's that snake for," he asked as he pointed to it.

"Well, if you had gotten here earlier, you would see a demonstration of faith."

"So, you're a snake handler, huh?"

"Third-generation."

"Mind if I handle your snake?"

The preacher nodded, and Eddie took the snake out of his cage and let it bite him directly in the chest, much like that time he had shown Kristin when they encountered that rattlesnake. He allowed the snake to hang on his chest and to bite him all over and the crowd all gasped in shock while a few people clapped.

"What are you?" asked the preacher. "You unholy beast."

"Like I said, I am a vampire."

"I recognize them!" shouted a woman in the audience. "They're the vampire killers from the news!"

People in the crowd started to gasp and scream and a couple people began to slowly get up and walk out.

"Guilty as charged," said Eddie as he took a bow with the snake still hanging off of him.

"You unholy servant of the devil!" Shouted the preacher as he began to fling holy water at Eddie's face and hold up a cross. "Take that!"

"Please," said Eddie as he wiped the water from his face and held up his own crucifix. "This is all Hollywood."

"Get back," said the preacher as he began to walk backwards. That was when Eddie lunged forward, took the snake and began strangling the preacher with it.

When everyone saw that they started to try to pile out of the tent, but Eddie jumped off the stage and began tearing people apart. The blood sprayed all over and the limbs went flying while Kristin stood on the stage smiling and laughing. "Oh Eddie Darling," she shouted into the microphone, "this is the best honeymoon ever!"

Eddie continued with his massacre as Kristen continued to stand on stage, took out her gun and began firing randomly into the crowd. This went on for several more minutes until most of the people in the tent were dead. A lot of them managed to escape by tearing through the tent walls and scrambling off. But that was when Kristen and Eddie heard the sound of police sirens.

"That sound means it's time for us to leave," said Eddie.

Kristin ran down from the stage and she and Eddie began to run towards the tent exit when 15 police officers piled into the tent from all directions with guns drawn. They were surrounded.

"Freeze, police!" shouted the head police officer. "Drop your weapons and put your hands in the air."

"What should we do Eddie?" Kristen asked as she kept her gun raised.

"There are too many of them," said Eddie, "and I can hear more outside and a helicopter coming. You aren't indestructible."

"Are you suggesting that we just give up?"

"This is your last warning," said the head police officer as he pointed the gun directly at Eddie who was standing in front of Kristen trying to shield her from any potential gunfire.

"Are you ready to become more famous than anyone in history," Eddie asked Kristin.

Kristin smiled, nodded and slowly placed her weapon on

the ground. "I love you Eddie."

"Until death do us part."

They both put their hands up and the police surrounded them. It looks like the human authorities had gotten to them first after all.

Chapter 32

Thomas and Reggie heard about Eddie and Kristen's apprehension from one of their vampire agents. The police and the National Guard had been present in too large of a number for any vampire to try and stop them without exposing himself.

Thomas immediately got on the phone with Whitaker.

"I was expecting your call," said Whitaker as soon as he answered the phone.

"You need to tell me where Eddie and Kristen are being held."

"And why exactly do I have to do that? My goal had never been to just catch Eddie, but to expose your entire kind."

"Do you think I did not anticipate that you would try this? That is why I went to the liberty of tracking down every family member and friend that you have in this world. If you do not tell me the whereabouts of Kristen and Eddie no one you know will ever be safe. I will kill every last one of them and then I will come for you. You don't want to start a war that you know you cannot win."

"Then I will make sure that everyone I know has police protection. I only need to keep them safe for a short while. Once the existence of vampires has been exposed, we will come for the rest of you. So I'm going to call your bluff. I think that I hold more cards than you do."

"Are you really willing to risk the death of all of your loved ones."

"And how safe would they be if you are kind continues to exist? I already lost a sister. And unless vampires are eradicated it's only a matter of time before your kind was going to kill off all of my loved ones anyway. I have been taking precautions ever since I first got involved with you. You can go to hell. The wrath of the Lord is immense. You may think that you can avoid death and avoid judgment, but I know you can be destroyed."

Thomas realize that there was no reasoning with Whitaker and just hung up on him.

"So what we do now?" Reggie asked.

"We go to all of the prisons in the area and fight our way inside."

"Isn't that rather risky?"

"We have no other option at this point. Eddie has already given himself up into custody and will soon expose us all. As long as we can destroy Eddie without anyone else being captured it doesn't matter how much circumstantial evidence they have of the existence of vampires. People's ability to deny things is strong and should not be underestimated. With just a few tricks a video and a couple of unusual corpses drained of blood are not absolute proof."

"But look how belief in vampires has risen just as a result of Eddie's killing spree."

"Belief is not going to destroy us. As long as there is no absolute proof this will all eventually be forgotten. So send out word. Eddie must be destroyed at any cost. Our very existence depends upon it. And time is of the essence. Whitaker is probably on the way to wherever Eddie is right now."

"I don't get it," said the police photographer. "None of the pictures of this guy have come out. I have tried different cameras, different film, and basically everything that could be tried. I'm starting to think that maybe he really is a vampire."

Eddie was in the interrogation room when Whitaker arrived. "Let me see him," said Whitaker as he entered the room.

"Well hello hello hello," said Eddie as Whitaker approached. "It seems another person has come to see the vampire."

"Close the door," said Whitaker. "I want to talk to Eddie alone."

"Are you sure you want to do that sir?" asked the officer on duty. "This man is very dangerous."

"So, he is handcuffed, I have nothing to fear from him."

The officer nodded and closed the door, leaving Whitaker face-to-face with the object of his obsession.

"I know what you are," said Whitaker.

"So you have seen the medical reports," said Eddie with a laugh of contempt.

"I don't need to see the medical reports. I don't know what it is that makes you tick, but I definitely intend to find out."

"Well, I'm fully willing to cooperate, just so long as I am assured protection from the rest of my kind."

"You're not exactly in a position to be making deals."

"You aren't interested to know the secret of immortality that I possess?"

"My only interest is in ensuring that your kind is eradicated from the face of the earth."

"Well, Sieg heil mine Fuhrer," said Eddie with a chuckle. "You know history doesn't look kindly on people that exterminate entire races of people, especially when those people possess the secret that everyone on Earth wishes to possess – the secret of never dying."

"Don't you dare compare me to that monster. It is you and your kind that are the monsters. You aren't persecuted victims, you are a race of parasites and predators. You sustain yourself through murder, and in your case wonton slaughter of innocent life. There is absolutely no redeeming quality to you."

"So you really aren't interested in immortality?"

"All I care about is exposing your kind to the world. Once that is accomplished, I'll see to it that you're the first of them to be destroyed."

"So no deal then?"

"No deal. I don't do deals with the devil. And as I said, you aren't exactly in a position to be making deals."

"Well, I think you're wrong about that. You see I am here solely because I felt that this was my best chance at survival. But I really hold all the cards. You see my imprisonment here is entirely at my discretion. And if I have no deal with you there is no reason why I should not just kill you off right now."

"That would be kind of difficult given that you are sitting there handcuffed to that chair." Whitaker laughed at Eddie and spat in his face.

Eddie started laughing hysterically.

"Why are you laughing?"

"You were laughing at me because I am handcuffed to the

chair."

"And why exactly is that funny?"

"This is why," said Eddie as he snapped the handcuffs.

"Oh shit," said Whitaker with a look of horror on his face. He turned to run, but before he could scream, Eddie had knocked him to the floor and was on top of him.

"I'm going to enjoy killing you," whispered Eddie as he began to strangle Whitaker. Eddie continued to press down on Whitaker's neck and then in a fit of excitement tore his head off and began drinking from it.

Eddie tossed Whitaker's head aside, then he kicked down the door.

"Freeze," shouted the officer at the door, as he pointed his gun at Eddie.

"No," said Eddie as he leaped forward and tore the officer to pieces.

Other officers began running down the hallway but Eddie quickly tore through them. He took a few gunshot wounds, but it's nothing a little blood won't cure. He was on a high. Eddie continued slaughtering officer after officer until the majority of them were dead. He then came over to Kristin's cell, and tore the door off.

"Eddie," she said with a look of surprise as she hugged him. She looked up at him. "I thought that we were giving ourselves up and revealing the existence of vampires to the world."

"Well, things have changed. I have realized that you cannot make a deal with humans. As soon as they prove that we exist they would destroy us. We have to get out of here now, while we still can. It won't be long before people come looking for us. Both human and vampire."

"But where are we going to go Eddie? We can never stay anywhere for any length of time. We can't keep this up forever."

"I know. Maybe we could go to Europe or some faraway area of the world where we will never be found. But right now we just have to get out of here."

Kristin nodded as she reached down and picked up the gun from one of the dead officers. "I guess I'll be needing one of these."

They ran down until they managed to find a police car. But

just as they approached it, Eddie could sense that someone was coming and paused.

"What is it, Eddie?" Kristen asked as she stopped in her tracks.

"I can smell Thomas and Reggie. Just get in the car. We have to go now!"

They got into the police car, put the sirens on and raced out of the prison. Following immediately behind them he could see Thomas and Reggie in their own car.

"What are we going to do now Eddie?" Kristen asked and Eddie could hear her heart beating in an accelerated pace.

"I don't know," said Eddie as he turned to look at Kristin, "just let me fucking think of something,"

"Watch out!" Kristin shouted. But before Eddie could turn around, he had crashed the police car into a giant crucifix right on the front lawn of a church, sending them both flying through the windshield.

Chapter 33

Eddie quickly got up and started looking around. "Kristin," he shouted. "Where are you?"

"Eddie," he heard a voice faintly say as he ran towards the direction where he saw Kristin lying on the grass.

"Kristin," he said as he ran towards her. As he approached her lying on the lawn, he could see that she was covered in blood, with a huge gash across her forehead. The sight of all that blood was driving him crazy but he had to restrain himself.

"No, no, no," said Eddie as he picked up Kristin. "I won't let you die."

"Eddie," shouted Thomas as he ran out of his car, "now is the time for you to die."

Eddie ran from Thomas and through the church doors. He kicked them open as he ran forward with Kristin.

"Eddie," muttered Kristin as blood ran down her mouth.

"Yes," he said as he shook her.

"I don't feel so well, Eddie."

"I'm not going to let you die."

"Eddie."

"Yes?"

"I love you, Eddie."

Kristen began choking on blood and her eyes were starting to roll back into her head. Eddie cradled her body in his hands and could feel the life draining from her. He knew what he had to do. He leaned over, bit Kristin's neck and injected his venom. He then placed her down on the altar.

No sooner than he had done that did he see Thomas running towards him. He leaped out of the way and Thomas fell into a pile of candles, which fell on the floor, igniting the carpet. Thomas soon came up and picked up Kristin's body over his head.

"Give yourself up Eddie, and I will spare her life."

"No, you won't."

"You're right," he said with a big smile, "I won't."

Thomas took Kristin's body and tossed it through the stained-glass windows like some rag doll.

"And now it is time for you to die Eddie."

Eddie could hear Reggie running up behind him, but he jumped out of the way, and tripped Reggie, who fell into Thomas knocking them both into the flames. They both rolled on the floor and managed to put the fire out as Eddie began to run towards the windows to go after Kristen. But before he could get there and Reggie and Thomas both dove on top of Eddie. Eddie managed to kick them off into the pews.

Thomas and Reggie both got up and took out stakes.

"It's two-on-one, Eddie," said Reggie as they both walked towards him.

"But you're forgetting one thing," said Eddie.

"And what is that?" asked Thomas

"I want to live more than you do."

Eddie ripped off a piece of the pew, took out his lighter and lit it on fire, giving him a burning stake. Thomas and Reggie began running towards Eddie, who leaped over them and onto the altar.

"Come and get me," taunted Eddie as he waved the flaming stake at them.

"I am sick of your shit Eddie," said Thomas as he began to dive at Eddie with his stake pointed forward.

"No," shouted Reggie. But it was too late, Thomas had dived at Eddie and just at the last moment Eddie dove out of the way and Thomas jumped right into the flames. Thomas stood up on fire and Eddie took his stake and knocked his head right off, turning him into a pile of dust.

Reggie stood back, holding his stake up at Eddie.

"It looks like it's come down to the two of us," said Reggie.

"Father and son, creator and creation," said Eddie.

"You are my worst mistake, Eddie. And it is a mistake that I intend to correct. I guess it's fitting that you should die in a church."

"It's your move," said Eddie as he stood on top of the altar and held up his stake.

"No," said Reggie and he began to walk away.

"Where are you going?"

"I'm going for Kristin."

A sudden rage filled Eddie and he started running towards Reggie without thinking, holding up his stake. Just as he was about to dive on Reggie, Reggie turned around, raised his stake and knocked the stake out of Eddie's hand. Reggie went to stake Eddie but Eddie grabbed the end of Reggie's stake, so that now they were each holding one end of the stake. Eddie let go of the stake, ran behind Reggie and grabbed him from behind.

"I'm not going to let you destroy Kristin," said Eddie.

"This ends now," said Reggie as he thrust the stake through himself and into Eddie's heart. "Goodbye, Eddie. Ashes to ashes, and dust to dust."

Eddie let out a shriek and they both turned into a pile of dust. The ashes of the creator mixed with the ashes of his creation as the church burned around them and the sound of police sirens filled the air.

Epilogue

The doctor took one look at Kristen's body and shook his head. "She is clearly dead. There are multiple lacerations on the body, a huge loss of blood and there is no pulse or a heartbeat. I would send her down to the autopsy room. I guess this is the end of the vampire killers. Did you find the other one?"

The officer talking to the doctor shook his head. "We are still investigating the cause of the fire. No other bodies were recovered, although some clothing was found at the scene. We'll have to get forensics to look at it."

The doctor put a sheet over Kristen's body and an orderly came and began to wheel her down to the autopsy room. That was when Kristen could hear all the sounds of the hospital buzzing to life like never before. She also realized that she had a new hunger. Kristin stood up and the orderly nearly fainted.

"Oh my God," said the orderly with terror in her voice, "she's alive." The orderly turned around to call the emergency room, but before she could do that Kristen had ran up to her and taken a good bite out of her neck. The blood tasted delicious and Kristen felt a greater intoxication and she had ever felt before. Never had taking a life been this exhilerating!

She decided it was best to sneak out of the hospital discretely. She managed to sneak out the back and walk off into the darkness. She wasn't sure where she should go first, but she knew that she didn't want to stay here. She walked over to the highway and waved down a truck.

"I need a ride," said Kristin to the truck driver.

"Hop in," he said.

Kristen got in and sat down next to him.

"Where are you heading," he asked.

"I won't know until I get there."

"Well, you're welcome to come with me as far as I can take you." That was when he noticed Kristen's clothing look all ripped up and covered in blood. "You don't look so good. Are you okay?"

"I feel better than okay. And I think that you look rather good."

"Oh yeah," the trucker said with a big smile.

"Yeah," she said with a big smile. "You look almost good enough to eat." And that was when she knew she couldn't help herself. She turned to the truck driver, bore her fangs and began to take the first full meal of what she hoped would be a very long and exciting new life.

Made in the USA
Lexington, KY
25 November 2013